With big dreams of being a published author since she was an eleven-year-old girl writing *Beverly Hills 90210* fan fiction before fan fiction was even a thing, **SHANN McPHERSON** has been writing angsty, contemporary romances for most of her thirty-something years.

Living in sunny Queensland, Australia, when she's not writing, Shann enjoys making memories with her husband and cheeky toddler son, drinking wine, and singing completely off-key to One Direction's entire discography.

# Also by Shann McPherson

*Where We Belong*

# Sweet Home Montana

## SHANN MCPHERSON

**ONE PLACE. MANY STORIES**

HQ
An imprint of HarperCollins*Publishers* Ltd
1 London Bridge Street
London SE1 9GF

First published in Great Britain by
HQ, an imprint of HarperCollins*Publishers* Ltd 2020

ISBN: 9780008381998

MIX
Paper from
responsible sources
FSC
www.fsc.org
FSC® C007454

This book is produced from independently certified FSC™ paper
to ensure responsible forest management.

For more information visit: www.harpercollins.co.uk/green

Printed and bound in Great Britain by
CPI Group (UK) Ltd, Melksham, SN12 6TR

*For Louis*

# Prologue

*Ten years ago . . .*

I'm the kind of girl who's been dreaming of her wedding day for most of her life. The dress, the flowers, the groom. When I was a little girl, I used to sneak up into the attic and play dress-up with my mom's wedding gown from the Seventies, twirling around in the beauty of the last light of day shining in through the tiny windows, catching the dust particles floating through the air like glitter. In that moment, as a wide-eyed ten-year-old with my whole life ahead of me, it was almost as if dreams could really come true.

Fast forward ten years, and here I am, staring at my own reflection, trying so hard to rack my brain as to who the woman looking back at me even is. Sure, she looks like me. She has my honey blonde hair, and the same gray eyes with flecks of blue and gold, but I don't know her. Standing there in a white dress, gripping a bouquet of wild flowers as if it's her lifeline, the woman staring back at me is a relative stranger, and for some reason it makes my heart jump up into the back of my throat. I can't breathe. It isn't right. There's something seriously wrong. This is my wedding. I'm marrying my best friend, the love of my life.

This is the day I used to dream about. I'm a bride. I'm supposed to be blushing, not barely breathing.

"You ready, sweetheart?"

I jump, pulling myself from the overwhelming thoughts consuming me from the inside. Turning, I find my father standing in the doorway, his imposing frame filling the space. He's dressed in an impeccable black suit, a matching Stetson—the good one he saves for formals and funerals alike—perched upon his head. He looks handsome, and proud, and my uncertainty quells when I meet his eyes to see such adoration within his penetrating gaze.

I manage a nod, swallowing the lump of trepidation that sits in the back of my throat. Bunching up the heavy lace train of my dress, I cross the room, staring at the hardwood floor with every tentative step I take. Dad stops me. Reaching out, he tucks his forefinger beneath my chin, forcing my eyes to his, and for a long moment he regards me closely, and I'm almost certain he can see straight through me.

"You know," he begins, his deep voice hushed as he continues, "you don't have to—" With an imploring gaze, he stops himself, silencing whatever it was he was going to tell me.

"What?" I press, my brows knitting together. I'm almost positive I know what he was about to say, but I just need to hear him say it. If he says it, then I know it can't be wrong.

But he doesn't say it. Instead, he presses his lips together in the semblance of a smile, shaking his head dismissively. "You look beautiful, sweetheart. Just like your mother."

My heart stops at that.

My mother.

I blink a few times as a hazy memory flashes through my mind.

I'm seven years old and I've just had a bath, the scent of my favorite bubblegum bubble wash lingers in the damp air. I'm sitting at the vanity in the bathroom and my mother is standing behind me, combing the tangles from my hair, a wistful smile playing on her lips, illuminating her effortless beauty.

"What do you want to be when you grow up, Quinny?" she asks.

I meet her eyes in the mirror, answering matter-of-factly, "A princess."

She laughs, a musical lilt resonating throughout the space, but then a sudden seriousness comes over her, one that she tries desperately to hide with a forced smile that doesn't reach her eyes. "Will you promise me something, darling girl?"

"What is it, Mommy?"

My mother sits down on the bench seat beside me, smoothing the backs of her delicate fingers over my chubby cheek, a faraway gaze in her eyes. "Promise me, whatever you do, never forget to chase your dreams."

I notice a sadness come over her, one I've never seen before. In her eyes there's a sheen that reflects the soft downlights shining from above the mirror. I blink at her, unsure what she means. And, because I'm only seven, I simply offer a smile, craning up to place a kiss to her cheek. "Okay, Mommy."

I wish I'd known more. Maybe I could have saved her. Maybe, just maybe, less than a year later she wouldn't have taken to her wrists with a razor blade.

"Sweetheart?"

I blink hard, shaking my head free of my memory, finding Dad looking at me, concern evident within his inky eyes. As Mom's haunting words echo throughout my mind, my chest heaves to keep up with my suddenly racing heart. A cold sweat beads at my nape. Tears threaten what little composure I have left. My eyes flit frantically from side to side, for what? I don't even know.

"Quinny?" Dad steps in, his large hands enveloping my upper arms and gently pulling me closer to him.

I find his eyes, the safety and familiarity within them, and just like that my anxiety dissipates enough for me to catch my breath. "I c-can't—" I shake my head. "I can't do this," I cry.

He stares at me a long moment, studying me, and then he simply nods.

3

I've left a bunch of times. I can't even count how many. In the three years I've been away at college, I've stood in this very spot in the center of the bustling departure terminal of Great Falls International so many times before, looking my father in his eyes as we fumble our way through goodbye. But never before have I stood here looking at my father with such a resolute finality. This goodbye feels like it might just be forever, and the more I try desperately to swallow that painful lump of emotion that's wedged its way into the back of my throat, the more the tears sting my eyes.

Dad clears his throat, glancing away a moment before meeting my gaze. He lifts a large hand, scrubbing his stubbled chin, for lack of anything else to do with his hands. "I'll see you for Thanksgiving."

I hesitate a moment, averting my gaze from his eyes, which have always been able to see straight through me. And, although I'm almost certain he knows, I can't risk him seeing the truth. That he won't be seeing me for Thanksgiving. That I probably won't even be home for Christmas. That I don't know if I can ever come back. Not after what I did yesterday. Call me a coward, but my leaving is what's best for everyone.

I nod once, lifting my chin again, and I force a smile through the overwrought sadness that's clawing at me from the inside. "Thanksgiving," I manage, my voice wavering.

He lifts his faded brown Stetson from his head momentarily, ruffling a hand through his salt and pepper hair, which is far more salt than pepper, nowadays, thanks to me. His dark, penetrating gaze steadies me, and in that moment, he says so much with just one look.

"In life, it doesn't matter where we go, or how long we're gone for. What matters is that we never forget where we come from, so no matter what, we can always go home." Royal Wagner is a man of few words. A stoic man who stands at six-foot-three. Imposing and intimidating in every sense of the word. And yet, I

4

find myself completely taken aback by what he's just said to me. So much so that I can't possibly stop my infuriating tears from breaking free, trailing down over my cheeks.

Dad closes the distance, his strong arms wrapping around me and pulling me to him. And I go willingly, holding on to him so tight, burying my face into his chest and breathing him in as more tears fall. When the final boarding call for my flight to Newark rings throughout the vast terminal, I find myself instinctively fisting the fleecy material of his vest, gripping it tight as if I can't bear to let him go. And I can't. I don't want to. But I have to.

"I'll call you," I say through a sob, my broken voice muffled by his flannel shirt. "Every day."

Dad presses a kiss to the top of my head, quietly shushing me, and I could stay like this forever in the arms of the man who has always been my hero. But I know I can't. And, reluctantly, I force myself to pull away. I have to. If I don't, I might never leave.

I swipe at the tear tracks staining my cheeks with the cuff of my New York University sweatshirt, unable to meet my father's eyes as I crouch down to collect my backpack from the floor. And with my gaze fixed on the shiny tile, I press my fingers to my lips, blowing him a quick kiss before turning quickly and hurrying toward my gate, unable to chance a single glance over my shoulder in his direction. Seeing him standing there will only break my already shattered heart. And despite the crippling, self-inflicted pain of leaving my father and my whole world behind, I know it's for the best. It has to be.

# Chapter 1

I navigate the Monday morning crowds treading the Fifth Avenue sidewalk, balancing a double-shot Americano, my designer handbag and a thirty-page new-build proposal I was supposed to have read over the weekend for today's monthly sales meeting. I didn't read the proposal. In fact, I didn't even take it out of its perfectly bound folder. And as I hurry into the marble lobby of my office building with a throbbing head, I wish I had read it. Especially last night, instead of consuming an entire bottle of pinot noir while watching *Real Housewives* reruns like the sad, single, almost-thirty-year-old that I am.

Once inside the packed elevator car, awkward silence ensues as we ascend, save for a few people obliging in amicable yet obviously forced conversation with others they'd probably rather avoid. My cell phone chimes loudly three times, bringing with it a few eye-rolls from the people surrounding me, but I ignore the new messages, flashing an apologetic smile at those around me when it chimes one more time. There's no way I can manage my phone, coffee, handbag, and documents. Whoever it is can wait.

I stare straight ahead at the mirrored doors, exhaling a defeated sigh of resignation when I'm forced to look directly at my own reflection. The morning rain has caused my honey blonde hair to frizz and my mascara to run. But I shrug a nonchalant shoulder. At least I managed to make it into the office today. My bed was feeling awfully warm and cozy when my alarm went off. I glance up at the floor counter above the doors, watching as it ticks by, mocking me with every floor we pass.

Do I hate my job? No. My job, my life is what most dreams are made of. The perfect apartment on one of the best cobblestone streets in Tribeca. An enviable designer handbag collection, shoes, too. But lately I've found myself trapped within a funk I just can't seem to crawl my way out of. I don't know what it is. I suppose it could be the dreaded three-zero looming right around the corner.

When the elevator car stops with a sudden and unexpected jolt, I'm knocked by the woman beside me, causing me to lose my balance. And, in a flurry so fast I can't possibly prevent it from happening, lukewarm coffee is soaking through the delicate silk of my shirt as the documents I was holding on to fall from my hand and scatter across the elevator floor.

I pan down to take in the state of my shirt, to the mess on the floor, as impatient people push past me on their way out of the doors, paying no mind to me or my obvious dilemma.

I sigh, my shoulders sagging in resignation.

Sadly, this is my life.

Did I mention I hate Mondays?

After attempting to clean myself up in the bathroom, I'm so late to the sales meeting, I can't help but feel all eyes on me, looking me up and down with thinly veiled incredulity as I make my way into the boardroom twenty minutes after go-time, slipping into the only available chair right by Mr. Hawkins, the chairman of one of the most prestigious brokerage firms on the East Coast.

My cell chimes twice, interrupting Keith from our marketing department, as he talks to a detailed presentation on the year-to-date advertising spend. When his eyes flit in my direction, I offer him an apologetic nod as I take out my diary, scribing some important points. But then I catch my assistant, Oliver, watching me with wide eyes and an obvious smirk pulling at the corners of his mouth as he assesses the glaringly obvious coffee stain on my shirt, accompanied by my frizzy, unruly hair. And it takes all I have not to throw my pen at his head from the opposite side of the glossy teak table.

"What on earth happened to you?" Oliver asks with a chuckle as he hurries behind me on my way out of the meeting.

I flash him a warning glare over my shoulder. "Don't even ask," I mutter through gritted teeth, trying my best to cover the brown stain on my silk shirt with my leather-bound diary. My phone vibrates, and I look down at the screen to see a blocked number calling. It's the sixth time so far this morning and they haven't even bothered to leave one message. *Take a damn hint, buddy.* I decline the call, noticing another three new text messages only adding to the myriad other messages already waiting for my attention.

"Is this Versace?" Oliver gasps incredulously, pulling my attention away from my phone as he tugs gently on my blouse.

"Yes," I answer sharply, stopping momentarily to collect a stack of copies from one of the interns' desks. "Can you please send for a new shirt from Saks. Black." I bark my order slightly more abruptly than I had intended before softening the blow with a wavering smile. "I'm sorry. I'm meeting Shareeq at eleven o'clock, and I can't show up like this."

With Oliver hot on my heels, I continue through the length of the bustling sales floor, toward my corner office. The office I've worked my butt off to secure. The office that means that I've made it. Glass walls, glass doors, floor-to-ceiling windows that look out over the concrete jungle that is Manhattan, providing an awe-inspiring view of the Chrysler Building reaching high up into the drab gray October sky. It feels like only yesterday I was tucked away in a cubicle by the fire escape doors, head buried in client cold-calling sheets. Now, here I am, in a glass box with a nice view, my name branded across the door in three-inch gold lettering.

"Someone's a little testy this morning," Oliver says from behind me, a teasing lilt to his voice.

"Yes. *Someone* is a little testy." I turn offering a droll look. "In case you haven't noticed"—I point to the stain on my shirt. "*Someone* didn't get to enjoy her morning coffee . . ."

Oliver chuckles.

My phone chimes again with another new text message and I hold it up in the air between us. "Is there a new listing I'm not aware of?"

He shakes his head with a shrug, taking my diary from me and placing it onto the console table beside the white leather chaise in the corner of the room.

"My phone is going nuts," I murmur under my breath, shaking my head to myself as I take my seat at my desk. I power up my computer, but when I click on my inbox, reading the subject line of my most recent email received less than an hour ago, an involuntary gasp escapes me, and suddenly it's as if I can't even breathe.

*Dear Miss Wagner,*

*I ran into Adam Delaney of CRTJ on Friday evening while I was dining with some associates at the Morrisey Club. We got talking about Prince Street. He raised some valid points about your suitability to take on the project. CRTJ specialize in the new-build market, and they have a dedicated project team for this type of listing.*

*Mr. Delaney also mentioned that he has firsthand experience with similar developments, particularly in the Tribeca area. He was also the sole listing agent for Broadway Towers, and sold more than 65% of all units at full ask or above within three weeks of the listing date.*

*Unfortunately, after much deliberation with my team, we feel it is in our best interest to go with Mr. Delaney and his team at CRTJ. I do hope there are no hard feelings. While I believe you're a tremendous agent, and I can't wait to work with you on future projects, we just feel Adam and his team will take better care of our needs during this time.*

*Please feel free to contact my assistant, Leilani, if you require anything further from me.*

*Kind regards,*

*Mihir Shareeq, Head of Operations, BSG*

"Son of a *bitch*!"

"What?" Oliver turns quickly, his face fraught with concern as he leans in closely, gawping over my shoulder.

"Adam Delaney . . ." I say his name in some sort of a daze as I scan the length of the email again and again, going through a plethora of emotions with each and every word. "He just– He just *stole* Prince Street."

I'm just about ready to grab my computer monitor and throw it straight through the damn plate glass window, down onto Madison Avenue. My heart races as panic begins to claim me from the inside out, and I look around for something, anything, I don't even know what.

"He can't do that!" Oliver shrieks indignantly, his voice pitchy and piercing. "BSG signed with *you*!"

"No." I shake my head as the weight of the world comes crashing down upon me. Burying my face in my hands, I could just about cry, and I probably would be crying right now if I wasn't so pissed off. "They *didn't* sign. That was my eleven o'clock with Shareeq."

Oliver says nothing as a tense and heavy silence rings through the air.

"Can you please go out and get me a coffee from the café downstairs?" I say, smoothing my hair back from my face as I take a deep, fortifying breath, hoping like hell it helps to provide some semblance of clarity so that I can deal with this situation effectively and rationally. "I need to figure out what the *hell* I'm going to do."

10

"I'll get Shareeq on the phone for you." Oliver moves quick smart, grabbing me a bottle of Fiji Water from the small refrigerator built into my closet. And that's what I love about him. He just knows what to do and when to do it. I don't even have to ask half the time. He's good in a crisis. Me? Not so much. In fact, I often have no idea what I'm doing. I'm just good at faking it.

I started at Hawkins Group fresh out of grad school with a drive like no other. And in that time, I've managed to work my way up the corporate ladder. From intern to assistant, to junior broker, to broker, to senior broker where I'm now in the top ten in all of Manhattan. I've fought hard over the years to make it to the top. I've sacrificed so much. Almost everything. And I'm damn good at my job. Ruthless at times, or so I've been told, but real estate is still very much a man's world in this city, and sometimes only the strong survive, which is why it is imperative that I keep my cool right now. I can't allow my emotion to show, despite my internal panic. I won't let Adam win.

Adam Delaney has had it in for me ever since a client chose me to list his thirty-million-dollar Columbus Circle penthouse, because my pitch was better. Adam went on social media and not so subtly insinuated that I wear low-cut tops and tight skirts just to get what I want. Misogynistic jerk. I began proceedings to sue him for defamation. Our lawyers settled out of court. I won, of course. And ever since then, he's been vying to take me down one client at a time.

And with this latest stunt, stalking the likes of Mihir Shareeq, coincidentally crossing paths with him at a members' only gentlemen's club in the Upper East Side and casually bringing the luxury fourteen-unit new-build development he knew I was signing into conversation, well, he may have just succeeded.

"I have Shareeq's assistant on the line," Oliver's voice rings through the silence of my office.

"Thanks." I press the flashing button on my handset and wait, ignoring my ringing cell phone as it vibrates loudly on the desk with that same blocked number. I turn it over. Face down, so it doesn't keep distracting me.

"Miss Wagner?" Leilani, Shareeq's assistant, comes through the line, her voice deep and sultry.

"Is he in?" I ask briskly, wishing my racing heart would calm to a more manageable thrum. The sheer inconvenience of a heart attack right now would be all I need.

"I'm sorry, Miss Wagner, he's out of the office all morning."

"Well do you know where he is? It is *vital* that I speak with him." I stand, waving for Oliver through the glass wall to stop him on his way out. He notices my flailing hand and pauses, his brow furrowed as he waits.

"He's meeting with Mr. Delaney for brunch at Illusions. I don't know the address but I believe it is in SoHo."

"It's okay. I know where it is. Thank you so much," I say, signaling to Oliver to forget about fetching me my coffee and to get me a car and a driver immediately before quickly ending the call.

My cell rings again as I collect my things, but I shove it and everything else into my purse. I hurry to the closet and pull out the blazer I keep in there for emergency situations such as this. After I shrug it on, it does little to conceal the coffee stain, but it's all I have right now.

"Hawkins wants to see you in his office," Oliver says as he opens the door for me, his hands held up in the air in surrender.

"Now?" I gape at him from the threshold.

He nods, and I can tell by the way he's biting down on his bottom lip that this can't be good. Mr. Hawkins knows. I just know it. I've just lost the biggest deal of my career. It'd be stupid to think it would be anything *but* bad. I release an almighty sigh and begin toward the glass stairs that connect the sales floor to the executive level.

"Quinn, I heard about the Prince Street deal . . ." someone says from deep within the bowels of the sales floor.

"It's nothing," I yell back over my shoulder, waving a nonchalant hand in the air, my quavering voice doing little to help dispel the obvious doubts of my colleagues. But I ignore everyone and everything, my jaw clenching hard as I proceed up the stairs and into the sleek lobby of the executive floor.

Mr. Hawkins' glamorous executive assistant glances up from her computer, and I almost expect her to stop me, to ask me what I'm doing, but she doesn't. In fact, all she offers is a look of condolence complemented by a pitiful smile as I continue past her. God, even she knows I'm about to have my ass handed to me. My clammy hands ball into trembling fists at my sides as I try to count to ten. I stop momentarily at the imposing double doors, knocking just once.

"Enter!" a booming voice from the other side demands, and I'm literally quaking in my pumps as I reluctantly step inside.

Edward Hawkins is an institution. A force to be reckoned with. At seventy-eight years old and standing at only five-feet-two-inches, with thick wire-frame glasses and sheet-white hair, he's the most unexpectedly intimidating person I've ever come across in this cut-throat industry, and that's saying a lot in a city like New York. He meets my eyes with a threatening glower, turning in his chair and reclining ever so slightly, his stubby fingers steepled beneath his white-bearded chin. But I remain defiant, my chin raised slightly higher in a show of confidence I sure as hell don't feel on the inside.

"Sit."

Now, let me get one thing straight. I'm definitely not a "yes, sir; no, sir" kind of gal. I'm a self-respecting, confident woman who just so happened to grow up in a house full of men and thus can take care of myself in almost any and every situation. But when Edward Hawkins fixes you with that all-penetrating and intimidating look in his steely eyes, and tells you to sit, then you better damn well sit your ass down.

"What is this I'm hearing about Prince Street?" he asks in his native New Yorker-accent.

I clear my throat, forcing a smile as I take a tentative seat in the chair across from his sprawling mahogany desk. "It's nothing more than a misunderstanding, sir."

My cell rings again from deep inside my purse and I do all I can to pretend as if I don't even notice it. But I do notice it. So does he. He glances at my purse, his bushy brows drawing together. I blink once, my face impassive as the loud vibration continues through the heavy silence.

"You told me on Friday night that the deal was done," he says finally, regarding me with a hard look over the top of his spectacles. "So, were you lying then or are you lying *now*?"

I swallow hard, carefully considering my words. He's got me there. When he called me, late Friday evening, I was so happy to be able to give him the good news, and of course I told him the deal was done. Because, as far as I was concerned, the deal was done. Shareeq and I shook hands, and where I come from that means something; all a man has is his word and his handshake. Clearly, I was wrong.

"I'm on my way to meet with Shareeq right now to get everything sorted."

Mr. Hawkins narrows one of his eyes, looking at me long and hard. "Do I need to remind you that this is a one-hundred-million-dollar deal?"

"No, sir." I shake my head.

He quirks a dubious brow. "And do I need to remind you what *losing* a deal like this can do to a person's career?"

I shake my head again, vehemently this time, not trusting myself to speak.

With one last lingering look of disappointment, he dismisses me without so much as another word, turning back to his computer, and I take that as my cue to leave, jumping up quickly and hurrying to the door.

"Wagner?"

I stop, my hand on the door handle, and I glance over my

shoulder to find him still staring at his illuminated monitor. "Y-yes, sir?"

"Don't bother coming back to the office without that signed listing contract." He flashes me a hard yet fleeting once-over. "Do I make myself clear?"

With one swift nod I slip out of the office as seamlessly as I can, fully aware of that same relentless vibration coming from the depths of my purse yet again. I hurry across the shiny floor, cursing out loud when I make it out into the silent foyer, and I frantically press that elevator call button over and over again, as if my life depends on it.

Illusions is a pretentious bistro in the thick of SoHo, and with the morning traffic against me, it takes more than thirty-five minutes to get here. It's quicker on the damn subway. By the time my town car pulls up to the curb out front, I'm a clammy, breathless mess as I cut across the sidewalk, bursting into the restaurant with such gusto, all heads turn to see what the commotion is about.

"Can I help you, miss?" The hostess glances up from her lectern, eyeing me cautiously.

I ignore her, scanning the dining room until I find a familiar head of perfectly highlighted hair, Mihir Shareeq's face falling in stark shock when he catches sight of me, causing Adam Delaney to turn and do an almost hilarious double take.

"You!" I yell, pointing a finger at Adam from across the room, because now is not the time for manners. "Outside. *Now!*" I storm back out to the bustling downtown sidewalk, taking my first real breath in what feels like forever.

"Quinn?"

I turn, finding Adam stepping out of the restaurant, buttoning his blazer, his brow raised in piqued interest as he looks me up and down. He pinches his bottom lip between his thumb and forefinger in an attempt to hide his growing smirk, and my anger increases exponentially.

"Don't give me that look, *Delaney*. You know full well what I'm doing here," I hiss between gritted teeth, stepping right up against him.

He barely bothers to conceal his smugness, leveling me with a single look. And I swear, it takes every last ounce of self-control I have left in me not to clock him with my surprisingly strong left hook. "What the *hell* are you playing at?"

He scoffs, innocently holding his arms out at his sides. "Hey, babe, it's just *business*." He glances up toward the sky, scratching his chin in mock-consideration. "Isn't that what you told me when you *stole* Columbus Circle?"

"First of all, *don't* call me babe!" I warn him. "Secondly, I didn't *steal* anything." I poke him in his chest. "I won that listing fair and square. I can't help it if you can't pitch to save your damn life."

He rolls his eyes indulgently before grinning down at me with that condescending smile I just want to slap right off his pretty-boy face. "Look, why don't you just come inside, we'll chat with Shareeq and maybe we can do a co-listing?"

I fold my arms over my chest, glowering at him.

"I don't know why you don't take me up on my offer to partner up. The two of us together could *kill* it in this city. Number-one agent—" He points to himself, pausing as he looks to me. "And what? Number . . . twelve?"

"Eight!" I seethe. "And I wouldn't partner up with you if my life depended on it."

He scoffs, quirking a brow. "That's not what you were saying a few months ago when you were sleeping in my bed."

I swallow back a string of profanities.

Yes. Call me a masochist, but Adam and I dated. I'm a sucker for punishment. I refer to our two-month tryst as an unfortunate lapse in judgment, a moment of insanity, something I've wished I could take back every day since.

"I swear to God, Adam—" My hand balls into a fist, but before I can do anything, my phone rings yet again, only this time I

16

choose to answer it in the hope it will stop me from killing this impossible asshole in broad daylight where there are far too many witnesses.

"What?" I snap abruptly as I hit the answer-call button.

"Quinn?"

My brows knit together in confusion at the sound of the familiar voice coming through from the other end of the line, crackly and muffled, nearly inaudible. I turn away from Adam, shoving a finger into my other ear in the hope of hearing over the excessive sound of New York City going about its usual business around me. "Hello?"

"Quinn, it's me, Cash."

I can't help but balk. I don't even remember the last time my big brother called me. "Cash? W-what's—"

"You need to come home, Quinny," Cash says with a heavy sigh of despondency.

"What? Cash! What are you talking about?" I shake my head in exasperation, glancing furtively over my shoulder to find Adam watching on like the nosy prick he is. He probably thinks I'm speaking to another client he can steal from me. I get back to my brother's confusing, cryptic phone call. "What is it? What's wrong, Cash?"

"Quinn, it's Dad," Cash's deep voice continues. "H-he's dead."

# Chapter 2

It's been almost ten years since I've been home. Ten years. And yet the two-hour drive from the city, following the banks of the Yellowstone as it runs through the mountains and the valleys, is a drive I know like the back of my hand. Every corner, every dip, every bump in the road is familiar. I could drive it with my eyes closed and never once take a wrong turn. And yet it's been ten long years since I've bothered driving this road because I'm too damn stubborn and proud.

As I navigate my Land Rover rental through the winding roads of the Rocky Mountain foothills, beneath the sky-high ponderosa pines, their branches creating a canopy overhead, my heart races as an unbearable anxiousness begins to consume me from the inside out, the closer I get to my destination. My palms are clammy. My stomach twists. Sweat beads on my brow. I can barely even breathe. I had no intention of ever coming back here. Not after everything. I shouldn't be here. It doesn't matter that it's almost ten years later. I'm still the girl who left Colt Henry at the altar. The girl who broke the heart of the hometown hero. To the people of Black Canyon, I'll probably always be that girl, no matter how many years have passed.

I still remember the look in his eyes when he came to find

me afterwards. When he forced me to tell him what I feared admitting out loud.

I still remember that look of betrayal, the hurt and the pain that I was responsible for inflicting upon him. I still remember it like it was yesterday, not ten years ago. Because that kind of thing will stay with you forever. That look in his eyes haunts me, flashing in my mind every time I close my eyes, as if to remind me of everything I once had, what I'll never have again because I was stupid enough to let it go in the first place.

I swallow the guilt and remorse that lingers at the back of my throat, reminding myself of my father and the reason that I'm here.

It still feels like some horrible nightmare. Except it wasn't a nightmare. It was real. It *is* real. A quick glance in the rearview mirror reminds me just how real it all is. The bruise on my forehead and the graze on my cheek that I suffered when I collapsed from shock, right there on the sidewalk in front of Adam Delaney, is real. The shattered screen on my cell phone from when it fell with me to the pavement, is real. And, the call that started it all was and still is, painfully real.

My father is dead. The one man I've looked up to all my life. My hero. My everything. The one man who has always been there for me, to protect me, to keep me safe, to make everything better. He's gone and I didn't even get to say goodbye or tell him that I love him just one last time. I lost the last ten years with him because of my mistake, and now there's nothing I can do about it.

I close my eyes for a beat and grip the steering wheel so tight my knuckles turn a stark shade of white. My chest constricts around my heart, the pain almost unbearable. Tears sting the backs of my eyes, begging for release. But I won't cry. I can't. I've spent the best part of the last twenty-four hours crying. I don't know how many tears I have left.

When the trees part and Black Canyon comes into view, for a moment my breath is taken away because in the ten years I've been

19

gone, I'd forgotten just how beautiful it is. Surrounded by thick, lush forest, rolling hills, and looming snow-capped peaks, the tiny town really is a beautiful little secret, hidden in the middle of nowhere. A diamond in the rough of the unforgiving wilderness.

A light rain drizzles down over the windshield as I make my way into the city limits and the dark, threatening clouds begin to envelop the mountains, casting an ominous hue over the town.

Releasing a trembling breath, I scrub a hand over my weary face, sniffling back the traitorous tears that continue to threaten me as I drive into the place that brings back so many memories, passing the familiar buildings that haven't changed one bit in the time that I've been away. Everything is still the same, and yet nothing is the same. I'm a different person to the one I was when I walked away from this place all those years ago, never even bothering to look back.

If I could go back and undo all the shitty things I've done in my life, I would. In a heartbeat. But I can't. And now here I am, ten years later and my whole world as I've known it is falling apart. I didn't expect to feel so sick to my stomach. But I guess that's what happens when you come back to the one place you vowed never to return to.

Ten or so miles along the desolate road that leads out of town and in the direction of the ranges, I pull into the familiar drive, glancing up at the sign hanging overhead as it swings to and fro with the violent wind of the fast-approaching storm: Wagner Ranch. Home. At least, it used to be home. It's not anymore. In fact, it hasn't been home for so long that even just driving through the gates and into the thirty thousand acres of expansive, sprawling land, I can't help but feel like I don't belong here. Like I'm an imposter. A trespasser at the risk of being shot by a ranch hand.

I follow the rocky drive, looking out over the fields to my left where what appears to be a hundred head of cattle are grazing high up in the hills, to my right where buffalo are roaming free. Wagner Ranch lies in the thick of the country, what feels like a million miles from the rest of the world, a whole lifetime away from the metropolis of New York where I've spent most of my adult life.

Thick, heavy clouds cover the mountains, and in the distance a deep rumble of thunder follows a violent fork of lightning, but thankfully, just as the rain starts to fall harder against the windshield, the main house comes into view up ahead and I breathe a sigh of relief. The imposing log and stone structure I grew up in, the place I used to pretend was my castle and I, its princess, is illuminated like a beacon in the darkness of the fast-approaching storm, each window aglow giving off an air of warmth and comfort like only a home can.

Pulling into a makeshift parking spot between a shiny Dodge Ram with the ranch's logo emblazoned across the side, a sleek Range Rover and a rusted F-250 pickup with a busted tail light, I grab my slicker and my handbag, leaving everything else in the car before making a run for it. By the time I make it up onto the porch, my sneakers are covered in mud and my jeans are soaked up to my knees.

Inside, the house is as I remember it, and as I take in the vast foyer, looking up at the exposed beams in the twenty-foot ceilings I'm struck by a million memories flooding through me at once, and despite my sadness, I can't help but smile. The mounted bison head that used to scare me as a kid and, quite frankly, still does, sits high above the stairs, its black eyes lifeless yet terrifying as they bore into me. Then a sudden wave of emotion crashes over me, tugging painfully at my heart, and never before have I missed my father the way I miss him right now. He feels so close and this place smells just like him. But there's something missing, and it's so obvious that despite everything that is so familiar to me, so much like him, he's no longer here, and that familiarity suddenly feels so empty and void.

With a defeated sigh, I hang my slicker on the hook by the front door before inviting myself in. The great room that steps down to the left is empty, the fireplace alight with a crackling fire that warms the cavernous expanse of the entire downstairs. The kitchen and dining to the right is empty, not a single thing out of place. I continue through to the corridor, stopping at the framed photographs of me, my brothers, my father, our mom lining the walls, and as I study the old picture of my parents on their wedding day, I reach out, gently stroking the glass with a resigned smile because I know they're together again in a better place where my mom is happy, but that doesn't mean it hurts any less.

Hearing the faint sound of a murmured conversation coming from my father's office at the end of the hall, I hesitate momentarily, smoothing my hair back from my face before heading toward the voices. I knock on the open door before walking nervously inside, and it takes a moment for my glassy eyes to adjust to the muted light in the room. But when they do, I pause on the spot when I find Cash standing by the floor-to-ceiling window, looking out over the land, his silhouetted form cutting a lonely figure that hurts my heart.

"What the *hell* are *you* doing here?"

I startle, turning in the direction of the desk, to the darkened figure standing so fast, the chair topples to the floor, big hands slamming down upon the glossy oak in a show of fury I hadn't been prepared for, which causes me to jump in fear for my life.

I manage to collect myself, clutching at my racing heart. "Hey . . . Tripp."

My twin brother looks at me in a way that stings like an abrupt and unexpected slap to the face. The disdain in his hard glare is unmistakable, piercing through the dim light of the room. He folds his arms across his broad chest, shaking his head at the sheer sight of me, his top lip actually curling up in disgust, and I can't say it doesn't hurt. It hurts like hell and it's an added pain I'm not sure I can handle right now.

22

"What do you think you're doing here?" he asks again between gritted teeth before looking to Cash for answers. "Cash, what's she doing here?" he demands, waving a hand in my direction.

"I called her," Cash says gruffly, turning, his eyes finding me.

I shake my head incredulously. What am I doing here? Is he actually serious? "My father is dead!" I exclaim, my eyes wide as I gape at Tripp. "You actually thought I *wouldn't* come home?"

"Like you give a shit," Tripp mutters, shaking his head.

"Are you *serious*? How can you even say that?!" I yell, my voice breaking from the overwhelming emotion coming over me at just how little he clearly thinks of me.

"We ain't heard squat from you in years!"

I balk at his words spoken with such vitriol, gaping at him.

Haven't heard from me? Yeah, well whose fault is that, Tripp? I want to laugh in his face. But I don't. He really does still hate me, even after all the time that's passed. But he's so wrong it's scary, and although it doesn't really matter at this time, I have to correct him. "I call him every single day. And every Sunday after church," I yell, my tears getting the better of me, which I'm quick to swipe from my heated cheeks with the sleeve of my sweater. "I sit on the phone with him for an hour every Thursday morning while he approves the payroll. Hell, I call him after every damn Packers game because I know how worked up he gets watching his team play!" I take a deep, racking breath trying so hard to calm myself, closing my eyes a moment to placate my emotion.

"Yeah, well, he's dead. You won't have to worry about calling no more," Tripp says, looking down at the desk, to the papers strewn across it.

I gape at him, at his brutally harsh words, tears blinding me. But I bite back my retort. He's hurting. We all are. I soften a little. "I came home to help." I glance at both of my brothers. "Any way that I can."

Tripp scoffs, a derisive laugh void of any humor ringing

through the air. "You're here to *help*? Or you're here sniffing around for your *inheritance*?"

My jaw actually drops, my heart stammering. His words are like a rusty knife to my stomach.

"Easy, little brother . . ." Cash warns, taking a step forward to stand between us.

Tripp looks from me to Cash and back again, murmuring a few choice curse words under his breath that I can't quite make out over the sound of the rain as it pours down outside.

I hold my trembling hands in the air in surrender. "Look, Tripp. I didn't come here to fight. I came here to say goodbye to my father . . ." Emotion gets the better of me, a sob bubbling up from the back of my throat, but I force myself to continue. "To help with the funeral, and—"

"We've been doing just fine without you, Quinny," he interrupts with a huff, looking me up and down, a scornful glint flashing within his steely eyes, a look that cuts straight through me. "We don't need no help. Especially not from *you*." And, with those parting words, he turns and storms out of the room, leaving an air of anger, sadness and loathing in his wake.

I stand there a moment, my shoulders falling in defeat. I'm not sure what I was expecting. I knew my return wouldn't receive the warmest of receptions, but I never expected my own brother— my *twin*—to ever look at me the way he just did. I swallow the painful lump that feels as if it's strangling me, sniffling back the emotion threatening to break what little composure I have left.

"He didn't mean that."

I turn, finding Cash's eyes watching me, and I exhale a trembling breath, pressing my lips together in the semblance of a smile. "Yes, he did, Cash. He meant every word."

Cash crosses the room, coming to stop in front of me, and I'm actually a little taken aback when he pulls me into his arms, enveloping me in a hug that just about knocks the wind out of me. I hesitate, because an embrace like this is foreign to me. It's

24

been a long time since anyone's held me in such a way. I tentatively wrap my arms around him, closing my eyes, and as I breathe in his familiar scent that reminds me so much of Dad, I realize right at that moment that this is exactly what I need.

"Well *I'm* glad you're here," he whispers into my hair before pulling away, his big hands resting on my shoulders.

I blink back my emotions, looking up at him with a small smile. "W-where . . . Where is he?"

"They took him to the city for an autopsy. He'll be transported back tomorrow."

I clear my throat. "When can I see him?"

"I'll take you to the funeral home tomorrow."

The words are all too real right now, and my knees feel weak. I reach a hand out, gripping Cash's in the fear that I might actually fall to the floor. He steadies me, and I meet his dark eyes that are so much like my father's it's almost frightening.

"What happened?"

Cash presses his lips together, shaking his head as he so clearly searches for his words. "He was out in the back paddock with Colt—" He stops himself, and it's as if he suddenly realizes what he's said. He flashes me an apologetic glance before averting his eyes and casting his gaze down to the floor.

For a moment even just the mention of his name causes my stomach to twist, my heart jolting in my chest, fighting against the vise-like grip my emotions have on it. "Colt . . ."

Cash nods, and I find some semblance of comfort knowing that it was Colt who was with my father at the time. That he wasn't alone. That Colt, the boy he loved like another son, was there to comfort him until help came, whether he knew it or not.

"They were out riding the east boundary, checking the fence. Colt said one minute he was fine, the next he just fell from his horse like a ton of bricks. Heart attack. The coroner called just before you got here to tell us he was most likely dead before he even hit the ground."

I close my eyes, trying so hard to process my brother's words but it's almost impossible. It's hard to believe because I don't want to believe it. I spoke to my father just two days ago. Two days. And two days ago he was fine. He said he was even thinking of finally taking me up on my offer and flying out to the East Coast to come visit me after years of begging him. I shake my head at that thought. It should have been me who came back here to see him. Why couldn't I just come home?

"God dammit . . ." I hiss under my breath, wiping at my damp cheeks.

"C'mere," Cash mutters through his own emotion, pulling me back into another embrace.

"I'm gonna go back into town." I swallow a sob, prematurely breaking our hug and taking a step back. "Grab a room at the Oakmont or the Lodge," I say with a casual shrug, smoothing my hair back from my face.

"No, Quinny, don't leave." Cash shakes his head, his face falling, and for the first time I can see a distraught sadness in his eyes, and it's heartbreaking to see my brother who has always been the strong one, stoic like our father, reduced to such a state of fragility. "Stay. This is *your* home. Dad would *want* you here."

More tears prick my eyes at his words but I blink them away. "I think it's best if I just stay away from Tripp for a few days."

"Don't worry about him. Come stay in the Foreman's House. It's just me, Shelby and CJ," Cash offers, his eyes hopeful. "Don't you wanna see your nephew? He's always asking about you."

"Of course I do! But . . . I-I just . . . I can't—" I shake my head, and while Tripp is my main concern, I'm also conscious of the fact that Colt is a permanent fixture around the place, living in my grandfather's old cabin on the property, and I just don't think I'm ready to risk facing that whole situation right now.

"I'll be back tomorrow. First thing." I nod, stepping around my brother and walking out of the office.

Continuing back down the hall, I see Tripp on my way past

26

the doorway to the kitchen, and I pause in my tracks. His eyes momentarily meet mine and I witness a flash of something I wasn't expecting to see in his glassy gaze, but whatever it was is quickly replaced by that same anger and pure hatred they'd possessed moments earlier, so I continue on my way down the hall toward the entry.

As I shrug my slicker on in the foyer, I can't mistake the sound of my brothers' voices arguing from down the corridor. They're fighting about me. I know it. But I choose to ignore their heated exchange, walking outside where I'm met with gusty winds and torrential rain blanketing down from the low-hanging clouds in the looming gray sky.

"Home, sweet home," I mutter under my breath as I pull my hood up over my head, making a run for it down the steps and through the knee-deep puddles, back toward the safety of my rental car.

# Chapter 3

Growing up, I was a daddy's girl. From the day I was born. Daddy's sweet little fair-eyed angel. His favorite; and those are his words, not mine. Hell, he used to say it all the time even in front of my brothers. I was his favorite. It was an undeniable fact.

When our mother lost her battle against depression, Tripp and I were only eight years old. Cash was twelve. Tripp seemed to be okay, following in his older brother's footsteps. Me? Well, I latched on to my father. I went everywhere with him. I was his shadow. He and I were so close. The best of friends. No one could make my father smile the way I could. I think it was because I reminded him so much of my mom. The two of us were inseparable. But then, I unknowingly went and broke his heart.

The first time I broke my father's heart was when I was fifteen. I asked him if he could drive me into town so I could meet Colt at Danny's Diner for ice cream. Of course he asked me what the hell I was doing meeting up with the likes of Colt Henry on a Saturday night without Tripp. I was honest, and I told him it was because Colt asked me. It was a date. My first. With my twin brother's best friend of ten years, no less. I'll never forget the look of resignation in my father's eyes that day. I think that was the moment he realized I wasn't his little angel

28

anymore. I had a new guy in my life. It was time for poor old Dad to take his seat.

When Colt asked me to be his girlfriend that night at the diner, of course my brother made a big fuss out of it, accusing me of coming between him and his best friend, of stealing Colt away. But I didn't steal Colt. In fact, it was Colt who began choosing to hang out with me instead of Tripp, when he wasn't busy working for my father on the ranch or playing football for our high school's varsity team. But that's what happens. Kids turn into teenagers, and teenage boys start to choose teenage girls over their best friends. I felt bad, but at fifteen years old I'd fallen head over heels for that green-eyed boy from the wrong side of town, and neither my father nor my brother could do anything to get in the way of a star-crossed love like ours.

The second time I broke my father's heart was when Colt asked me to marry him. He'd surprised me on the five-year anniversary of that first date, with his grandmother's ring tucked into the pocket of his pants. Colt, dressed in his Wrangler jeans and pearl-snap shirt, and the big shiny belt buckle he'd won at some rodeo a few months earlier that had secured him the money to be able to fly out to New York, looking so out of place in the city. He got down on one knee right there by the fountain in the middle of Washington Square Park and asked me to be his wife. And of course I said yes. I loved him. More than life itself. He was my all. My everything. I couldn't imagine my life not being with Colt, and I immediately started to plan a June wedding at the ranch for when I would be home that coming summer.

Despite his reservations about ultimately being replaced as the man in my life, my father was happy. Even Tripp was okay about our engagement. In fact, everyone was excited for us; mine and Colt's wedding was the talk of the Canyon, the event of the year. The wealthy rancher's daughter and the boy from the wrong side of town. We were *that* couple. Two people who were born for one another. Our love was a love that people depended on.

It gave them hope that true love really did exist, and that it was more than a myth read about in fairy tales.

But then the doubts started creeping into the back of my mind. I loved Colt. Irrevocably. I knew I'd never be able to love anyone else the way I loved him. But was I really ready at twenty years old to legally commit myself to one man for the rest of my life? I was still a kid. I had my whole life ahead of me. I'd dreamed of business school, and then I planned on building a career for myself in the city. But Colt hated city life. He had no intention of ever leaving the Canyon. Was I supposed to marry Colt, forfeit my dreams, and live happily ever after as nothing more than a rancher's wife who gave up everything for the man she loved?

I couldn't do it. Anytime I so much as considered it, my mind would wander back to that time just before my mother's death, when she made me promise that I would chase my dreams. I couldn't stay. She gave up on her dreams to stay with my dad and raise a family, and look how that turned out. Granted, she was unwell, but I just couldn't risk ending up like that. I owed it to my mother to live my life and chase my dreams, despite my love for Colt.

My father was the only one who stood by me through my decision. Sure he told me what I did was wrong. But he still stood by me. And that was the third and final time I broke his heart. When I left. He could see it in my eyes when I said goodbye to him at the airport that day. He knew I wouldn't ever be coming back, and that broke his heart.

Maybe my father's death wasn't my fault, but I'd broken his heart so many times it was fragile because of me, and I can't help but feel as if my hands are stained with his blood.

I pull up to a parking spot in the middle of town, the rain relentless as it thunders down onto the roof of the car, so loud it's almost unbearable. And, for the first time since getting onto the Delta flight back at JFK, the weight of everything that's happened over the last twenty-four hours, the last ten years, comes crashing down around me. I grip the steering wheel so tight as if it's my lifeline, bowing my head as a sob racks through me, hot tears falling onto my cheeks as I cry over everything I've lost. My father. My brother. My home. Everything my life was once about is gone. In one day it feels as if my whole life and everything I've ever known has literally been ripped right out from underneath me, and all I can do is cry.

After a moment or two I somehow manage to pull myself together as best I can, sitting up a little straighter and wiping away my tears with the back of my hand when something catches my attention, flickering in the reflection of the rearview mirror. I turn, glancing over my shoulder, my bleary eyes finding the familiar neon sign of Duke's flashing on and off through the darkness of the gloomy gray afternoon. With a deep breath that trembles through my emotions, I grab my handbag, pulling my hood back over my head, and I force myself out into the rain. I swear I've never been so desperate for a shot of whiskey in my life.

Duke's Saloon, the main bar in town, is the kind of place that can turn pretty nasty after dark when the cowboys show up to drink away their troubles. But it's also a lot of fun. We used to come here when we were kids. Duke, the owner, would serve us even though he was friends with most of our parents and therefore knew our ID's were blatantly fake. It didn't hurt that I was the daughter of Royal Wagner. Growing up in a town like Black Canyon, where everyone knows everyone else, it was difficult to get away with too much trouble, but Duke let it slide. Many a night was spent underage drinking, dancing to the live band while having the time of our young lives right here at Duke's, and I can't help but smile at the long-forgotten memories playing through my mind as I walk into the saloon.

Inside is quiet. Just a few die-hard locals perched at the bar nursing beers while an old country song twangs softly from somewhere in the background. I continue with my head down because I'm not sure I'm ready to risk showing my face around here just yet. If my own brother can't even stand the sight of me, then I doubt the rest of the town will be very welcoming.

I take one of the stools at the far end of the bar, placing my handbag onto the counter while I scan the shelves of liquor, sniffling back my earlier tears. I rifle through my purse, pulling out a fifty-dollar bill and gripping it with a trembling hand while waiting for service, which is when a curvy brunette with one arm completely covered in tattoos walks down from the opposite end of the bar, an enviable sway to her rounded hips.

"What can I get ya, doll?"

I clear my throat. "Crown. Straight up." I place my money onto the bar. "And keep them coming, please."

She nods, an impressed glimmer in her eyes as she regards me a moment before grabbing a clean glass and the bottle of Crown Royal from the selection of colorful liquor bottles. She expertly pours my drink right in front of me, sliding it over with a smile. I drop it back, wincing at the afterburn as it trails its way down my throat, tapping the empty glass against the walnut counter, which she quickly refills.

"You're not from around here, huh?" She smirks at me, quirking a perfectly microbladed brow as she fills a second glass for herself.

"What gave it away?" I ask with a perfunctory shrug, sipping my whiskey this time.

She leans forward, looking over the counter, assessing me. "Gucci sneakers. Chanel purse."

"Girl knows her designers," I say with one arched brow.

"What can I say? I keep up with the Kardashians." She laughs lightly, meeting my eyes as she drops back her own shot of Crown.

"I *used* to be from around here." I shrug again, offering her a small smile I know doesn't reach my eyes, and something passes between us. I can tell she senses my sadness. "Not anymore . . ." I add dismissively.

She stares at me, pressing her lips together, before holding her hand out. "I'm Rylie."

I look down at her long, pointed nails, glittery and perfectly painted. I meet her eyes once again, noticing the precise winged liner and thick lashes that must have taken her forever to apply. She really does keep up with Kardashians. And I like her. Not because of the Kardashians, but because she obviously chooses not to conform with a place like the Canyon. Tattoos. Winged liner. Neon nails. I like her a lot. I could be friends with a woman like Rylie.

"Quinn." I shake her hand.

"So, Quinn . . ." Rylie leans forward, resting her elbows on the bar, steadying me with a penetrating stare. "What's a Gucci-wearing gal like you doing in a dive like this?" She waves a hand in the air, indicating Duke's Saloon.

"I like this place." I take in the familiar surrounds. "It reminds me of home."

Rylie watches me for a beat, and I know she can tell there is so much more to my story. But, like a well-trained bartender, she doesn't pry; she simply waits until I choose whether or not I feel like she's a complete stranger I can trust. Bartenders get this a lot. It's part of their job. A prerequisite. To listen to drunk fools bitch and moan all day long about their problems while pretending to care.

"Can I ask you something, Rylie?"

She nods, offering a casual shrug as she tops up both of our glasses.

I hesitate momentarily before suddenly asking, "Do you believe in redemption?"

She blinks at me, and I guess the topic of redemption is pretty heavy for four-thirty on a Tuesday afternoon. So I add, "Like, if a person's done something terrible in their past, do you think they can really redeem themselves?"

Rylie takes a sip of her whiskey, glancing up to the low-hanging beams in the ceiling for a moment. She narrows one of her eyes as if to seriously consider my question before finally meeting my stare once again. "I think it depends."

My brow furrows. "On what?"

"On whether or not the person is an asshole."

I stare at her, not having expected such a brutally honest response.

"I mean, you're either an asshole or you're not," she continues. "Good people do shitty things. It doesn't necessarily make them bad." She shrugs again. "So, if you're not an asshole, then I think you can definitely redeem yourself. But, if you are, then you may as well just keep on being an asshole, because nothing's gonna change the way you are."

I press my lips together, looking down at my glass. No words have ever resonated with me more.

"But, Quinn?"

I glance up again, meeting Rylie's eyes with my own. She cocks her head to the side, offering an ever so subtle smile. "You're not an asshole, doll. I can tell."

She offers me a conspiratorial wink before turning and heading over to a customer holding his empty glass in the air, and I breathe a sigh of relief because there's just something about Rylie; I trust her. I like her. And, she's right. I'm not an asshole. I just hope I can redeem myself. I need to at least try to make things right—for my father, my brother, for myself.

But, right now, before I begin making anything right, I need to get drunk. I need to forget. And as I down yet another shot of whiskey, that is exactly what I intend on doing. Redemption can wait until morning.

34

# Chapter 4

Two, maybe three hours later, I'm drunk as sin. So drunk, in fact, I can't even find my damn lips to drink from the bottle of Miller Lite my cute new cowboy-friend bought for me at the bar after offering me a panty-dropping grin I'm sure works for him most nights with all the girls.

That's the great thing about cowboys. They come and go, from one town to the next, so often, a woman like me is a literal nobody to them. He doesn't know me. He doesn't know I'm Royal Wagner's daughter. He doesn't know I'm the girl who left Colt Henry at the altar. He has no idea the unimaginable pain I've caused to some of the people I love most in my life. This guy knows nothing about me, and I know nothing about him. He could be an ex-con for all I know, running from a jaded past like most cowboys who come through the Canyon. He could have a damn wife and kid back in some trailer park somewhere. Who knows? We're strangers, he and I. And right now that's just what I need. To be a stranger. A nobody. To forget everything, even if only for one night.

Outside, the earlier downpour is nothing more than a few deep puddles on the ground, but the air is icy cold and thick with the threat of more rain. I shiver, my teeth involuntarily chattering together as I try to smoke the cigarette my cowboy has kindly given me. I don't smoke. But I guess I'm smoking tonight. I'm doing a lot of things I wouldn't normally do tonight, such as barely managing to keep myself upright, swaying unsteadily as I breathe a plume of toxic white smoke up into the inky night sky.

Inside, the band continues playing an emotional, guitar-heavy tune that rings through the air, the music comforting on a night like tonight. But, out here, I'm all alone with my cowboy as he stands so close, one arm wrapped around my waist, keeping me from falling to the ground. And as the sad song drifts out through the saloon doors, I keep thinking back to the way Tripp looked at me back at the ranch. I'm not an idiot. I could see it in his eyes. He doesn't just hate me. He despises me. In fact, I bet he'd rather I was dead right now, instead of our father. I know I hurt him with what I did all those years ago, I know what I did was wrong. I hurt Colt, I hurt my brother, I hurt everyone with my decision. But haven't I paid enough for my mistake?

"You okay, sugar?"

I lift my chin to see the cute cowboy looking down at me, his lopsided grin faltering momentarily. And it's at that moment that I realize I'm crying, my cheeks damp from my silent tears. I sniffle, shaking my head. I'm not okay. I'm far from it. My father just died. He's gone. I'm not going to ever talk to him on the phone again. I'm never going to hear his gruff chuckle, the laughter he tries to hide through a fake cough. He's just gone. And I'm here, drunk on a darkened street corner, with some random cowboy who so clearly just wants in my panties, smoking a damn cigarette.

This is the last place I should be, right now, and it's time for me to go before I do something I'll no doubt have to add to the already long list of my life's regrets. But as I turn, murmuring a goodbye, I start to walk away, but his hold on me tightens, and I stumble against his reluctance to let me go.

"Whoa." He takes the opportunity to wrap both his arms around me, pulling me even closer to him in the process. "I've got you, sweetheart."

Normally those words might sound sweet, endearing. He's *not going to let me fall*. He's *got me*. But there's something in the way he's looking down at me. Something in his darkening eyes. Something in the way his hands move down to my hips, holding me almost indecently, like a man shouldn't hold a woman he's only known for fifteen forgettable minutes.

"I s-should go," I stammer. "I need to get home . . ."

"Home?" He scoffs derisively. "I thought you had a room here in town . . ."

I try to move away, but his hold tightens so much that I'm almost sure my skin will bruise. I meet his eyes and when I catch something dangerous within his hard stare, something I don't like, my fight-or-flight responses begin to stir, and I know I have to stand up for myself or else he's going to think he's won.

So, with as much force as I can muster, I shrug out of his grip, causing him to falter just enough to lose his cool. And suddenly, my cute cowboy with the lopsided grin is replaced by a pissed-off jerk with fire in his eyes. He puffs his chest out, looking me up and down, and it's clear within his dark gaze that no woman before me has ever fronted up to him. Lunging forward, he grabs my wrists, pulling me so close I can feel his hot breath on my skin, and it is at that precise moment that I'm reminded we're out on a dimly lit side street, all alone, and I can't help but think I might be in way over my head.

"Let me go!" I yell, forcing myself not to cower beneath the weight of his intimidating glower, but it's difficult. I consider myself a strong woman, but the look in his eyes alone is terrifying.

He doesn't say a word. Instead he throws me back against the side of the truck parked at the curb, flanking my petite frame, each of his hands planting on either side of my head. On the inside I'm petrified. I've never been in such a position. I know this could turn bad at any moment. But I'm also drunk. And with the alcohol comes Dutch courage that is strictly for show.

"What are you gonna do, huh? You gonna hit me? Rough me up a little?" I quirk a brow, challenging him with a wavering smirk.

He slams his hand against the metal right beside my head. "I'm gonna teach you a lesson, you little *bitch* . . ."

"What did you just call me?" A sudden burst of fury sears my skin, bubbling just beneath the surface from his words, alone. Call me whatever you want, but bitch? That is one word I simply will not accept. Immediately, I see red. My trembling left hand balls into a fist at my side, and before I can even consider the consequences, that same fist is connecting to the side of his face, knocking him senseless, even if only for a moment.

Unlucky for me though, he manages to collect himself with little effort, and before I can prepare myself for the impact, a big, calloused hand connects with my cheek with such force I can taste the metallic pang of blood in my mouth as silence rings through my head and my knees finally give way. With one slap he's knocked me out of it. I can't even see straight. It feels as if the entire left side of my face is on fire. But he keeps me upright, pinning me back against the truck, the back of my head slamming violently against the metal.

His steely eyes blaze through the darkness, his top lip curling as he looks down at me in disgust. And I know this is it, this is my demise, but for some reason I can't help but laugh. Maybe it's the liquor. Maybe it's everything that's happened over the last couple of days, the last ten years, but I laugh still, the sound empty, hollow, void of any humor.

"Do it!" I hiss, tears spilling onto my cheeks, despite my maniacal laughter.

With the way he's looking at me, I'm almost certain he's going to do it, whatever *it* might be. I've never been looked at in such a way. Like he could happily finish me, leave me for dead right here in the gutter, and sleep like a damn baby afterwards.

But, before he can do anything, a shadowy figure lurches out from the darkness, and in what appears to be slow motion, the cowboy is taken down in one fell swoop.

What the hell?

I stagger sideways, breathless as I try to compose myself, looking down at the two men grappling with one another on the pavement to the soundtrack of muttered curse words and bare-fisted knuckles connecting with bone. My mind is a haze of liquor, confusion and emotion. But then, my savior comes into the dim light of the nearby street lamp, looking up at me with one of his arms wrapped tightly around the cowboy's neck, holding him in place. And everything stops.

I'm rendered speechless, breathless, and everything in between.

Colt.

He forces the cowboy to look up at me, blood pouring from the man's nose as he chokes against the thick, sinewy arm strangling him.

"Do you know who that is?" Colt's gruff voice breaks through the silence of the night, a threatening growl. He pummels the cowboy once more in his gut with his relentless fist until he answers him.

"Who? Her?" The cowboy shakes his head, his eyes wide with fear. "What the hell are you talking about? I don't know—"

"I'll ask you one . . . more . . . time!" Colt says slowly, continuing his incessant assault. "Do you *know* who that *is*?"

"No!" the cowboy cries, and I almost feel bad for him.

"Tell him!" Colt shouts, not looking at me. "Tell him who you are, Quinny."

I stare down at the cowboy, his strength diminishing with every one of Colt's strikes. His eyes bore into mine and I hold his gaze as I spit the remnants of blood from my mouth to the ground right beside him. "Quinn . . . Wagner."

Recognition washes over him at the mention of my surname, his face suddenly falling in stark surprise. Oh he sure knows who

I am now. "I'm s-sorry. I'm— I didn't know, I—" He splutters through his words.

Colt's fist connects with the cowboy's face one final time before he releases his hold of the man's bloodied shirt, leaving him in a heap on the ground as he makes his way up to his feet, brushing his hands over his jeans. Calmly smoothing his chestnut hair back from his face, he blows out a breath between his lips, casting a furtive glance up and down the empty street. He turns to me, barely even indulging me with one single look, doing everything he can to avoid my eyes, his own evidently conflicted.

"Come on, I'll take you home," he mutters in a low voice, shaking out the swollen knuckles on his right hand. He turns and stalks up ahead, disappearing around the corner with nothing but the threatening air of anger left in his wake.

I cast one final glance down at the cowboy as he clutches at his side while whimpering in pain; sorrow and regret clear in his eyes when they meet mine. "I'm sorry," he groans.

I stare at him long and hard, shaking my head dismissively before hurrying as quickly as my drunken feet can carry me to follow after the ghost of my past.

Main Street is dark. Everything is so still. It's almost as if the whole world is asleep. Eerily silent. Icy cold. Ominous. The only sound ringing through the air is that of my sneakers as they squelch upon the wet pavement, through the puddles. Adrenaline, alcohol and something else races through me as I try to catch up to Colt, his long strides almost impossible to keep up with, even with the unsteady gait caused by the limp of his left leg. I stop then. A painful lump balling into the back of my throat at that thought. I caused that limp. That was my fault. I broke him. My heart suddenly hurts, but I try so hard to ignore the pain, running after him.

"Jesus, will you slow down?" I huff.

Of course, he doesn't slow down. In fact, I'm almost certain he speeds up. And that's it for me. If I wasn't drunk, I probably would just do as I'm told and follow him, but the whiskey in my veins fuels the stubbornness I inherited as a Wagner, so I stop right there in the middle of the wide empty street, glaring at the back of Colt's head as he surges toward the same shiny Dodge Ram emblazoned with the Wagner Ranch logo that had been parked back at the main house earlier.

I can't help but wonder . . . was he there when I was there?

Colt must sense I'm no longer following because he pauses, glancing over his shoulder at me, and when his eyes find me planted to the spot, a deep crease pulls into his brow. "C'mon, Quinn. I'm not playing."

"I'm not going back to the ranch." I shake my head defiantly. "I'm staying here. In town."

Colt guffaws, holding his hands out at his sides incredulously as he looks up and down the dark, empty street. "Where you gonna stay, huh?"

"The Oakmont," I answer matter-of-factly.

"They're closed for renovations, genius."

*Of course they are.* I'm in no state to get behind the wheel and drive across town to the Lodge. I curse under my breath. "Well," I begin, shrugging. "Then I'll just sleep in my rental."

He offers a sardonic look, quirking a brow.

"There is no way in hell I'm going back to that place." I shake my head vehemently. "I'm pretty sure Tripp is going to kill me in my sleep."

Colt looks up to the dark night sky, pinching the bridge of his nose. He seems to hesitate, considering something, then he curses out loud, meeting my eye with a no-bullshit look as he approaches me, stopping just a few feet away. "God dammit, Quinn. I ain't got time for this shit."

"So go!" I yell, throwing a hand in the air.

"You're still a stubborn piece of work," he grunts under his breath. But before I can even think of a retort, he crouches down and I'm suddenly being lifted off my feet, into the air, thrown

41

over his shoulder like a sack of potatoes, the whole world literally turning upside down, which isn't helping my current state of intoxication.

"What the— Let me down!" I scream, hands and feet flailing. But he ignores my demand, carrying me in the opposite direction of my rental car.

I hear the sound of metal hinges creak in objection before being up-righted and placed into the cab of Colt's truck. I go to say something, but he just slams the door right in my face, glaring at me through the foggy window before moving around the front and silently making his way up into the driver's seat. The loud engine comes to life, roaring thunderously through the night and drowning out the palpable silence between us.

"You know, I didn't ask for you to swoop in and save me back there."

He scoffs once under his breath, shaking his head to himself, and without saying a word, he shifts the truck into gear and pulls out onto the road and we drive in an uncomfortably steely silence through the pitch black of night.

The air between us is thick with tension, but I take the opportunity to glance at him from the corner of my eye, the dashboard lights illuminating his face, highlighting his infuriatingly striking features. I'd almost forgotten how beautiful he truly was. And wow. It's as if he's gotten even more so over the years. His strong jaw is now shadowed with a few days' growth of scruff. Those dimples are still there, the ones that pull into his cheeks each time he rakes his teeth over his full bottom lip; something he's always done whenever he feels awkward as hell and doesn't quite know what to say. A prominent nose, with the slightest bump on the bridge from when he broke it after coming off a bucking bronco for the first time when he was just sixteen years old. Thick lashes frame eyes that capture the glow of the muted lights, reflecting peridot and gold and silver.

He looks exactly the same as he did ten years ago. Maybe a few extra lines and creases at the corners of his eyes, his widow's peak a little more defined now than it was when we were younger, but he's just as handsome as I remember him, and the years have been kind. The sheer sight of him brings back those same overwhelming feelings I spent the last ten years of my life trying to get over. Or maybe I'm just drunk.

Colt suddenly casts a fleeting glance across to me, catching me ogling him, and I snap myself from my reverie, clearing the bubble of emotion from my throat while shifting a little awkwardly.

"You know, I could've kicked that guy's ass myself. I was doing just fine on my own."

"Yeah, you really looked like you were handling it," he murmurs sarcastically, his eyes focused intently on the road ahead, his grip on the steering wheel tight, causing his split knuckles to glisten as fresh blood seeps from the painful-looking cracks.

"Why do you care, anyway?" I scoff, leaning an elbow on the doorjamb to rest my chin upon my hand. I exhale a heavy sigh. "You *hate* me."

"I don't hate you."

At that, my brows knit together in confusion and I turn to look at him. He flashes me a casual glance, the anger in his eyes replaced by nothing more than an impassive indifference, blank and hollow, void of any semblance of emotion whatsoever.

He shakes his head once, shrugging one of his shoulders as he turns back to the road. "I stopped hating you a *long* time ago."

"Y-you did?" I gape at him, sufficiently confused, and maybe even a little more excited than I'd ever admit out loud.

Colt nods, momentarily meeting my gaze once more. "I don't care enough about you to hate you, no more."

My shoulders fall at his words. I stare at him, blinking once as a million and one thoughts race through my mind.

*Damn.*

I've never felt more dejected in all my life.

I'd almost prefer he did hate me; I'm pretty sure it would hurt less.

# Chapter 5

I wake with what can only be described as the taste of trash in my mouth. I don't necessarily know what trash tastes like, but I'm assuming this is it. Pure trash lingers on my sandpaper tongue, as does the taste of blood, while pixelated memories of the night before come over me in nauseating waves. When a vision of Colt flashes through my mind, I think I might actually be sick. But I'm startled by the faintest murmur of a cheeky giggle that sounds light years away, pulling me back to the now and rendering me frozen.

*What the—?*

One heavy lid opens, my eye scratchy as I search the dimly lit darkness surrounding me.

Where the hell am I?

Suddenly, warm breath fans over my cheek, followed by a wet tongue slobbering all over my face. I jump up, screaming out, pushing what feels like a furry beast away from me, but after a moment I come to enough to realize the weird-as-shit situation I'm actually in; I'm hungover as hell, in a dark room where I don't know where I am, and a freaking dog is licking my damn face.

I manage as best I can, pushing up to my elbows, finding a German shepherd almost as big as me, panting in my face, next

44

to a shaggy-haired boy who looks exactly like Cash did in the photos from when he was a little boy.

"CJ . . ." I rasp, scrubbing a hand over my face, managing the best smile I can right now.

But he just squeals, deafeningly so, scampering out of the room as quick as his little legs will carry him, his loyal four-legged friend following closely behind.

I scrub another hand over my face, rubbing my gritty eyes before taking a look at my surroundings. I'm still dressed in what I was wearing yesterday, covered with an afghan, on a sofa in the den of the Foreman's House where Cash and his small family currently reside. Stretching, I stifle a yawn before forcing myself up. My head throbs causing me to wince, but I push through the pain as I make my way to my unsteady feet, stopping to find what little balance I can collect before continuing out of the room.

The house is quiet, warm, and I can see outside it's raining again, making the morning appear dark and gloomy. I make my way through the short corridor and into the big kitchen, which is where I find my nephew perched at the table, his eyes smiling at me as he eats a bowl of cereal, giggling quietly to himself. I stop when I find Shelby, Cash's beautiful wife, standing at the island, a mug of something steaming in her hands. Her ebony eyes go wide when she notices me, gawping at me, and I linger on the spot realizing I must look a state.

"Hey . . ." I croak, waving my hand awkwardly.

Shelby's eyes remain wide as she stares at me, her face stark, and while I try not to take offense, it's not easy when you're being looked at like you're a circus freak.

"Cash Junior!" Shelby says in a chastising tone, turning to her son with bulging eyes. "What did you *do*?"

I glance between Shelby and CJ, my brow furrowing in confusion, but before I can say anything, Shelby places her mug onto the counter, grabs her cell and comes toward me, her phone held up in my face right as a bright flash goes off, almost blinding me.

"What the—" I rub my eyes with my thumb and forefinger, seeing spots as I blink frantically before slowly focusing on the screen held in front of me, finding a picture of myself from seconds ago, my face covered in what appears to be Magic Marker doodles.

"CJ Wagner!" Shelby chides her son.

"It's okay, it's just marker," I placate her with a light chuckle, walking over to the kitchen sink and dampening a handful of paper towels. I scrub at my cheeks, which makes me hiss out in pain, and the memory of being slapped into the middle of another decade last night comes rushing back to me, and I close my eyes tight a moment, taking a few deep breaths.

"I'm so sorry, Quinn." Shelby's voice startles me, and I turn to find her standing right there.

"It's fine, don't worry about—" I stop when I notice the sadness in her eyes, and I realize she's no longer referring to the Magic Marker on my face. I manage a tight-lipped smile, fully aware of CJ curiously watching us from the table. "It's fine," I say again, nodding once before allowing Shelby to take me in her arms, hugging me tight for a moment.

"Coffee?" she asks while pulling away. Emotion is thick and heavy in her voice as she crosses to the shiny coffee machine sitting on the island, and she clears her throat to even her tone.

"Yes, please." I amble across the kitchen, pulling out the chair next to CJ.

"How do you have it?"

I meet CJ's curious gaze with a salacious wink. "Black. Like my *soul*," I say in a deep voice directly to him, his eyes widening at my words as he continues shoveling Cheerios into his mouth.

Shelby joins us, placing a mug onto the table in front of me, taking the seat opposite her son. She leans over, ruffling his messy hair with her hand, smiling at him, and he giggles, focusing intently on his breakfast.

"Are you doing okay?"

I nod, shrugging noncommittally, fleetingly glancing at CJ. I don't know if he fully understands what has happened. That his grandfather is dead. So, I tread carefully. "I think it's still sinking in . . ."

Shelby regards her son. "Hey, baby, do you wanna take your breakfast into the living room and watch your cartoons?"

CJ's brown eyes light up. "Can I?"

Shelby nods, helping Cash Junior off the kitchen chair, handing him the plastic bowl. "Don't spill it."

He grips the bowl carefully, looking down at it with every step he takes, disappearing through the doors and into the sitting room. Seconds later, the *Paw Patrol* theme song can be heard from the next room, and I can't help but smile.

"How are you, *really*?" Shelby asks, and her hand on my arm causes tears to sting the backs of my eyes. I meet her kind gaze, her smile soft and genuine. I don't know her that well, despite the fact she's my sister-in-law and has been for six years. Our only communication has been via a Skype call every week, ever since CJ was born. I hate that I didn't make it home for his birth, or the wedding. But I just couldn't bring myself to get on that damn plane. It was just all too much. Yes, it was a coward move on my part, and an added regret to my long list of regrets. Cash wasn't happy with me. But Shelby managed to turn him around, made him understand. She's one of the kindest women I know. And the empathy within her inky eyes right now is warm and sincere.

I shake my head. "I still can't believe it. I mean, I was only speaking to him on the phone a few days ago. And now he's . . . he's gone." I stare down at my coffee, tracing the rim of the mug with my finger. "It's so unreal. This place just doesn't feel the same, now. It's like it's some alternate universe. The same, but different in a way that I don't like because it's missing the most important person." I shake my head. "What are we supposed to do without him?"

I chance a glance at Shelby, finding her watching me with sadness in her eyes.

"He was the glue that kept this dysfunctional family together. Without him . . ." I shake my head again, at a loss for words, but thankfully she gets it. She shifts a little closer, covering my hands with hers, and we just sit there for a moment, saying nothing, as CJ's cartoon fills the void of the words neither of us can seem to find.

"So, anyway . . ." I break the silence, taking a sip from my cooling coffee. "Where is my brother?"

"He went into town to get your car," Shelby says, quirking a brow at me from over the rim of her coffee mug as she takes a small sip. "What the heck happened last night, anyway?"

I blink at her.

"You passed out in Colt's truck." She smirks, a knowing glint shimmering in her eyes. "He carried you inside, and when Cash questioned him about it, he went all broody and Colt-like, and stormed right outta here."

My eyes widen as I remember back to last night, Colt's words reverberating through my head: *I don't care enough about you to hate you . . .* Those words sting even more now that I'm sober. Well, semi-sober, at least. I take a big gulp of my coffee, wincing as it burns its way down my throat, but the burn brings with it some semblance of clarity. And I shift a little in my chair, meeting Shelby's questioning gaze. "I was at Duke's. He showed up. Brought me back here." I shake my head dismissively. She doesn't need to know the rest, and I don't want to relive it and think about just how badly it could have ended.

"You were at Duke's?"

I nod.

"And Colt was there, too?" Her brows furrow.

I shake my head. "No. He just found me outside . . ." I say no more, purposely avoiding anything about being attacked by a cowboy, press my lips together, and an overwrought silence seems to follow my words. And as I stare into Shelby's eyes, I can tell her mind is working overtime.

"What's his deal, anyway?" I ask as casually as I can. "He's still living in the cabin . . . Is he married?"

"Nope." Her response is short. Curt. And for some reason, her silence speaks volumes, and I know there's something she's not telling me.

"Girlfriend?"

"No." She shakes her head, looking down at her coffee. "He's single."

Before I can press her any further, the sound of tires crunching over loose gravel outside interrupts the moment, and we both glance out through the bay window to see my rental pull up, Cash hopping out and jogging toward the house through the rain with his head down. Moments later, my brother walks through the door that leads from the mud room, through the laundry and into the kitchen, raindrops clinging to his dark hair. His eyes find me, his brow furrowing as he studies my face, the Magic Marker clearly still glaringly obvious.

"CJ saw fit to color your sister's face." Shelby answers his unspoken question.

"O-kay . . ." Cash shakes his head, dismissing his confusion. "Well, we're going to see Dad at ten o'clock." He offers me a knowing glance, and I check the time on the clock above the wall oven, realizing I have less than an hour to get ready if we're going to make it into town by ten. I thank Shelby for the coffee and take my mug to the sink.

CJ suddenly bursts into the kitchen, squealing in delight and launching at his daddy with his arms outstretched.

"Hey, buddy." Cash effortlessly lifts his son into the air, kissing the top of his head, and I smile watching their exchange, despite the weight of what's going to happen today hanging over my head.

"I think you should head back up to the main house." Cash moves in closer, his voice low.

"What?" I gape at him. "Why? You don't want me *here*?"

"Of course that's not it." He swallows hard. "I just . . . I think

Tripp could use someone up there with him." He scratches at his bearded chin. "I'm worried about him."

I gauge him a long moment, considering his words. I know what he's saying. What he isn't saying. And, although I can't be certain my twin brother won't stab me the second I step foot inside the front door, he's still my brother, my blood. I can't stand the thought of him being up there in that big house all alone.

I sigh, nodding once. And, with a quick glance at Shelby, I manage a smile, reluctantly taking the car keys from my brother.

The main house is silent when I walk inside with my duffel bag slung over my shoulder, pulling my oversized wheelie-case behind me. Inside the great room, the fireplace is void and cold. In fact, the whole house seems frigid and dark, and heartbreakingly empty. I continue through the main foyer, to the bottom of the stairs, listening out for any sign of life. But I'm met with piercing silence. Nothing.

"Tripp?" I call out.

Still nothing.

With my case weighing almost as much as I do, I begin up the stairs, cursing under my breath with every impossible step. Breathless, sweaty, and exhausted by the time I make it to the landing, I continue down the hall toward my old bedroom, which is when I'm stopped by the unexpected yet obvious sound of sniffling coming from the other side of the door to the master suite.

I pause, standing there a moment as I consider my options. Sure I could ignore the sound of my brother, a grown man, crying. Or, I could go in there and check that he's at least okay. Either way, I'm sure I'll be the bad guy for whichever choice I make. Cracking my knuckles, I go over and over the two options in my head before giving up and slowly pushing open the door, entering the room without so much as knocking.

"Tripp?" I poke my head around the door, finding my brother

50

sitting on the edge of the big bed, hunched over, holding what appears to be one of Dad's button-downs in his hands.

He jumps, clearing his throat loudly before violently swiping at his tears with the back of his hand. When his eyes meet mine, they're red-rimmed and glossy, the whites painfully bloodshot, and I wonder if he's even slept a wink since it happened.

I was Daddy's girl. Cash was almost like his protégé. But Tripp . . . Tripp and our father never really saw eye to eye. They were always butting heads. Arguing. Fighting. I remember when we were seventeen, Cash was away at college, and Tripp and Dad got into a disagreement that turned so quickly, Colt actually had to pull the two apart. I don't know what it was about. Like all of their quarrels. I've never understood the differences between them. All I know is that they each love hard, but they fight harder. Wagner men, through and through. But it's heartbreakingly evident that the residual pain of their volatile relationship is making Dad's passing so much more difficult for Tripp.

"What do *you* want?" he asks, his voice gravelly and broken. He turns his back to me, busying himself with placing the shirt he'd been holding into the suit bag lying on the bed.

I step tentatively over the threshold. "A-are you all right?"

After a moment he mutters something about being fine, but I know it's a lie. He's anything but fine. I can see it in the way his hands tremble, the way in which his broad shoulders seem so small and frail, like the weight of the world is causing him to just about break. But at least he isn't yelling at me.

"You know I'm here if you need—"

"God dammit!"

I cower instinctively at his brash words, but then when I see him struggling with the zipper on the bag, I breathe a sigh of relief when I realize his outburst isn't directed at me for once.

"Here, let me," I say, hurrying across the room.

He mutters something unintelligible under his breath, stepping away, and I carefully fix the stuck zipper, slowly pulling it closed,

51

taking a moment to look down at the black bag that holds the clothes my father is going to be wearing while he spends the rest of eternity buried six-feet deep in the cold ground. I release a stammering breath, emotion rearing its ugly head. But I manage to blink back my tears, maintaining what little composure I have. I turn slowly to find my brother staring down at the bag, fresh tears sliding down over his cheeks. And never before have I ever felt someone else's pain the way I feel his right at that moment.

Tripp looks at me, meeting my eyes just as a sob bubbles out from the back of his throat. And suddenly, as he falls apart right there in front of me, I quickly close the distance between us, wrapping my arms around him and pulling him close. He cries on my shoulder, sobs inconsolably, and I smooth a hand over his racking back, our differences set aside in that moment, for now at least.

# Chapter 6

I guess you could call me one of the unlucky ones. In my twenty-nine years on this earth, I've been unfortunate enough to witness firsthand the terrifying reality of death more times than a person my age should have to witness such a thing.

When my mother died, I was eight years old. Old enough to realize, yet slightly too young to understand fully. And because of that in-between state of my mind's maturity, Mom's death was something that has stuck with me ever since. The sadness she felt leading up to her death still resonates with me. And the shocking details of her suicide, the bits and pieces I've discovered and put together over the years since, haunt me every day. Her death is something I was sheltered from, but by sheltering me from it, I think it made dealing with it as I grew up so much more difficult. I love my mother. But I also hate her for what she did. And I'm not sure I'll ever move past that.

My grandfather died a few years after my mom. When I was thirteen. He was old with the onset of dementia, so when he finally passed away, he was a shell of the man I'd grown up with. He wasn't himself, and so his death was a welcome cure to the sickness that took him away long before he died.

So, while I've dealt with the grief of losing people, I should be used it by now. Everyone leaves sooner or later. But Dad's death is different. Maybe it's because I'm older, now, and I truly understand what it means to lose someone. Maybe it's because it was so sudden, because I didn't get to say goodbye. Maybe it's because I feel like I missed so much time with him, like I was robbed of the years I'd spent taking for granted that he'd be around forever.

Whatever it is, nothing could have prepared me to deal with the crippling emotion of losing my hero, of seeing him lying lifeless and cold, and so empty. And as I stand here, the silence in the cold room overwhelming, I wish I'd been a little more prepared. I never imagined I would ever see someone who was once so strong, whose strength was so all-consuming, suddenly look so hollow. Someone who was once so imposing, who could command the attention of an entire crowd without effort, suddenly not even the shell of the powerful man he once was. But that's just it; as I look down at him so gray and still and void, I realize that it's not my father. My father is gone and this is all that's left.

It's a sobering moment, one I'm sure will stay with me for the rest of my life. I should be remembering all the good times, all the times I shared with him that brought a smile to my face. All the times he made me feel like his little princess. All the times I looked up at him like he was the hero from all the fairy tales I read as a girl. But I don't think about the good times. As I stand there staring down at him, my heart still and barely beating, all I keep thinking about is every time I ever said or did something so unimaginably hurtful to the one man in my life I naively thought would be here forever.

Like the time he caught me and Colt in my bedroom with the door closed. It was a hard rule. No closed doors if it was just the two of us. We were only kissing. But Dad still kicked Colt out on his ass, literally dragged him down the stairs, out the front door, and pushed him from the verandah where he landed on the grass with a thud. After that, I was forced to muck out the stables for a whole month, and Colt and I weren't allowed to see each other for a week. So, I did what any sullen and impulsive fifteen-year-old girl might do. I hid horseshit in every nondescript crevice in my father's truck. For an entire week he couldn't figure out where that stench was coming from. He ended up having to get the whole cab reupholstered, and the cost came out of my pocket money.

When I was seventeen, Dad and I had a huge fight over colleges. He wanted me to stay close. But of course I had to apply to schools on the other side of the country because my dreams were in New York City, and Mom made me promise to chase my selfish dreams. I remember looking him dead in the eyes and telling him that I wanted to get the hell away from this town so I didn't end up slitting my wrists like my mother.

That was the most horrible thing I've ever said to him. Granted it was after I found out that Colt was staying in the Canyon. That he wasn't coming with me to New York. That he, in fact, had zero intentions of ever leaving like we had planned all along. I was probably more upset with Colt, than my father. But the pain in Dad's eyes was heartbreakingly obvious in the wake of my words. And the worst part of it all is that I meant what I said. I meant every last one of those words.

Over the years I said and did some unforgivable things to my father. I was young and stubborn, and ever since my mother's passing, I was living with a crippling pain I'd never dealt with. But I was also taking advantage of him because I knew I could get away with it. I knew, no matter what, Dad would still love me, in spite of what I said or what I did, and he would always be there for me, always on my side. But now he's gone. He's not here. And all those mean, horrible, downright nasty things I said to him when I was an ignorant, arrogant little girl, I can't take back. But that's the thing about fathers; you expect them to be around forever. But now he isn't here and I can't apologize, and he can't accept that I truly am so sorry from the bottom of my heart for everything I ever put him through. And that may be the saddest part in all of this.

A single tear trails down my cheek, and I sniffle, the sound echoing throughout the silence. I lift a trembling hand, hesitating momentarily before tentatively placing it against my father's chest. He's cold. Stiff. Empty. Blinking hard, I heave a heavy breath, searching the face that is so familiar yet so unlike the face of my father.

"I'm so sorry," I whisper, gently patting the white sheet covering his naked torso.

And I am sorry. For everything. Sorry I didn't stay. Sorry I never came back. Sorry that I left him without ever even considering that it may very well be the last time I saw him.

I'm sorry.

I always will be.

For everything.

"You okay?"

I startle from where my head is resting against the window, tearing my blank gaze away from the side of the road as it whizzes by in a blur. I meet Cash's dark eyes in the reflection of the rearview, managing a nod. I can't trust my own voice. The emotion threatening to break me is far too real. I'm not okay. In fact, I'm far from it. I keep seeing my father lying there, dead. I keep imagining what his final thoughts may have been. I know the coroner said he was most likely dead before he hit the ground, but what if he wasn't? What if he was just lying there, so scared, realizing he was never going to see me or my brothers ever again?

I keep thinking that I'm never going to see his name flash up on the screen of my cell phone. Calling me at the most inconvenient time, like he always did. But I would smile regardless, while I eagerly hitting the answer button. But I won't have that again. His name won't ever grace the screen of my cell again. He's gone.

And he's never coming back. So, no. In answer to my brother's question, I'm definitely not okay.

"What about you?" Cash glances at Tripp in the passenger seat. "You all right, little brother?"

Tripp says nothing, offering a noncommittal shrug, and I go back to watching the sky-high fir trees whizz past, trying so hard to rid the vision of my cold, gray father from my deeply conflicted mind.

"I need you guys to sign a few papers with me. The lawyers are stopping by in the morning," Cash continues, but I'm not really paying attention. "Quinn, are you available at nine?"

*Like I have anything else to do.*

I nod, but then my ears prick when I hear Tripp murmur, "It's got nothing to do with her."

My brows knit together as I glare at the back of my brother's head. "What's got nothing to do with me?"

"The ranch." Tripp throws a scornful glance over his shoulder, and I assume the moment we shared earlier in our father's bedroom where he literally cried on my shoulder for five minutes, is long forgotten.

"It's my *home*!" I guffaw because, quite frankly, he's deluded if he thinks the ranch has nothing to do with me.

"Your *home*!" He laughs a derisive laugh, shaking his head at me. "The place you left ten years ago? The place you never even bothered coming back to visit? The place where Cash and I have been working our asses off since the day you were still playing with your damn dolls?"

I stare at him, blinking once.

"The ranch ain't none of your damn business, Quinny. You can get that thought right outta that pretty little head of yours."

I know he's just upset. And I should let it go, let him think whatever it is he wants to think if it makes him feel any better. We can talk about it when he's calm. But screw him. "The ranch is my business just as much as it's yours and Cash's!"

57

"Like hell it is!" Tripp's voice booms, reverberating through the silence of the cab. "Your name may be on the deed, but that's all you got. You stay the hell out of this!" He turns back around, and, just like that, I'm supposed to accept that the conversation is over. He's so much like our father, it's uncanny.

I catch Cash's eyes in the mirror once again, and I can see a desperate pleading within his stare. He's begging me to leave it. To let it go for now. But the thing is, I'm like my father, too. And I can't let it go.

"You really do think I'm only here for my inheritance, don't you?" I scoot forward on the back seat, poking my head through the break in the front seats, and I'm so close I can see Tripp's jaw tighten, despite his passive exterior. "You know, it might come as a surprise to you that I've actually done quite well for myself in New York. I'm one of the top-ten real-estate brokers in the whole city. I own a three-million-dollar apartment. I've got money. Hell, if it came down to it, I wouldn't even *need* my inheritance."

Tripp scoffs with a dramatic roll of his eyes, still staring out through the windshield. "Fine, then sign your share over to me and Cash."

Cash chuckles lightly at that and I throw him a warning glance before zeroing back in on Tripp. "No, I won't." I shake my head. "I won't do that, because as much as you care to disagree, this ranch is my home, too. And, whether you like it or not, I'm . . . I'm staying."

"You're stayin'?" Cash suddenly pipes up, looking at me briefly, his brows climbing higher in surprise. And to be honest, I'm almost as surprised as he is at my declaration. "For how long?"

Tripp shifts in his seat, turning to look at me, his eyes dark and narrowed, and I meet his hard stare with one of my own, shrugging one shoulder. "I haven't decided yet . . ."

"Why?" Tripp quirks a dubious brow, a malevolent smirk pulling at his lips, one void of anything but menace. "Are you looking to fool some other poor sucker into falling for you just so you can leave him at the altar, too?"

My jaw drops of its own accord as a heavy silence thick with tension settles in the wake of his words.

Cash clears his throat, shifting awkwardly in the driver's seat, his grip on the steering wheel a little tighter.

Tripp sniggers to himself, a look of satisfaction in his eyes as he turns to focus back out on the road ahead.

I just sit there, gawping at him, in some kind of shock. I'd like to think he didn't just say that, that I was imagining it. But I'd just be fooling myself. Whoever said *sticks and stones might break my bones but words will never hurt me* is a damn liar. Tripp's words are like weapons and he knows exactly how to inflict the worst possible pain on a person with the vitriol that spills out of his mouth.

"Cash, stop the truck."

Tripp's smirk morphs into a smug, cocky grin. He knows he's beaten me. He knows he's just cut me deep down with those words. And I hate that he can affect me so easily. But I remain impassive, my threatening gaze like daggers as I continue staring at his smug profile.

"I'm not gonna stop the damn truck—we're miles from the house," Cash says with a bored tone.

I glance furtively at the rifle secured into the rack above the passenger door, and I briefly consider pulling it down, and taking off the safety, to show him just how serious I am. But I don't. "Cash, stop the damn truck or I swear to God . . ." My shrill voice echoes throughout the cab, but I trail off because I don't want to admit out loud that I'm seriously about to stab my brother with my nail file moments after seeing our dead father.

Cash quickly veers off the gravel road, pulling up to the side of the ditch that lines it. Before we even come to a complete stop, I have my door open, and I jump out, landing with an unsteady stumble. I'm quick to compose myself enough when my brothers turn to look at me through Cash's open window.

"You're really gonna walk?" Cash asks, looking down at me with a quirked brow.

"Just leave her ass," Tripp mutters, that infuriating smirk still lingering on his lips.

"Shut up, idiot," Cash chastises his little brother.

I flash Tripp my middle finger, turning my back as the truck pulls away, its tires skidding in the gravel, leaving a cloud of dust circling around me. I glance briefly over my shoulder, watching as they disappear around the tree-lined bend, and I release a heavy breath of frustration.

I carefully skid down the ditch, climbing through the gap in the wire fence. Fighting my way through the waist-high grass, I continue through the field and far away from the makeshift road, heading down toward the river that runs through the middle of the ranch, the river that leads the way back to the main house. It might take me an hour or two, maybe even more, but I guess I could use the time to cool down or else I seriously might murder my twin brother.

Forty minutes later and I'm exhausted. My feet hurt, I'm desperate for a drink, and my anger still hasn't subsided. Not even the lulling trickle of the flowing river eases my mind. In fact, I think I'm even more angry now than I was.

Tripp's words continue to replay over and over in my head like a broken record. My past is no joking matter. I know what I did. The whole damn town knows what I did. I don't need him reminding me of just how badly I messed everything up.

He's such a dick. He hasn't always been, though. Tripp and I used to be so close. We weren't just brother and sister; we were best friends. Twins. The same damn person. I used to tell Tripp everything. I'd confide in him. Hell, he was the one I told when I first got my period. He had no idea what to do, of course, but he gave me his flannel shirt to tie around my waist when it had unfortunately made its appearance while I was at school wearing a white jean skirt. He accompanied me to the school nurse. He even went in and bought my first box of Tampax from Gordon's Grocery after school that day because I was too embarrassed, and

I was terrified Mrs. Gordon was going to make a big deal out of it in front of the entire store.

Once upon a time, mine and Tripp's bond was unbreakable. But then a boy with green eyes and dimples inadvertently came between us. After Colt, our relationship changed. And, ever since, Tripp and I have never been the same.

I huff an exasperated sigh, stopping for a breather and looking out over the river, to the thick forest of trees on the other side, the snow-capped mountains looming high up into the clouded sky in the distance. I take a seat, pulling at a long weed, smiling fondly as I remember back to when we were kids, when we used to swim in this very river when the summer sun perched itself high up in the hazy August sky. Just Cash, Tripp, and me. Before our mother's sadness. Before Colt became a permanent fixture in all of our lives. Before the ranch started to take over the boys' lives. Before dreams of a whole other life started to take over mine. Those were the days. God, I miss them.

I'm pulled abruptly from the fondness of my reverie by the sound of rustling leaves coming from the bushes on the other side of the water, and when I hear the distinct sound of a growl, my heart leaps up into the back of my throat when I realize I'm suddenly no longer alone.

I stay as still as I can, despite my fight-or-flight responses battling deep down inside of me. My mind tells me to calm down, that it's probably just a curious raccoon, but my gut tells me to get the hell out of here, and that that curious raccoon is more likely to be a damn grizzly bear, hungry for lunch.

When I hear another growl, and the sound of a twig snapping followed by more rustling, I make my way to my feet, my trembling hands brushing down the back of my jeans. My eyes flit from side to side, searching the darkness of the forest. And then I see it. Or, them, rather. One wiry gray wolf, followed by another, their steely eyes glaring at me from across the river, each of them baring their teeth with a threatening snarl.

Shit.

I take one careful step back, praying I don't trip on a rock, not once breaking eye contact. But then, to my left, another wolf, black as night with flaming amber eyes, comes from out of nowhere, braving the shallows of the water and edging closer and closer, snapping its jaw violently as one of the grays lets out an almighty howl that rings through the air.

Growing up on the ranch I've encountered a plethora of dangerous animals in my time. Rattlers, cougars, bears, even wolves. But never on my own. And never so unprepared. I don't even have my pepper spray. It's in my handbag, in Cash's truck. And I suddenly blame Tripp. I'm going to die. And it'll be all his fault.

The two grays have followed the leader of their pack, and are now on my side of the river. A little more hesitant than the black dog, but still taunting me, intimidating me with the occasional glimpse of their sharp teeth. I keep a steady gaze on all three of them as they edge closer and closer. If I stay, I'll be mauled to death. If I turn and run, the wolves can run faster. I'm as good as dead.

In the flash of an instant, my life doesn't fly before my eyes like they say it does. In fact, my mind is blank, eerily so. It's a strange feeling. Blank, nothingness, accompanied by the deafening sound of my heartbeat whooshing in my ears. But just as I'm about ready to admit defeat, my father's voice comes into the nothingness in my head, and he reminds me of who I am. A Wagner. Relentless. Stubborn. And strong-willed. And I know at that moment that I have to fight, that, in some weird way, maybe he's here with me, ready to go into battle with me. So, with everything I have, I have to fight if it's the last thing I do.

I take a deep, heaving breath. It rattles through me. I glance from one wolf to the others, mentally psyching myself up, preparing myself for what? I don't even know. My left leg shakes as I silently count *one, two, three,* and with another deep breath on the fourth count, I let out the most feral, ferocious, intimidating sound that I can muster from deep down in the pit of my belly, turning on the ball of my foot before taking off as fast as I can.

But then, suddenly everything falls silent in the wake of the sound of a gunshot erupting throughout the stillness of the valley like an almighty explosion.

I stop.

The wolves stop.

Everything stops.

# Chapter 7

Am I dead?

Is this what death feels like?

I gasp for a breath, feeling the air fill my lungs.

I'm not dead.

I turn quickly, frantically searching for the wolves, but with a few yelps and howls, I see the hint of a bushy black tail disappearing into the shadows of the thicket of trees across the river. I clutch at my thundering chest, looking out at the fields, searching, which is when I see a horse galloping furiously toward me from the distance, a familiar figure mounted upon its back, rifle in hand, propped in the air, the barrel still smoking.

"What the hell are you doing out here?" Colt yells, his voice booming.

He doesn't even wait for an answer before jumping down from the saddle, stalking past me to check the coast is clear of the dogs. Without warning, he lets off another shot, and I cower, covering my ears with my trembling hands as the eruption ricochets through the air.

"You can't be out here, Quinn!" He comes rushing back to me, his eyes full of concern as they study me, looking closely for any sign of injury, and something about his concern comforts me. He still cares about me. At least enough not to want to see me eaten by wolves.

A big, strong hand grasps my shoulder. "You all right?"

Through gasping breath I manage a nod, although my heart screams no. *No, I'm not all right. I almost died!*

Colt exhales a ragged breath, taking another careful look around, his hand still resting upon my shoulder. But just as I'm thinking about how warm and contradicting his gentle touch is, it's as if he's realized too. He removes his hand quickly and obviously, stepping away from me as silence settles heavy and thick between us.

I take the chance to look at him. Really look at him. From head to toe. Scuffed riding boots. Jeans that look as if they were made to fit only him, pulling perfectly in all the right areas. A flannel shirt that skims his strong upper body and tightens ever so slightly over his broad shoulders, the sleeves rolled up to his elbows.

Huh. Tattoos. Covering the majority of both arms. He was never one for tattoos before. I can't help but wonder what changed over the years.

He removes his Stetson, wiping at his sweat-beaded brow with his shirtsleeve, before replacing the hat again, dipping it low to shield his gaze from the muted light of the afternoon.

"What?" He glances at me from the corner of his eye, his jaw clenching momentarily.

I avert my gaze. "You keep saving me."

"Well, stop getting your stupid ass into shitty situations and you won't need no damn saving," he says matter-of-factly, his voice deep and gruff and brutally honest.

*Touché.*

He turns to me, clearing his throat. "C'mon. I'll walk you the rest of the way back to the house."

I follow him to his horse. Instead of pulling himself up into the saddle, he grabs the reins and begins to walk the buckskin, glancing over his shoulder at me to check I'm following. And I do. I don't need a repeat of last night. I'm not drunk. And I also don't want to see what happens if those wolves come back.

We walk in silence for a while. Neither of us speaking. And it's an uncomfortable silence, awkward and thick with an obvious tension that makes me nervously crack my knuckles. I stare intently at the ground, but every so often I see him glancing at me in my periphery, although he pretends to be looking out over the paddocks, to the fields in the distance, I can feel his eyes on me; his gaze penetrating and palpable, and so familiar.

"I'm sorry about Royal . . ."

I snap my head up then, finding him staring straight ahead into the distance, sincerity in his eyes.

I swallow the sudden emotion balling at the back of my throat, considering my response, but what am I supposed to say to that? Thanks? Me too? It all seems so pointless. Pointless words void of any true meaning, just spoken for the sake of it.

"You okay?" he asks.

I think for a moment, before answering, "No. Not really."

I stare out at the mountains as memories of my father come flooding back to me, all the times he took me out on his horse, showing me every last corner of this land, telling me that one day it would all be mine and my brothers'. And now it is. But I'd give it up in a heartbeat if I could just have him back.

I sigh in resignation, forcing myself back to the now. "I'm sorry you had to see it."

Colt shrugs a shoulder as if it's no big deal, but it is a big deal. It's a huge deal. He was the last person to see my father alive. He heard his last words. Witnessed his final breath. As terrifying as that moment would have been, I've never been more envious of someone before. But I don't press him, and he says nothing more as we continue ahead, consumed by that same overwrought silence.

"So you're still here working at the ranch, huh?" I ask with a small smile, in the hope of lightening the heavy air between us.

"Yep," is all I receive in response.

I press my lips together, considering another approach. "Do you still ride?"

"Not after the accident." He's just as short this time, but only now there's a sadness in his eyes and I really wish I hadn't brought it up.

*Of course he isn't competing in rodeos anymore, you idiot.* He's lucky to be alive. I mentally facepalm.

"How are you?" I ask after a few beats, as soft as I can. "After . . . the accident, I mean."

Colt just shakes his head, his jaw clenching to the point of painful. "Ain't none of your concern no more, Quinny."

I look down to the ground, raking my teeth over my bottom lip. I guess I deserve his hostility after what I did. This man loved me with all he had, and I broke his heart. But his obvious disdain toward me hurts more than I think I could have ever been prepared for.

My memory wanders back to that night, a few months after the wedding. I was up late, or early, studying for an economics final. It was after two in the morning when I got the phone call from my father telling me that Colt had wrapped his truck around the trunk of a fir out off Old Prairie Road. I remember sitting in my dorm in a heap on the floor, staring at the study notes I'd pinned to my wall, tears streaming down my face. It felt as if someone had literally ripped my heart right out of my chest while it was still beating, showing it to me while violently squeezing the life out of it. I was empty and void, and devastated because I'd lost the love of my life before I had the chance to go home to tell him that I'd made a mistake, that I loved him, that New York wasn't my dream, and that a happy-ever-after with him was. But I was too late.

I release a trembling sigh at that memory, watching as Colt leads the way. I study the way his strong shoulders look as if they have so much resting upon them. The way he drags his feet a

67

little, his limp painful and obvious, a constant reminder of every-thing he lost. The way his head seems to be forever bowed, tilted downward, like he can't be bothered keeping his chin held high like he used to. He just seems so defeated. It's a heartbreaking sight to see; a stark contrast to the confident, slightly cocky young cowboy I remember him to be.

"Can I ask you something?" I ask despite my reluctance.

He scoffs, shaking his head. "What do you wanna ask me, Quinn?" He releases a frustrated sigh, and when he steadies me with a hard gaze, I find his eyes are dark and cold, nothing like how I remember them. "What?" he continues. "You wanna know how I've been doing? What I've been up to? What my life's been like for the last ten years? You wanna catch up on old times?" His tone is mocking, and I avert my eyes, looking down at my hands.

And I know I should just keep my mouth shut, but I can't help myself. My voice seems to have a mind of its own. "Do you ever wonder how different things would be right now if I . . . if I never left?"

"Nope." His answer is curt and definitive. And it hurts. A crease pulls between his brows. I know he could say a lot more. But he doesn't.

"I do . . ." I admit quietly under my breath in the hope he doesn't hear me.

Colt stops suddenly.

Oh, he heard me all right. In fact my words affect him so much that he stumbles ever so slightly, but he tries to cover his misstep with taking a better hold of the mare, as if it were her fault, smoothing his hand down over her nose. And, although his face remains impassive, his jaw tight, it's his eyes that give him away, blazing beneath the muted light of the afternoon sun hidden behind thick, gray clouds.

"God damn you, Quinny," he hisses through a tightly gritted jaw.

I gape at his words.

Cursing under his breath, Colt pulls himself up onto the horse, shaking his head and muttering a string of curse words under his breath.

Panic begins to settle low in my belly. "W-what . . . Where are you going?" I stammer.

"You can make it the rest of the way." He grabs the reins, and without so much as a fleeting glance in my general direction, he presses the heels of his boots into the sides of his horse, forcing her to pick up to a slow trot.

I furtively look around at the wide-open field around me. I'm still at least a good mile from the house. I'm a sitting duck. "B-but . . . what if the wolves come back?"

"They ain't comin' back."

"What if they do?" I cry out to Colt as the horse picks up speed.

"Run!" he yells over his shoulder, before hissing loudly, the mare tearing off into the distance, leaving me all alone with nothing but the memory of my past regrets, and the fear of wild dogs eating me alive, to keep me company.

By the time I make it back to the house I'm a dirty, breathless mess.

Shelby is standing next to a proper-looking lady, holding a big vase of orchids, and she does an almost comical double take of me, her eyes widening as she stares down at the big mud stain covering the front of my sweater.

She gasps. "What on earth happened to you?"

"Don't ask," I mutter through gritted teeth, continuing to the front steps.

"Quinn, this is Julie." Shelby stops me, gently tugging on my sleeve. I turn to see the proper-looking woman holding out a perfectly manicured hand. "Julie works with Mr. Jenson at the funeral home. She's here setting up . . . for tomorrow."

At the mention of tomorrow, my shoulders fall and a knot tightens in my belly. But I quickly close the gap, shaking Julie's proffered hand.

"I'm terribly sorry for your loss." Julie bows her head, and I can tell she's well versed in what to say and how to act in such a situation.

"Thank you." I manage a small smile at the woman.

"I'll be upstairs, cleaning myself up," I say to Shelby. And with a polite nod to Julie, I turn and continue up the stairs and into the house, which is when I'm hit by the overpowering fragrance of the fresh flowers that appear to be placed all through the downstairs living area.

I stop, looking out over the sprawling great room as sadness consumes me. The place looks like a damn botanical garden, and I can't help but shake my head. My father wouldn't want pretty flowers and a woman like Julie organizing fancy hors d'oeuvres and black-tie servers. He'd want a bottle of whiskey, and some football game playing on a muted television, to the tune of Bob Dylan's greatest hits. But, who am I to have a say?

I sigh in resignation, turning and heading for the stairs.

When I get to my bedroom, I take a breath for what feels like the first time in forever. Resting my head back against the closed door, I squeeze my eyes shut for a moment, collecting myself. I'm still shaken by the disdain in Colt's eyes, the way he looked at me before riding off on his horse, leaving me all alone, literally thrown to the wolves. It hurts to see him the way that he is now. He's changed so much from the cocky go-getter he was when we were kids, to the brooding, sullen shell of the man he is now. It breaks my heart. Am I to blame for the demise of Colt Henry, or is there more to his change than just me?

Pushing my hair back from my face, I continue through to my bathroom, stopping on my way to kick off my ruined Gucci sneakers. Tripp can replace them. And my cashmere sweater. Dick.

I spend at least twenty minutes in the hot, steaming shower, trying so hard to scrub the guilt and the shame off my skin. But it's no use. It doesn't budge. All I keep thinking about is Colt. The sadness in his eyes that were once so vibrant and full of determination. He's half the man I remember him to be, and I hate that I played a part in beating him down to what he is now. I know what I did was inexplicably wrong. I wish I could take it back. With everything I have, I wish I could go back and change it all. But it's been ten years. So much can change in ten years. I'm a different person.

I've spent the last ten years of my life living far away in a big city, with all intentions of becoming just another face in the crowd. A city where I could fade into the background. A city where I wouldn't be *that* girl. But in those ten years, I didn't just become another face in the crowd; I lost the person I was. The old Quinn was left here, in the middle of nowhere, Montana. Forgotten about. And I miss her. Because despite her faults, she was the best part of me.

# Chapter 8

I take a seat at my dresser, still wrapped in a towel, my wet hair dripping down over my bare shoulder, causing me to shiver against the cool chill hanging in the air.

Looking at myself in the mirror, I sigh. My gray eyes are tired, weary, the whites slightly bloodshot from a combination of lack of sleep and stress. My honey hair is dull and flat. Pale skin. Washed-out lips and cheeks. I'm a shadow of the woman I was only a few days ago. Well, the woman I thought I was a few days ago. Being home in the Canyon has taken its toll on me while also causing me to question myself and everything I've lost over the last ten years of my life.

I think back to Rylie from Duke's Saloon, to what she told me. That I can redeem myself because I'm not an asshole. When she told me that, I wasn't so sure. I mean, I've done some pretty asshole-ish things in my time. Leaving the love of my life at the altar really tops the list, I'd say. But there was more. Many things I'm not proud of. But one thing I know for certain is that, deep down, I have a good heart. And how do I know that? Because I was raised by a man who made sure of it.

I glance at the photos lining the mirror of my dressing table. Happy snaps from what feels like a lifetime ago. And I guess it was a lifetime ago. A whole other life. In every one of the photos I find an enviable smile beaming back at me. That girl was happy. Sure, she used to dream of getting the hell out of here, away from the Canyon, but here she was happy. Her happiest. I need to find that smile again.

I zero in on a photo of me and Colt, pulling it down from its stickum to inspect it closely. We were only sixteen. It was taken at his first ever real-life rodeo. He was so nervous. He'd been practicing for so long in the corral here at the ranch before and after his shifts as a junior hand. The ranch hands would coach him, spur him on from the fences, telling him where to hold on, how to tuck his chin in tight to his chest. But it was my father who saw a raw talent in Colt. He backed him financially, sponsoring him by paying his entry fee, and getting him kitted out for a professional competition.

That night, Colt won his very first belt buckle after staying on a terrifying mustang for almost nine seconds. In the picture he's smiling so wide, his eyes shining and dimples popping as he holds up his shiny buckle, and I'm beaming proudly by his side, wearing his hat. His arm is wrapped tight around my shoulders. I remember that night so vividly. It was one of our best nights. Colt was on top of the world, and I was his girl. In that moment, it honestly felt like everything was exactly how it was supposed to be. From that night on, Colt Henry was the Rodeo King of the Canyon, and I was his Quinn. King and Quinn. The two of us together were an unstoppable force to be reckoned with. We thought our reign would last forever. God, I can't help but laugh. Look at us now.

I carefully stick the photo back up against the glass, smiling at all the memories I've stuck up over the years. My dad. My brothers. Colt. My old dog, Lucky. A lifetime of happiness that suddenly makes me question why I was ever so desperate to get away from it all in the first place.

Why wasn't it enough?

Life in the Canyon wasn't so bad.

Why couldn't that girl in the photos just stay?

I envy her, but I resent her even more. She ruined everything, and a really messed-up part deep down inside of me can't help but blame my mother.

Dressed in a pair of my old Uggs I found deep in the closet, thermal leggings and a flannel shirt, I walk downstairs, carefully scoping out my surroundings for any trace of Tripp. I'm not sure I can risk seeing him tonight, not after what he said to me today. I'm not sure I can keep my cool. I'm not sure I'll be able to stop myself from flipping him the middle finger if he so much as glances in my direction.

I poke my head into the kitchen, finding it empty and dark, the only light coming from the rays of the setting sun poking through the clouds as it melts into the west mountains. My shoulders sag in relief, and I continue inside, pulling open the big refrigerator and assessing its contents. It's packed full with anything we could ever need. After I left for college, I made sure Dad hired a cook. Someone to come in and do all the meals for him and my brothers. Shop for groceries. Do all the things the housekeeper didn't do. All the things I did when I was living here. I couldn't leave with the thought of the three of them surviving off steaks off the grill every night. A cook looking after them offered me some semblance of comfort, knowing they were eating well while I was gone.

But as I scan the shelves inside the fridge finding beef, beef, and more beef, lasagna, fresh vegetables and fruits, I'm literally spoiled for choice, and yet I find nothing that interests me. Actually, I'm not even hungry, despite the fact that I've barely eaten anything all day.

When I hear the faint yet distinct sound of Bob Dylan floating like a murmured hum caught in the breeze, I close the fridge, turning to see the glow of fire coming from the pit out back. I cross the kitchen, stopping at the glass doors, looking out to see my brothers and Colt sitting around a fire, each of them with a glass of liquor in their hands. I feel like I should be out there with them. That's where I belong. With my brothers and my . . . Colt. But I find myself hesitating, knowing I could start something with Tripp unintentionally just by simply going down there. But I stifle that doubt and grab a coat from the hook by the door, shrugging it on. Its warmth envelops me, and it smells of my father. I bask in the familiarity it provides. It's almost like he has his arms wrapped around me, protecting me, keeping me safe. And I pull it tight around me as I step outside.

The night air slices through me, but I follow the verandah, walking down the three steps, crossing the patio and stopping at the wooden Adirondack chairs. Colt avoids even so much as a casual glance in my direction, and that stings. But I ignore his obvious avoidance, and my eyes tentatively meet Tripp's from across the fire, the dancing flames illuminating his face. And in this light, he looks just like me. Me and our mother. I half-expect him to tell me to piss off. But, he doesn't. He definitely considers it; I can see it in his contemplative stare. But instead, he reaches down and grabs a glass from the tray on the ground beside him, filling it with liquor from the fancy crystal bottle. He stands and slowly walks around the fire, holding the glass out to me.

I cast Cash an uncertain glance, but he simply nods once, taking a sip from his own drink, so I accept the glass from Tripp, knowing it isn't tainted, and I take a seat on one of the empty chairs.

Tripp sits back down in his seat, stretching his long legs out on the lawn in front of him, resting his head back and closing his eyes a moment. I take a sip from my glass. Whiskey. I'm shocked at just how smooth it feels on my tongue, how it warms my body on the way down instead of burning my throat.

"This was Dad's." Cash holds his glass up. "He bought this bottle back when he first took over this place from Grandpa."

I glance down at the glass in my hand, at the amber liquid

as it reflects the flames of the fire, and a sudden sadness rakes through me, a sadness I'm not prepared for.

"He said he was going to wait and drink it with his kids when he passed the reins over." Cash pauses, and I watch as he bows his head a moment before looking up to the inky night sky, holding his glass in the air. "This one's for you, Dad."

I cast Colt a sideways glance, and he does the same to me. Then I meet Tripp's eyes once more across the fire, and something passes between us, something void of anger and hate. He juts his chin at me, lifting his glass, and I meet his gaze with a small smile. "To Dad."

We each down the contents of our glasses, and a moment of silence settles between us as one Bob Dylan song stops and another begins. Tripp tops up his glass, handing the bottle to Colt. Colt fills his before passing around to Cash, and Cash does the same, and I hold mine out for a top-up. I pull my knees up to my chest, wrapping an arm around them as I sip my drink, watching the flames lick up into the dark sky as the fire crackles and hisses violently.

After an hour or so, we're all sufficiently buzzed, remembering the good times with our father, and I cannot stop smiling at the memories as they play through my mind like an old home movie reel.

"Remember when Dad was away and you threw that party?" Tripp says, a smile on his face as he looks at our big brother.

Cash chuckles, bowing his head, his shoulders trembling with his laughter.

I smile as I remember back to that night. "Everyone drank all the beers." I laugh. "And then you tried replacing it the next day but Duke was out of town and the bartender at the saloon wouldn't serve you!"

Tripp and Cash both laugh. Colt chuckles quietly.

"Dad came home and was all like, *Where's me dang beer?*"

Tripp exclaims, his hands in the air, imitating our father's drawl down to every minute inflection.

"Hey! It was mostly you two little pricks who drank it all!" Cash points an accusatory finger at Tripp and then Colt. "Y'all were fourteen years old, for Christ's sake!"

Tripp just shrugs, grinning to himself, but Colt's smiling gaze lands upon me. I'm suddenly lost in the memory of that night, my cheeks heating from more than just the flames of the fire.

I stayed away from the party that night, knowing that Dad would be none too happy about it if he found out. Instead, I sat up in my room with ice cream and my favorite book, losing myself in the pages of my latest fictional obsession, which is when I was startled by a gentle rapping upon my door before it opened just enough for Colt to stick his head through the gap, smiling at me. He'd asked me what I was doing, and invited himself in. He was drunk. I could tell. I could smell the stale scent of beer on his breath. But he was sweet. Funny and goofy, and nervous.

He sat on the other side of my bed, laughing at the fluffy green socks I was wearing, which had eyes on the toes, made to look like frogs covering my feet. He kept finding ways to touch me. My foot, my knee. When I flinched away from him, he realized I was ticklish, and took the chance to tickle my sides, which is how we ended up lying together on my bed, me on top of him, breathless as we stared into each other's eyes.

Everything changed between us with that one moment. That was the very first time I ever realized my feelings for him, and nothing was ever the same after that.

Colt and I share a meaningful glance at one another. And I know he feels that memory right now, just as much as I'm feeling it. And I can't help but smile when the corners of his lips curl up ever so slightly, a dancing sparkle in his green eyes.

"Remember when he was teaching us how to drive, down in the back field?" I look at Tripp, smiling knowingly. "He got so frustrated with me and my gear shifting. He was like, *Get out, darlin', let me show you how it's done!*" I try to imitate Dad's deep voice, my own laughter getting the better of me. "Then he reversed the truck into the damn river!"

Cash throws his head back, laughing out loud. He wasn't there. He was at college. But Tripp and I called him and told him all about it as soon as we made it back to the house. We stayed on the phone for an hour, just laughing.

"And then he got out and tried to push it outta the water, and fell face first in the mud!" Tripp cackles loudly, downing the last of his whiskey.

I continue sipping from my glass, smiling at the funny times we've shared.

Cash laughs again. "Remember how he used to watch the Packers games with the sound turned down. Because he couldn't stand that no-good announcer—"

"*Rex yella-belly Rubben!*" Cash, Tripp, and Colt all chime together in unison with Dad's country accent, thick and twangy, breaking down into fits of laughter.

"Rex Rubben?" I smile between my two brothers, to Colt, but they don't respond, too busy laughing with one another to notice my confusion.

I don't know what they're referring to. I'm assuming this was something that happened after I left. A memory I'm not privy to. I bet a whole heap happened after I left. So many memories I'm not a part of. Memories I can't laugh along with. Memories I missed out on.

"Hey? You okay, Quinny?"

When I snap myself out of my thoughts, I find Cash looking at me, his eyes full of concern. And I know immediately that I'm crying, the night air cool as it whips gently against my tear-stained cheeks. I sniffle, quick to wipe my eyes with the sleeve of Dad's coat that I'm wearing.

"You all right?" Cash asks again, his brows drawing together as he studies me.

78

"Yeah." I nod, forcing myself to smile before tipping my head back and finishing my whiskey. "I'm just thinking of all the memories I missed with him over the last ten years." As I admit it out loud, another tear falls, and then another, and then suddenly the emotion is all too overwhelming. It feels as if it's strangling me. I can't breathe through the sob that bubbles at the back of my throat.

"All the memories I missed out, because I was too damn selfish and proud, and *terrified* to come back here!" I bury my face in my hands, hunching forward, crying for everything I've lost, everything I've missed out on. Everything that's gone, that I'll never get back.

I feel an arm wrap around me, and I jump ever so slightly, looking up through bleary eyes to see Cash right there by my side, his own eyes glassy. And, for a moment, I'm disappointed. I wanted it to be Tripp. I wanted him to be here for me, like I was there for him this morning. I wanted him to lend a shoulder, like the one I gave him to cry upon. But Tripp isn't here. He's still sitting across from me, staring at me through the flames of the fire, his face eerily blank.

"Remember the time . . ." Tripp begins, his voice quiet, raspy as he continues, "When you left this place, and Dad couldn't even manage to drag his sorry ass outta bed for three fuckin' days straight?" His steely gaze fixes on me, resentment flashing within his hard stare.

I blink back my tears, watching him as he glances from me to Cash and back again, his brows pulling together in anger.

"Tripp, don't—" Cash warns.

"Remember the Christmases he used to hang your stocking above the fireplace, in the hope that you'd surprise him and miraculously just show up on the doorstep, even though deep down he knew you wouldn't?" Tripp glares at me.

"Hey, c'mon, man." Colt reaches across, clapping his best friend's back. "Don't do this. Not now."

I sniffle, my shoulders trembling as an overwrought emotion consumes me from the inside out.

"*You*. It was *you* who left, Quinny." Tripp stands abruptly to his feet, staggering ever so slightly as he lifts the crystal bottle to his lips, finishing what's left of Dad's beloved aged whiskey. "You're the one who didn't come back," he splutters, pointing an accusatory finger at me. "You've got no one else to blame but your fuckin' self." And, with that, he throws the empty bottle into the fire, the flames causing the glass to crackle before exploding into a million shards. And then he turns, stumbling over his own feet as he walks away, his silhouette disappearing into the darkness.

I turn to Cash, my bottom lip trembling as tears stream down my face. But he just shakes his head, squeezing my shoulder. He leans in a little closer, placing a kiss to the top of my head. "I should go after him . . ."

I want to tell him no. That he shouldn't go after him. That he should just let him go. That he should stay with me. But, I don't. Instead, I nod, and watch through bleary eyes as Cash jogs off, disappearing in the same direction Tripp took off to.

I pull my knees up to my chest, wrapping Dad's coat around me as tight as I can, and I bury my face into the warmth of the fluffy wool collar, crying.

I don't bother looking up when I feel the warm hand on my shoulder. I know his touch all too well, even after ten years. It's firm yet gentle. Strong and protective. And it's actually exactly what I need right now.

Another sob racks through me, and before I even know what's happening, Colt's hand moves from my shoulder, and his arms come around me, pulling me to him.

Glancing up through my tears, I stammer a breath, finding his gaze set on me as he holds me so close.

"Thank you," I manage through my emotion, sniffling back my tears.

He manages a small smile, shaking his head to dismiss my

gratitude. He presses a soft yet lingering kiss to the top of my head as I bury my face into his chest, gripping his jacket so tight like at any moment he might pull away before I'm ready to let him go. I need him right now. More than anything. Even if only for this one, fleeting moment.

# Chapter 9

I sat through the meeting with the lawyers. Signed what I had to sign. Listened as Cash took control of Tripp every now and again, reined him in and kept him in line, while saying what needed to be said. He's always so in control and collected. An enviable quality. Where Tripp and I are hotheaded like our father, but are both fair like our mother; Cash is just like Mom was, yet the spitting image of our father. He'll make a good landowner. Dad would be so proud of the way he's handling everything.

Dad had set aside trusts for each of us, and ownership of Wagner Ranch is divided. Cash gets forty percent. Tripp and I get twenty-five each. But what shocks me most of all is that remaining ten percent. When the lawyer read out that entitlement, I couldn't help but shed a tear.

*"To Colt Edward Henry, for his years of loyalty and sacrifice. For his dedication and commitment. And for being a damn good kid. I couldn't be more proud to call you my third son."*

I really wish Colt had been there for the reading. I'd have loved to see the look on his face.

So, Cash will be moving into the main house, as landowner; he'll take over control of the ranch, and Tripp will be his foreman, just as Cash was for Dad.

Colt will continue on as lead hand.

Me? Well, I guess I'm just expected to take my trust fund and go back to New York. To my big, expensive apartment in Tribeca. To my closet full of designer heels and handbags. To my dream life. But, right now, after everything that's happened, as I sit here on the bed I slept in as a teenager, dressed in a simple black dress, preparing to say goodbye to my father once and for all, I'm not sure that's what I want anymore. To go back to New York. New York City is like another world, now. A different world. A world that might not be meant for me anymore. A world that, perhaps, was never meant for me.

I sigh a heavy sigh full of conflict and emotion, battling with myself to keep what little composure I have left dwindling inside of me. Half the damn town is expected to show up at Royal Wagner's funeral, and I refuse to cause a spectacle of myself. If I can just make it through today without falling apart in front of anyone, I can come back to the house and fall apart in private.

A gentle tap sounds on my door.

"Come in." I smooth down the skirt of my dress, standing.

Cash steps in, dressed in a crisp black suit, a black Stetson perched on top of his head, beard neatly trimmed. His eyes are sad, and with one look we share something only two siblings can share on the day they're laying a parent to rest. He clears his throat, pressing his lips together in the hint of a smile, lingering in the doorway as he takes a look around my room, and I can tell he's flustered, that there's something else on his mind.

Tripp.

"You ready?" Cash asks, straightening his tie.

I nod. "Where's Tripp?"

He shakes his head, looking down to the floor a moment. "He was drinking . . . *again*." He shrugs, shaking his head when he meets my gaze once more. "He stormed off in a huff when I told him to pull himself together."

Infuriatingly, my heart stammers in my chest at the thought of

83

my brother out there, all alone at a time like this. Drunk, emotional. He's not handling it. It breaks my heart to see him hurting so much. And I hate it. I hate that he can make me feel this way. It's as if Tripp can do and say whatever he likes to me without consequence. He can hate me, mock me, pick at me and pick at me until there's nothing left to pick. But still, he's all I worry about, and if I'm being honest, I'd die for him. I just want my brother back.

"He'll be fine, Quinny. He just needs some fresh air," Cash says as if he can read my thoughts.

I take a deep breath that trembles through me, crossing the room, and I stop in front of my big brother, smoothing my hands down over his suit jacket, looking up at him before we wrap our arms around one another, holding each other tight in an embrace I can feel he needs just as much as I do. And then he takes my hand, leading the way.

I wasn't wrong. By the time our black car rolls to a stop at the very top of Wagner's Bluff, a clearing overlooking the sprawling ranch, to the mountains in the distance, it appears almost the entire town of Black Canyon has congregated by the small family cemetery where my mother, my grandparents, great-grandparents, all my ancestors are buried.

"Are you okay?" Cash looks at me from the other side of the car, and I nod. A lie. He offers a knowing smile, opening his door and getting out.

The driver opens my door for me, taking my hand and helping me out of the SUV. I thank him with whatever sorry excuse for a smile I can manage, taking a deep breath before continuing around the car. I stop when I suddenly find all eyes on me in some kind of hushed reverence, like they can't possibly believe I'm actually here, as if the estranged Wagner girl couldn't possibly come back for her father's funeral. The shock and confusion are palpable through the air, but I keep my chin high in a show of confidence I don't feel.

Cash is waiting for me, and I look only at him because he provides an assurance of safety and protection. He takes my trembling hand and we continue through the crowd of people, some of whom are smiling pitifully at me, others who are outright glowering at me, the girl who left Colt Henry at the altar. As Cash shakes hands with, and nods to the people he passes, I keep my eyes firmly planted on the ground, intimidated if nothing else.

At the end of the walkway we're met by Reverend Jackson and Shelby. Shelby hugs me first, holding me a moment, and I relax in her arms, closing my eyes, but when I open them, I'm immediately drawn to Colt walking toward the cliff's edge, head bowed, his hands shoved into his pockets. He's dressed in an impeccable suit, a matching black Stetson on his head. And that's when I notice Tripp cutting a lonely, silhouetted figure, staring out over the view of the rolling mountains and lush green valleys of the ranch. Colt stops next to his friend, placing a supportive hand on his shoulder, their backs to us, and I find some relief in the fact that Tripp still has his best friend after all these years. I know, no matter what, with Colt by his side, Tripp will be okay.

"Let's get this over with." Cash touches my shoulder.

I nod, reluctantly following him, trying so hard to avoid the curious glances coming my way. I take the seat next to him, and Tripp staggers over with assistance from Colt's steady hand, dropping down into the seat next to me with a huff. I take the chance to study Colt, from the disheveled hair beneath his lopsided hat, to his untucked button-down and loosened necktie. He's a mess, in more ways than one. I want to reach out, to grab a hold of his hand, but I don't do that because I doubt I'd be able to take his rejection.

"Royal Wagner was a simple man. He asked for nothing, wanted for nothing. He was a fearless man. A man I looked up to my whole life. He showed me everything I ever needed, ever wanted to know. He had the kindest heart, but my God, was he stubborn."

The congregation laughs at Cash's words, causing him to stop momentarily. He manages a smile, focusing back down on his notes. "But it was Royal Wagner's relentless and unwavering stubbornness that was his greatest asset. He knew how to fight, how to challenge, and how to win. But he also knew how and when to admit defeat. Because with his stubbornness came a humility that not a lot of people are lucky enough to possess nowadays."

From the corner of my eye I watch Tripp bow his head, his shoulders trembling, and it takes all I have not to reach out and gently touch his arm in a show of support. Just to let him know that I'm here for him. But, again, I don't. I leave that support to Colt on his other side, hoping like hell he's holding him up as best he can.

"Dad used to say, one day, son, this'll all be yours." Cash waves a hand in the direction of the land. "You need to know how to take care of it so, one day, you can hand the reins over to your son. And now, as I stand here, a father myself, I finally know what he meant back then. This is our father's legacy, his life, his whole world." Cash pauses, his eyes finding Tripp and then me. He nods. "It's up to us to keep that legacy going, so that the memory of Royal Wagner lives on in this land that he worked so hard to hold on to his whole life."

Cash takes a moment, looking down at his notes, clearing his throat, and I can tell the emotion is getting the better of him. He looks up one last time, and this time his eyes meet mine, holding me steady with his gaze. "Dad always said that in life, it doesn't matter where we go, or how long we're gone for. What matters is that we never forget where we come from, so that, no matter what, we can always come home."

My jaw falls open and tears sting my eyes as I gawp at my brother, remembering my father's words spoken almost ten years ago when I left Black Canyon. I manage a smile through my tears, nodding at Cash with a look of gratitude, because I had no idea how much I desperately needed to hear those words. And now, they mean even more than when I first heard them all those years ago in the airport.

"This here, this is our home, and right here, among the memories of our mother, and our grandparents, our ancestors, this is where we will ultimately end up, because it's here where we belong. Home," Cash continues. "Royal Wagner is survived by myself, Cash Wagner. By my brother, Tripp Wagner. And, our sister, Quinn. And, Dad, this is our promise to you." He pauses, looking down at the mahogany coffin laden with native wild flowers, so beautiful and rustic, just the way he would have liked it. "For as long as we grace this land of yours, we will never let your memory die."

Silence ensues, and Cash tucks his notes away into the inside breast pocket of his suit jacket. On his way past, he places a hand on the coffin, stopping a moment and closing his eyes, whispering a few hushed words we're not privy to before continuing back to Shelby, taking CJ from her.

Tripp shifts off his seat, staggering a little to find his feet. He chuckles to himself as he sways ever so slightly with every step he takes to the lectern. I didn't know he was speaking, and suddenly panic is settling low in my belly. I cast Colt an uncertain glance, and he meets my gaze with one of his own, fleeting, yet full of worry. I bite down on my bottom lip, watching as my unstable brother fumbles with the microphone, looking out over the gathering. He removes his hat, raking his fingers through his mussed, sandy blond hair, and his eyes are glossy, the whites painfully bloodshot, his gaze full of pure and unsettling disdain as it fixes on me, and immediately my skin pricks, because that is a look I know all too well.

*Please, Tripp, no.*

"Royal Wagner, huh?" Tripp begins with a chuckle. "What a guy!"

*Shit . . .* I glance at Cash, his face ashen, jaw tight as he watches our brother with what appears to be bated breath, knowing exactly what drunk-Tripp is capable of.

"You know, not many people know this, but the only reason I'm even here today, gracing God's big beautiful earth, is because I shared a womb with my sister, Daddy's little angel, Quinn."

Have you ever heard a pin drop? That's the sound that trails Tripp's spiteful, spluttered words.

I close my eyes a moment as a few people in the crowd gasp audibly, whispering to one another as an awkward silence full of tension settles heavily in the air.

"Yeah." Tripp nods, wiping his sniffling nose with the back of his hand. "Mom and Dad wanted a daughter to complete their *perfect* little family. They never wanted another son. I was an added extra. A bonus. An unfortunate mistake. Collateral damage. I guess that's why my whole life I could never do anything right, no matter how hard I tried. It was always *Tripp's* fault. *My* fault I left the barn open when we were ten and a pack of wolves got in and killed two of the horses." Tripp blinks at me, and I flinch under the weight of his scowl.

I know exactly what he's referring to. But it had been my fault. The wolves. I left the barn open. Tripp covered for me. He took the blame. I never asked him to, he just did it, but I never spoke up. I could have. It was nothing more than a careless mistake. I could have told the truth, but I didn't, and it was my brother who had been punished for my mistake.

"It was always *my* fault. My fault when Quinn left. *My* fault she never came back." Tripp scrubs a hand over his face, sniffling. "I was *nothing* compared to my *darling* sister. Daddy's precious little favorite. Which is funny, because it was *me* who stuck around. I stayed. I was the one who gave up every damn thing I ever had: college, a future someplace else. But I forfeited everything, just to stay and help keep this damn place running while she went off and chased her dreams."

At that, both Cash and Colt quickly get out of their seats, carefully approaching the lectern, one on either side of Tripp, forcing him away. But he doesn't go without one last mention of me, struggling against his brother and his best friend to turn, pointing an accusatory finger in my direction. "I hope you got everything you ever wanted, Quinny!"

My shoulders tense with the undeniable feel of everyone looking at me, their judgmental eyes boring into the back of my head. Shelby reaches out and takes a hold of my hand, but her reassuring touch is pointless. Tripp has succeeded yet again in tearing me down. But, the worst part of it all is that his words are nothing more than blatant, painful truths, and I can't help but feel less than an inch tall as I sink further down into my seat.

After a moment or two, Tripp is wrangled off to the side, out of ears' reach by Colt and Cash. Reverend Jackson tentatively approaches the microphone, offering a faltering and awkward-as-hell smile over the congregation, his gaze zeroing in on me. "Would . . . anyone else care to say a few words?"

I quickly shake my head once, looking down at my trembling hands in my lap, feeling my cheeks flame. I just want this to be over. I need to get the hell out of here, and quick.

# Chapter 10

Sometimes, a house can feel most empty when it's full.

Sometimes, it's when you're surrounded by people that you feel more alone than ever.

After the incident at the funeral, I've managed to keep out of the way for the most part of the reception. Buried in the small space beneath the stairs, on the bench seat where we used to store our rain boots as kids. The same glass of wine in my hand that I've been holding since we got back from the cemetery, just watching everyone as they eat our food, drink our liquor, and talk about my father as if he was their dearest friend. I can't help but roll my eyes. My father hated most of the people in the Canyon. He kept to himself mostly. He had a few friends, like Duke from the bar, and Robert Whatshisname, who owned the Lodge before it was purchased by a big city corporation that turned it into a fancy country club for the wealthy landowners to sit and drink together and talk about how much money they have.

This ranch was my dad's whole life. His best friends were the horses and his cattle. He found solace in his land.

Most of the people in this house right now barely even knew my father. They're only here for the status. Royal Wagner's funeral.

It's almost laughable. But still, I remain quiet and out of the way, because I don't feel like dealing with any further drama right now.

Tripp is off somewhere, probably halfway through another bottle of whiskey. Cash is doing the rounds. Shelby is being a good little hostess. CJ is curled up in my father's old chair, sleeping like a baby; I wish he was awake so I could at least have him to keep me company. Hell, I'd even let him draw doodles all over my face again. But sadly, I have no one.

I finish my wine, and glance around carefully, zeroing in on a server by the fireplace holding a tray of fresh glasses filled with rosé. I calculate how many steps it will take to swoop in, exchange my glass for a new one, and come back to my secret little alcove. My eyes furtively flit from side to side, surveying the possibility of damage, the threat of awkward encounters. But just when I think the coast is clear, I step forward, and immediately I'm approached by Ms. Winslow, a total gold digger who was trying desperately for years to make her way into my father's bed, and his will.

"Quinn, *darling*, how are you?" She looks down her surgically enhanced nose at me, circling the tip of her index finger around the rim of her crystal champagne flute.

"Ms. Winslow." I manage a tight-lipped smile.

"Oh, darling." She waves a manicured hand in the air. "Call me Sarah. We're practically *family*."

She's referring to the one date my father obligingly took her on, and I bite down hard on the inside of my cheek to stop myself from laughing at her ridiculousness.

"How does Colt feel having *you* back in town?" she continues, leaning in, speaking low so only I have the privilege of hearing her utter bullshit. "I'm sure it hurt like hell to see *your* face again."

I blink at her.

"I mean, you *are* the woman who ruined his *life*, after all." She sips her champagne, eyeing me over the lip of her glass. "Broke his heart. Forced him to the bottle. It must break his heart all over again to see you swan into town like you've done nothing

91

wrong." She clicks her tongue, shaking her head, and I catch the flash of something in her gray eyes, a glint of malevolence, and I know she's goading me. I made her life hell when she tried dating my father. Now, the tables have turned, and it takes all I have not to launch at her.

"Ms. Winslow."

I turn quickly at the sound of the familiar voice over my left shoulder. Colt standing there to my left, smiling politely down at Sarah Winslow, his eyes momentarily flashing to me before focusing back on the horrible woman. "Ma'am, do you mind if I steal Quinn away for a moment?"

Ms. Winslow clutches a hand to her chest, her fingers deftly toying with the string of pearls around her neck, cheeks flushing profusely as Colt flashes her his dimpled smile. "Of course. Y'all go." She waves us away, offering me an indulgent wink, and my hand balls into a fist before Colt takes hold of my elbow, leading me away.

The moment I step outside into the cool afternoon air, I release the breath I've been holding in the hope that it would keep me from losing it at Ms. Winslow. I throw my hands up into the air, shaking my head at the woman's insolence.

Turning, I find Colt standing there watching me, his hands tucked into the pockets of his trousers, the hint of a knowing smirk lingering on his lips, and I can't help but laugh. "Is that woman for real?" I yell through my incredulous laughter. "I mean, who the hell does she think she is?"

Colt lifts a hand, scrubbing it over his lips in an attempt to stifle his grin while nodding. "Yep, she's something else, all right."

"I swear, I could've shanked her!" I exclaim, holding up my empty wine glass for emphasis.

Colt steps forward, removing the glass from my vise-like grasp and placing it onto a nearby fence post. "That's why I stepped in. I could see it in your eyes. It was like Davina Bradford's after-prom party, all over again."

I laugh out loud, suddenly remembering back to the night I

almost threw down with Davina Bradford after prom when she was clearly trying to get her hands on Colt. She tried to tell me that my friend Taylor was looking for me. I went all over her huge mansion trying to find Taylor, and when I did, she just looked at me like I'd grown another head, telling me she wasn't looking for me at all, that she was too busy making out with Brady Mason. I marched right back to the recreation room to find Davina in a compromising position with *my* boyfriend, Colt's hands held innocently in the air while she was outright trying to give the poor guy a lap dance to a Beyoncé song.

She never even saw me coming when I launched at her and ripped out three of her ratty, bleached blonde extensions. And I can't help but cringe at the thought of that memory. I always was a little crazy when it came to Colt Henry.

"Don't worry about Sarah Winslow," Colt says with a shrug, pulling me back from my memory.

"Did you hear what she was saying?" I ask, hoping like hell he didn't.

He nods slowly.

I swallow hard. "I'm sorry. I—"

He shakes his head, dismissing my apology. "They're all the same in this town. You know how it is more than anyone."

This time it's me who nods. Because I do know how the people in this town can be. Better than most. I look up at Colt as he glances out at the mountains, and I take him in. He looks handsome as hell dressed in his suit, a crisp white shirt underneath, the top few buttons since unfastened, his black necktie loose, hanging casually. A glimpse of his chest is showing, and the same silver cross he's been wearing since we were kids flashes when the light hits it. As if he can sense my eyes on him, he removes his hat, combing his fingers through his hair as if he felt he needed to do something with his idle hands.

"Once again, here you are saving my sorry ass!" I laugh humorlessly, rolling my eyes at myself.

"Yeah, well . . ." He shrugs, putting his hat back on and stuffing his hands back into his pockets. "I wasn't gonna just stand there and watch her talk to you like that."

I manage a smile, meeting his eyes momentarily. "Thanks."

He presses his lips together, the hint of a smile causing his dimples to pop, his eyes zeroing in over my shoulder, gazing off into the distance.

"I don't even wanna go back in there," I say, glaring back at the house. "That undeniable sound of what feels like a million people whispering about you behind your back . . ." I trail off, feeling Colt's eyes on me. And I look to see a crease pulling between his brows, hesitation obvious within his green gaze.

But then he speaks, shocking me with his words. "Let's go for a walk, then." He juts his chin in the direction of the trail that leads down to the river.

"A-are you s-sure . . .?" I ask, my brows knitting together in tentative uncertainty.

Colt nods for me to follow, and I do, desperate to get away from that house and the people inside it.

"So, how's everything in New York?"

Colt and I have been walking for a while, slow enough for me to keep up in my heels, fast enough to get the hell away from Sarah Winslow and the rest of the unforgiving Canyon folk inside my dead father's house. We've been otherwise quiet, save for the amicable chitchat spoken just to fill the void of the awkward silences that keep settling between us. But this is the first time he's asked about me, and I'm slightly taken aback by his question.

"Um . . ." I search for my words, kicking at a loose pebble on the ground. "It's– It's okay."

"Just okay?"

I shrug. "I mean, it was great, at first. I loved it."

"But now?"

I lift my gaze from the ground, feeling his eyes on me, but

94

I avoid his curious stare, choosing instead to look out over the valley that was once my home. "It's funny. I can stand right here in this one spot, staring out at these mountains, with no one around, nothing. Nobody. And I feel whole." I glance sideways at Colt, finding him watching me intently. He nods for me to continue. "But New York—a city of eight million people—there's just something about it that makes me feel so lonely. So empty."

We stop on the hill, looking down over a huge herd of cattle grazing the rolling fields. Colt stands beside me, saying nothing, folding his arms over his chest, and together we just watch the world pass. The breeze blowing through the trees. A bird of prey circling high in the sky up above. The gray clouds rolling in with the threat of snow, enveloping the highest peaks of the mountains. It's breathtaking, in every sense of the word. But, being here, staring out at what was my father's pride and joy, it brings back all the memories, all the feelings, all the emotions.

"God, I miss this place," I whisper under my breath.

I feel Colt look at me and I can't help but smile. "I mean, obviously I miss my father. I miss my brothers. I . . . I miss *you*." I don't look at him, I can't risk him seeing the tears in my eyes. The tears that are for him, and for everything else I was stupid enough to lose along the way. "I miss my home." The emotion racking through me gets the better of me, and a tear falls over the edge, hitting my cheek, and that one singular tear is my downfall, causing a sob to bubble up the back of my throat. "I lost so much. I lost everything. I miss it all and it's all my fault. I just . . . I just wish I could take it all back," I cry, burying my face into my hands.

After a moment, a familiar warmth presses against me from behind. An immediate feeling of safety and comfort comes over me. A familiar strength wraps around me. A familiar scent inundates my entire being. Colt stands behind me, his arms wrapping around me, holding me. I feel his lips press against the top of my head in a tender kiss, lingering as he gently shushes me. I breathe him in—a trembling, racking breath—my tears still falling. And suddenly, in that moment, despite my tears and the raw emotion consuming me from the inside, everything is okay. But that's the thing about Colt. He always makes everything feel as if, no matter what, it's going to be okay. His strength, and his warmth, and the comfort of his familiarity is all I need right now. In his arms, it truly does feel as if everything will be right again.

We stand there for a long time. Just the two of us. I don't even know how long. Me resting back against Colt's strong chest, his arms protectively wrapped around me. I relax my head back against his shoulder, staring out as a violet sky settles overhead, dusk falling, turning the air cold and icy as it blows down from the mountains.

"Did Colt talk to you about the lawyers?" I ask quietly.

"No." He moves, and I know he's shaking his head. "What about?"

I know I should let my brother tell him. But I can't help myself. I want to see the look in his eyes. So, I turn in his arms, glancing up at him through my lashes. His jaw remains tight, in that way he does so as to not give himself away. And while his arms remain around me, his gaze is set intently straight ahead, focused over my head, out over the valley.

"My father's will," I begin, biting back my smile. "He left you ten percent of this place."

I feel him stiffen. His chest stops rising and falling. He isn't breathing. He doesn't even blink. In fact, the only thing giving anything away is the reflection of the setting sun causing his eyes to glisten with the tears he's so clearly trying to hold back.

"He loved you," I continue, and I know those words affect him. I can feel it in the way his hands grip me a little tighter.

Colt doesn't remember what it was like to feel the love of a parent. His grandmother loved him. But the love of a grandparent differs significantly from that of a parent. And Colt never had that love.

96

"We should head back to the house," he finally says, his raspy voice breaking the steely yet companionable silence.

I crane my neck, looking up at him, his arms still secured around me, like he can't bear to let me go even if he wanted to. I stare into his eyes, finding a conflicting emotion deep within his gaze. He's scared, nervous, and everything in between. And so am I. It's obvious. Something suddenly feels different between us. I can't be imagining it. I know he feels it too.

But there's something else in his eyes. His secrets. His past. Whatever it is he's not telling me. He's guarding himself because he knows it's safer. He knows the pain I'm capable of inflicting upon him, and that tears at my heart, shredding at it with sharp, violent claws.

After a few beats I nod, my stomach twisting at the thought of going back there to the Sarah Winslows of the world and I can tell he notices my apprehensions.

"I'll walk in with you." He offers the hint of a smile, and, for the first time since I've been back, I witness that magical sparkle within his emerald eyes, and it momentarily knocks the air out of me. "Strength in numbers," he adds with a casual shrug.

I nod again, pressing my lips together in the hope of stifling my smile at least a little.

His arms move from around me, and I feel a brief sense of loss, but then he offers his elbow, and I meet his gaze for a moment before linking my arm through his. He smiles again, leading the way, and with that one tiny gesture, my heart is whole.

# Chapter 11

I'm helping Shelby tidy up once everyone has finished eating our food and drinking our drinks, piling out of the house in drunken hordes. The servers are doing all the hard work, but I had to do something. I was about to send myself crazy, completely over-thinking my moment with Colt back on the hill. Even now, as I'm collecting discarded wine glasses from the great room, my gaze is intently focused on the man himself as he sits with Cash, the two of them in the middle of what looks to be a rather serious conversation, Colt gripping a copy of Dad's will in his hands.

"He misses you, you know?"

I jump at the sound of the hushed voice so close to my ear, almost dropping the glasses in my hands, causing them to clang together loudly. Cash and Colt glance over at me, but I turn away quickly, my eyes bulging when I find Shelby standing right there, a knowing smile playing on her lips as she looks from me, to Colt, and back again, quirking a brow.

"What?" I hiss, my brow furrowed. "What are you even talking about?"

"Oh, like you haven't spent the last forty minutes staring at him longingly from a distance?" Shelby chuckles quietly. "CJ is more discreet than you. And he's only four years old."

I roll my eyes. "I have no idea what you're talking about." I turn and head back up the few steps, hurrying the hell out of the great room, Shelby hot on my heels.

"Don't think I didn't notice you two disappear for an hour," she whispers loudly as we walk into the kitchen. "Where'd you go?"

I stop, placing the glasses onto the island counter before I do drop them, searching the room for the possibility of anyone who might care to eavesdrop. The coast is clear, save for two servers oblivious to us as they pack away their empty trays, and I take a deep, fortifying breath. I glance at Shelby, finding her staring at me incredulously, her eyes wide and desperate for an explanation. And, I mean, if I can't trust Shelby, who the hell can I trust?

"We went for a walk." I shrug, as if it isn't a big deal. "I'd been *attacked* by Sarah Winslow—"

"Ugh," Shelby groans with disgust, interrupting me. "She's such an old cow."

I bite back my laughter. "Colt saw it happen. He stepped in. Pulled me away before I killed her with my bare hands."

Shelby cups her hands to her chest, right over her heart. "He *rescued* you!"

For the third time in as many days, but I don't dare divulge that piece of information. "You read far too many romance novels." I roll my eyes again.

She guffaws. "So? What happened on your *walk*?" She waggles her eyebrows suggestively.

"Calm down, Shelby." I balk at her reaction. "I just buried my father. It's not like I took Colt to the back barn and got it on in the loft!"

Her cheeks flush as she smiles to herself, loading the dishwasher. "I need a life."

I lean against the island, watching her, her words repeating over and over again in my head. "What did you mean when you said that he misses me?"

She stands, looking at me, and she's suddenly serious, her

eyes flitting from side to side, checking the coast is still clear. She moves a little closer, resting against the counter beside me. "Promise you won't tell anyone I told you?"

I nod, my heart rate increasing from the secretiveness within her whispered tone.

She leans in even closer, so close I can smell the scent of her sweet vanilla perfume. "Cash walked into the bunkhouse to speak to the ranch hands. Colt was coming out of the bathroom, dressed only in a towel . . ."

My brows lower, pulling together in uncertainty as to where the hell *this* story is heading.

Shelby's eyes widen to the size of saucers. "He's got your name tattooed right over his chest. Right where his heart is!"

I blink at her, processing her words.

Colt has my name tattooed on him?

A permanent reminder of me etched right over his heart?

Now I don't quite know what to think.

"Cash didn't say anything to him about it," Shelby continues as she goes back to loading the dishwasher. "He just pretended he didn't see it. But he told me as soon as he came home. I swear that big, burly man is a true romantic on the inside . . ." She smiles wistfully at the thought of her husband.

I glance back in the direction of the great room, trying so hard to wrap my head around this. Sure, the tattoo could be old. But he sure as hell never had it before things ended between us. And then he had his accident. He was in a coma for nine weeks, and intense physical therapy afterwards for an entire year. He hated me for so long. Why on earth would he have his skin permanently branded with my name?

"Shelby, can I ask you something?"

She secures the dishwasher door closed, pressing a button before standing back up, meeting my eyes. She nods with a kind smile. "Sure, go ahead, honey."

"Is there something I should know about him?"

Her brow furrows in confusion.

"I know there's something going on." I shake my head. "He's still here, working at the ranch, living in the cabin. He's not married. He's single. He *hated* me. And, after what I did, I deserved that hate. But now you're telling me he has my name tattooed over his heart. The same heart that I *broke*?" I laugh once, emphasizing my exasperation. "It just doesn't make sense."

Shelby goes to say something, but then she hesitates, gauging me.

"I know you know." I implore her with my eyes. "I could see it yesterday morning, when you asked me about him bringing me back to your place . . ."

"It's not up to me to tell you, Quinn." Shelby looks down at her hands before meeting my eyes once again. "You should speak to Colt." She wipes her hands with the dishtowel, offering me a sad smile. "I gotta get back to the house to relieve the sitter. Little bitch charges triple after ten, just to eat all our damn food." She touches my arm, squeezing gently before turning and walking out.

I stand there in the silence of the empty kitchen thinking about what she said, allowing her words to sink in. Pulling myself up onto the counter, I release a heavy breath and look down at my hands.

Could I really stay here for good? Could I really give up my life in New York and come back to the Canyon? I mean, I've got nothing left in the city. No job. My reputation has probably taken a serious nosedive since being let go by Edward Hawkins, himself. I've received countless text messages and voicemails from Oliver, asking how I am, if I need anything, telling me that he's keeping my client list serviced in the hope that I return. He's literally all I have back in that city. One person in eight million.

But can I really go back there now, after everything? In three days it feels as if so much has changed. My father is gone. Cash is in charge of the ranch. Tripp has completely lost his mind. Colt has my name tattooed over his heart. As much as I wanted to get out of here all those years ago, I can't deny that this place is my home; maybe this is where I need to be right now. Maybe it's where I've needed to be all along.

I'm not sure how long I've been sitting here in the kitchen, on the island countertop, considering everything, but I'm pulled abruptly from my thoughts by the blur of Cash as he runs past the doorway, followed by Colt chasing quickly after him.

My brows knit together as I push myself off the counter, slowly walking out into the hall in time to see the two of them disappear into Dad's office.

"What's wrong?" I call out, picking up pace after them.

When I enter the office, Cash has the safe door open, and I watch on as he takes out a few bundles of cash.

"Um . . . *Excuse* me? What the hell is going on?" I raise my voice, stepping inside.

Colt glances at me, his face fraught with concern. "Tripp's in jail."

My heart kicks into gear as panic sets in. "What? What do you mean he's in *jail*?"

"Got into a damn fight. Sheriff took him in." Cash moves past me, tucking the money into the back pocket of his dress pants. "I'll deal with it."

I grab his shirtsleeve before he can get away. "Cash! You have a wife and a kid. You stay. I'll go."

"Over my dead body you're goin' out there on your own . . ." Cash shakes his head, and I can see the frustration in his eyes as he pinches the bridge of his nose.

I gawp at him, placing a hand on my hip. "I am a grown-ass woman!"

"God dammit, Quinny!" he snaps, and I stiffen, hearing a tone in his voice I've never heard before, one that sounds just like my father.

Colt quickly steps in between us, glancing down at me. "It's all right. I'll go. You can come with me."

102

Cash relents with a heavy sigh, handing Colt the money. And I grab Colt's arm, pulling him toward the door, my heart racing as fraught desperation takes over. I have to go get my brother. He's in jail. He needs me.

The drive into town is silent. The air between us is obviously thick with something I can't quite put my finger on. Tension and something else. Something not completely unbearable. It feels so weird to be sitting in Colt's truck, in a position I've been in so many times before, but now, ten years later, after everything, it feels so different. But, at least this time I'm sober.

I shiver, wishing I'd stopped to grab a coat on my way out of the house. But we'd been in such a rush, I didn't even think about it.

"You cold?"

I flash Colt a glance as he focuses intently on the dimly lit road ahead, his face impassive, illuminated by the lights of the dash.

"Yeah." I rub my arms through the thin wool of my dress.

He reaches forward, twisting the dial, and warmth blasts through the vents, heating my cheeks, and I can't help but sigh in a contented relief as it stifles the chill coursing through me.

"I feel so bad," I confess, looking down at my hands in my lap. "After the funeral . . . I thought Tripp had just passed out in his apartment. I didn't know he actually *left*."

"He's not really dealing too well with it all," Colt offers in slightly more than a murmur.

"I'm worried about him." I sigh, my shoulders falling.

"He'll be okay. I'm looking out for him."

I jump a little, startled by the sudden and unexpected feel of Colt's hand as he reaches over, gently squeezing my shoulder. My eyes move from his hand, meeting his eyes before he quickly turns back to the road, but his hand remains in place for a moment longer, and I take the opportunity to place mine on top of his before he takes it away. Another silence follows, this one a little more confusing than the last, the only sound that of the tires treading the uneven country road, and the warm air blowing out through the vents.

"Is Dwight still sheriff?"

Colt huffs, a combination of an exasperated sigh and an incredulous laugh, and I look at him to see him shake his head. "No. He retired a few years back." He casts me a sardonic glance in my direction. "You remember Robbie Shepherd, from school?"

"Yeah . . ." Dread sinks low in my belly.

"He's sheriff, now."

"You have *got* to be kidding me!"

Colt shakes his head.

Robbie Shepherd made Tripp's life hell through school. He made all our lives hell. It all started when Tripp kissed Robbie's girlfriend at the spring dance in sophomore year. Robbie kicked Tripp's ass. A few months later, Robbie made up a horrible rumor about me, something about giving him a hand job in the boys' bathroom during third period. Tripp beat Robbie's ass, and then Colt jumped in and finished him off. After that, Robbie planted weed in Tripp's locker and got him suspended for a month. It was a vicious cycle that went on and on until graduation, and then some.

"Is he still a *dick*?"

"Why do you think Cash gave me three grand?" Colt scoffs with a shake of his head.

I gawp at him. "You have to *bribe* him?"

He nods, his jaw clenching.

"Asshole . . ." I whisper under my breath, glaring straight ahead.

Colt chuckles softly, and we continue into town with a slightly more companionable silence settling between us; our mutual hatred for Robbie Shepherd bringing us just that little bit closer as we hurry to bail Tripp's stupid drunk ass out of the county jail.

# Chapter 12

The sheriff's station is on the outskirts of town, with nothing and no one around.

I shiver against the night air as I get out of the truck, following Colt up the neatly landscaped path to the front door. He presses the after-hours buzzer, looking at me over his shoulder as we wait impatiently for someone to let us in. When the click of the latch sounds, he doesn't hesitate before opening the door, standing aside and allowing me to enter first.

Inside, the fluorescent lights overhead sting my tired eyes, but I proceed to the counter with my game face on, ringing the service bell not once, but four times to show that I mean business. I know they know we're here—there's security cameras all over—but I ring the bell anyway, and then once more in the hope of annoying Robbie Shepherd as much as I possibly can.

The glass door opens, and a somewhat familiar face appears. I'd know those shifty eyes anywhere. Although he's at least thirty pounds heavier, and clinging on for dear life to the thin smattering of hair that barely even covers his head, Robbie looks like the same piece of shit he was in high school.

"Well, well, well . . ." He flashes a smug smirk, looking me up and down. "The wayward Wagner returns."

I roll my eyes, throwing my head back in dramatic exasperation.

"And with the poor sucker you left standing at the altar." He laughs a high-pitched cackle, his eyes flashing to Colt over my shoulder.

I feel a sting from his words, but I do all I can not to show it, deadpanning and arching a brow while folding my arms over my chest. "Where's my brother?"

"Drunk tank." Robbie nods back in the direction of the lock-up, chewing on a toothpick. "I'm not letting him go tonight. He's a goddamn threat to society."

"He just lost his father," I exclaim. "*We* . . . We just lost our father."

He doesn't even flinch; heartless bastard.

Colt leans over me, placing the wads of cash onto the counter. Robbie's eyes linger on the neatly stacked money, and I can almost see him mentally calculating how much is there. He flashes me a dubious glance.

"Three grand." I sigh. "More than enough for your . . . *troubles*." My eyes rake up and down his lofty form, to where his buckle is straining against his rotund waist.

He picks up one of the stacks, flicking through each note, his gaze remaining on me. "You know he beat a guy with a pool cue? Broke his nose."

"He has a temper . . ." I shrug nonchalantly. "You of all people should know that."

"He picked up a barstool and smashed it over some other unsuspecting guy's head."

I blink once. "He's a Wagner."

"He's completely lost his shit."

"That's for me to worry about." I rest my hands flat on the counter, leaning forward, my eyes never once leaving his. "You want me to sign a bail sheet, or what?"

Robbie regards me, slowly looking me up and down, the ghost of a smug smirk playing on his lips as he turns, retrieving some paperwork from the filing cabinet behind him. He slams the forms down in front of me, takes the pen from the chest pocket of his neatly pressed shirt and holds it out. I snatch it from him and commence filling out the documentation, fully aware of his eyes trained on me, watching my every move. His gaze is weighty, uncomfortable, and as if Colt can sense my unease, he steps forward, staying close, a tentative hand coming to rest upon my shoulder, and I can't help but release a shaky breath of relief at his presence.

When I'm done, I place the pen onto the papers, sliding them over, glancing up at Robbie as he picks up the forms and studies them closely, which I can tell he's only doing to waste more time and further aggravate me.

"You got your money, *Shepherd*," Colt speaks up. "Quit being a dick and just bring Tripp out here."

I force myself to walk away, knowing if I stand here any longer, looking at Robbie's smug face with his red cheeks and sweat-beaded receding hairline, I'm going to say or do something that's only going to give him reason to assert his power and throw me in the cell along with my brother. So, I turn, and walk back outside, braving the cold in the hope the night air brings some semblance of relief to the skin prickling at the back of my neck.

A plume of white smoke billows out with my heavy breath, snaking up into the night sky, and I wrap my arms around myself, looking out at the silhouetted mountains across the way, darkness looming overhead. I can't even begin to fathom everything. Here I am, standing outside the sheriff's station at eleven o'clock on the night of my father's funeral, freezing my ass off while waiting for my brother to be released on bail. Where did it all go so wrong?

Robbie was right; Tripp is losing it. My brother. My twin. My other half. The one person in my life that I used to be able to feel and sense. I don't feel him anymore. The person I knew almost as well as I knew myself. I don't know him anymore. This is the guy I've shared some of my deepest, darkest secrets with. Once upon a time, I used to turn to Tripp for everything. He was the one I went to when I couldn't go to Dad. Now, he can't even stand the sight of me, and it's almost as if he's a stranger.

Behind me, the door opens before closing heavily, followed by inaudible cussing and grunting. I turn quickly to see Colt walking out, struggling with a clearly unsteady Tripp trying to break free of his hold. But he stops struggling the moment his gaze lands on me. In fact, he stops altogether, gawping at me, his eyes darkening.

"Are you okay?" I ask, taking a tentative step forward, noticing the nasty gash above his left brow, taped together with bloodied butterfly clips.

"Pfft." He scoffs dramatically, swaying on his feet. "As if you give a shit." His voice is hoarse, gruff, and laced with disdain.

"I'm here, aren't I?" I hold my arms out at my sides. "Only hours after laying our father to rest."

Tripp's eyes flash with anger and he lunges at me, sticking his finger right in my face, causing me to cower instinctively. "Don't you dare fuckin'—"

Colt stops him. "C'mon, Tripp, brother . . ." He hisses under the weight of my brother, trying to pull him away and lead him down the path. "Let's get you back home."

"Let me go. I ain't your fuckin' brother!" Tripp suddenly erupts with an explosive fury, shrugging out from Colt's arms. But then he launches forward, pushing his best friend in his chest.

Colt, barely affected by the assault, collects himself, taking a step away, a step closer to me, his hands held in the air in surrender. He's clearly doing all he can to avoid fighting with his best friend when he's so drunk and broken.

Tripp's cold eyes dart between the both of us, his brow furrowed. "Awww," he coos mockingly. "Will you look at y'all," he continues with a teasing lilt. "It's like a blast from the past. History fuckin' repeating itself!"

"Tripp—" Colt warns, his teeth gritting together.

I gauge my brother, taking him in from his hollow cheeks, pale, clammy face. Glassy eyes, with little to no emotion left within them. He's the shell of the man I remember him to be, and it's a heartbreaking sight to behold.

"Just like old times." Tripp laughs a chilling, humorless laugh that echoes through the quiet night. He points to Colt as he continues, "Before you were a pussy." His accusatory finger then lands on me, resentment clear and evident in his hard stare. "Before you were a *bitch*."

I rear back from his words. It's as if he's slapped me. I find myself instinctively reaching up to touch my cheek, just to make sure he didn't strike me without me realizing.

Tripp chuckles to himself, pushing past Colt and me and staggering down the path toward the truck parked in the lot. And sure, I could say something. Stand up for myself. But he's drunk. He's a mess. What's the point? He's not going to remember what I say tonight when he wakes up in the morning with a hangover from hell.

"C'mon," I say to Colt. "Let's just take him home."

I turn to follow my brother, but suddenly I'm being pushed out of the way by a force so strong, I almost fall to the ground. I collect myself in time to see Colt launching at Tripp from behind, crashing into him like a freight train. And, with an almighty thud, it all happens so quickly. Colt has Tripp on the ground, pummeling him to within an inch of his life, the two of them cursing one another out, grunting and crying through their violent tussle in a flurry of fists, elbows and knees, right there on the immaculately manicured lawn outside the damn sheriff's station.

What the hell is even happening?

"What are you *doing*?" I scream, running toward them. "Stop!"

But I can't do anything. There's no way I'm big enough or strong enough to come between these two brutes. I'm forced to just stand back and watch the two of them fighting on the ground, punching one another with everything they have. But the longer I watch, the more I realize that maybe this needs to happen. Colt and Tripp are like brothers. They love hard, and they fight harder. And there's obviously a lot of unresolved emotion in the air between them—it's almost stifling.

I flinch when Colt's fist connects with Tripp's face, when Tripp's knee finds its way to Colt's groin, each of them groaning out in pain. I can't bear to watch them hurt each other. It's sickening.

The door to the station behind me opens and an unexpected laughter rings through the air, causing me to swing around and watch as Robbie Shepherd stands in the doorway with two of his officers, all three of them watching on with bemused smirks, cheering and clapping as if they're at a damn boxing match in Las Vegas.

"You're really just gonna stand there and watch this happen?" I yell back at the three of them.

"We're on a break," Robbie says through a smarmy grin, shrugging casually as he takes a sip from his coffee mug.

I throw my hands in the air in resignation, glancing up to the sky before cursing under my breath as I step around the two grown-ass men fighting on the ground like teenage boys.

"Hurry the hell up," I throw over my shoulder on my way back to the truck. "I'm not standing out in the cold while y'all fight like a pair of damn idiots."

# Chapter 13

I smooth a hand over Tripp's back before pulling the bedsheets up over his shoulders, watching as he snores softly, oblivious to my presence. He passed out in the back seat on the way home, after Colt dragged him by the scruff of his collar once the two had sufficiently kicked each other's asses.

As I watch my brother sleep somewhat peacefully, his left cheek swollen and bruised, his chin grazed, nostrils bloodied, my mind is reeling from everything that's happened today. Today, we laid our father to rest. Today, I learned that my brother is on the verge of losing his mind altogether. Today, I found out that Colt has my name tattooed over his heart.

When did my life become the messy, screwed-up situation that it is now?

I wish my dad were here. He'd make everything okay again. Without him, it truly does feel as if things are completely falling apart.

With a heavily resigned sigh, I lean down, and I place a kiss to the top of Tripp's head, gently smoothing his sandy hair back from his face. And, with one last glance to check he has everything he needs—water, Tylenol, his cell charging on the side table next to him—I turn and leave the room, switching off the light on my way out.

I walk upstairs from Tripp's basement apartment to find the rest of the house dark and silent. A soft glow from the dwindling fire in the great room lights my way as I continue down the hall, and I stop at the landing, finding Colt sitting on the couch, his elbows resting on his knees, head buried in his hands. He looks so defeated, staring down at the rug on the floor, tearing his fingers through the longer lengths of his hair.

"He's asleep," I say, stepping down into the room.

Colt looks up, his face illuminated by the flickering flames of the fire, and I can barely contain my own gasp as I take him in, not having realized until now the extent of the damage my brother had caused. His left eye is almost completely swollen shut. A bloodied split cracks through his bottom lip. But beyond the physical damage his eyes tell the story of the deeper damage, the damage that can't be seen at first glance, the damage I know goes a lot deeper than just my brother's drunken fists.

I stop, clasping my hands together nervously. "Are you okay?"

He manages a nod, but when he makes his way to his feet, he winces out in pain, clutching a hand to his left side, and I hurry to him, holding him steady with a strong grip on his arm. I study him closely, racking my brain with how I can help him, but when our eyes meet, there's a sudden shift in the air between us. I see tears in his eyes, one winning the battle and slipping over the edge when his lashes flutter. It hits his swollen cheek and slides painfully slow down his face, and he makes no effort to wipe it away.

"Colt?" My voice falters. "What do you need? Ice? Pain meds?"

He shakes his head, closing his eyes tight, more tears slipping free, and I know in that instant more than medication and pain relief, more than anything else, all he needs is me.

I lean up on my tiptoes, hesitating momentarily before wrapping my arms around his neck, coaxing his head down to rest upon my shoulder. His hands grip my waist so tight as he buries his face into the crook of my neck, crying so quietly that his

112

trembling shoulders are the only thing giving him away. I smooth my hands over his hair, shushing him.

After a moment or two, slowly he lifts his head, looking at me with red-rimmed eyes, tear-stained cheeks, a heartbreaking fragility radiating from him, causing my own tears to threaten to break me. But, then, in the flash of an instant, I see the look in his eyes change right before me, his big hands moving up over my arms, my shoulders, following the curve of my neck until they're cradling my face, cupping my cheeks so tenderly, so carefully, it's as if he's afraid I might break.

And, at that moment, I can't even breathe.

At that moment, as I stare into his eyes, it's as if my whole world stops.

At that moment, it's just the two of us.

Colt leans in, his gaze flickering between mine, lingering so dangerously close I can feel his breath as it dances over my skin before, tentatively, his lips press against my forehead, pausing there a moment as if he's scared to move. But I want him to move. God, I've never wanted anything more in my life. And my breath trembles when he does move, peppering slow, languid kisses down over my temple, my cheek, before finding the corner of my mouth, just shy of my lips, driving me insane with his trepidation. It takes all I have not to pull him closer as he teases me, before taking my bottom lip between his teeth and gently sucking it into his mouth.

When a whimper escapes me, he takes that as permission, inundating me with a kiss so all-consuming it takes a few seconds before I fully come to. My hands instinctively find their way into his hair, my fingers tearing through the soft lengths as his tongue pushes its way into my mouth, the two of us reduced to nothing more than a flurry of hands, lips, and inexplicable emotion. I thrust my tongue into his mouth, desperate for him. For all of him. It's been too damn long, but the familiarity is like home. A kiss has never felt so right.

Colt groans, a gruff, animalistic sound that only further ignites the flame burning deep in my belly. I moan, his hands moving down, lower and lower, fingers toying with the skirt of my dress as he grips my ass through the delicate wool. I can feel him pressing into my stomach, and it makes me weak at the knees, so much so, I wrap my arms around him so tight, scared I might crumble to an obliterated heap right here on the floor if I don't hold on for dear life.

When he pulls away, his fingers working their way up my back, kneading my skin before finding the zip at the top of my dress, I meet his eyes. They're dark and full of wanton desire that makes my stomach dip and clench. He tenderly kisses my forehead, my cheek, ducking down to nip the very tip of my nose, moving to the shell of my ear and sucking gently on the lobe as he begins slowly unfastening the zip, pulling it lower, and lower, until my back is exposed. His fingertips trace down over my spine, causing me to shiver against his featherlight touch, my skin erupting with goose bumps.

He ducks down, his lips kissing the curve of my neck, his tongue lapping at that one spot that drives me completely crazy, my toes curling. And I'm like putty in his hands, craning my neck to the side to give him better access as stars begin to dance around my head.

"God, I missed this," he murmurs against my skin, his voice gruff and raspy, and everything delicious.

I moan from his words alone. I needed to hear that. More than anything, I needed to hear him admit that he's missed me just as much as I have irrefutably missed him over the last ten years. In fact, that's all I need to know. I don't need anything else; right now, all I need, want, is him. We stumble our way to the sofa, finding the edge of the cushion, and Colt pulls away from me, his heavily hooded eyes watching me with such intent it's almost intimidating. But I keep a hold of his gaze with my own as I sit, pulling my dress down over my shoulders, making quick work of my plain cotton bra, his eyes darkening even more as he watches me while tearing at the buttons on his shirt, desperately shrugging it off before tossing it across the room. And, it is at that exact moment that my eyes find my name inked in the most beautifully intricate script, right there where Shelby said it was. On his chest, right over the jagged scar across his heart, the scar he received from the emergency surgery that saved his life.

I'm rendered momentarily breathless. I reach up, hesitating for a split second before ever so slightly and gently tracing the letters with the tips of my fingers. He almost flinches, as if he's afraid of me, afraid of my touch, and the thought that I can scare him with just one touch, breaks my heart.

"I'm sorry," I whisper, holding my hand against his chest, feeling the thick scar beneath my fingers, feeling his heart race.

Colt continues watching me, his hooded eyes stormy. I don't think I've ever been looked at the way he's looking at me right now. Not by him, nor by anyone else. He's looking at me as if I'm the only woman in the world. As if no one else can possibly compare. The sheer look of want, need and adoration in his eyes might very well be my undoing, but there's a stark trepidation also, and it's that foreboding look in his gaze that reminds me of just how terribly I hurt him. His hand reaches out, tenderly cupping my jaw, the pad of his thumb tracing the plumpness of my bottom lip, and he offers a small smile so full of something I hadn't been prepared for. I lean into his touch, exhaling a contented sigh, my lashes fluttering closed.

*God, I love you . . .* I think to myself.

But, just like that, everything comes to a spectacular stop.

Colt tears his hand away from me as fast as if he's burned himself. I almost fall against the sofa with how fast he lets me go. My skin is icy cold from the loss of contact, and when I look up at him, that expression I'd seen in his eyes only seconds ago has been replaced by nothing, an emptiness, that same painful indifference that stabs me right in the middle of my chest. And I know, with that one look, I've just gone and ruined everything.

"Y-you *love* me?" he asks, a hard crease etched between his brows.

Of course I went and said it out loud.

*Shit.*

"You love me?" This time, he asks the question with a derisive scoff before quickly refastening his belt buckle.

"W-what are you doing?" I stammer, feeling very naked all of a sudden. I hold my hands up to my chest, covering what I can of myself with my dress. "Colt. Stop. I-I can explain, I didn't mean it! I—"

He doesn't stop to hear me out. He doesn't stop at all. Instead, he turns away from me, finding his crumpled shirt on the floor, picking it up and throwing it over his shoulders, not bothering with the buttons on his way up the steps toward the foyer.

"Colt, stop!" I yell, chasing after him, one hand still covering what I can of my breasts.

He turns when he reaches the front door, facing me, this time his face masked with disgust as he regards me like I'm nothing more than a piece of garbage. "You love me, *now* . . ." His steely gaze cuts through me, hard and blunt. "Why couldn't you love me back then?"

I gape at him, shocked by his words. "But, I-I *did* . . . I—"

"God, I'm so fuckin' stupid," he murmurs to himself, shaking his head with another humorless laugh. "You almost went and fooled me again, Quinny."

I wake in the morning after a broken sleep, my head throbbing, my stomach knotted, and my eyes dry, swollen and itchy from crying myself into that broken, sorry excuse for a slumber. I spent all night replaying that moment over and over again in my head, the look in Colt's eyes, how it had changed so drastically when I'd stupidly gone and said that I loved him.

What an idiot.

Do I love him?

Without a sliver of doubt. All I know is that he's still the one for me. The one I was stupid enough to let go. The one I've spent ten years of my life trying to move past. The one I've spent ten years of my life resigned to the fact that, no matter what, he'll always be the love of my life. But that's the trouble with love; the heart wants what it wants, and for ten long, infuriating years, all my heart has wanted is the one whose heart I broke.

*I love you?*

God, of course he would run. I broke Colt's heart in so many ways, and he's terrified I'm going to do it again. Or, maybe I read him completely wrong. Maybe he doesn't want anything more from me than one final hoorah. Maybe it was closure he was after, closure after ten long years. But that tattoo. My name. Inked into his skin as a constant reminder.

I bury my head in my hands, closing my eyes, racking my brain. I have to see him. I have to talk to him. I need to see the look in his eyes when he tells me he wants nothing to do with me; Colt may be a closed book to most people, but I've always been able to see the truth in those eyes of his. I want to see him tell the truth, or lie to my face. At least then I'll know.

I jump out of bed and run through to the bathroom. No time to waste.

# Chapter 14

I'm met with another gray and dreary morning when I step outside. I zip up my leather bomber jacket, tuck my hands into the front pockets, and duck my chin down into the blanket scarf I wrapped around my neck three times. I missed this kind of cold. It's different to New York. Where New York's cold is stark and brutal, Montana's cold is stark yet refreshing.

I glance out over the ranch from the vantage point high up on the verandah, where Dad used to stand in the mornings with his coffee, looking out over what was his. From up here, you can almost see forever. The stables. The paddocks, all the way down to the river, to the rolling hills and looming peaks in the distance. My gaze sets upon Cash standing over by the fence, watching one of the ranch hands try to break a horse on a longline in the corral, the wild animal running circles around him, its chestnut mane flowing majestically in the breeze.

I continue down the steps, crossing the front yard. Cash casts a brief glance over his shoulder in my direction as I approach.

"Morning." I step up onto the fence rung to get a better view of the beautiful horse.

"How'd you sleep after last night?"

*Oh, if only you knew, big brother.*

"Not so good." I sniffle against the cool air. "Where is he?"

"He's gone to Jackson Hole with one of the ranch hands to pick up a colt."

*Colt.* I swear, that name will haunt me for as long as I live.

"Did he tell you about the fight?"

"At the bar?"

"No." My eyes widen. "With his best friend of almost twenty-five years."

Cash's brow pinches.

I shake my head in exasperation. "I don't know what the hell is going on with those two, but they almost killed each other . . . Right there, on the lawn in front of the sheriff's station."

Cash removes his hat, ruffling a hand through his hair, looking down to the ground, and I can see his mind working overtime, his jaw tensing.

"What is it?" I press.

"They've been fighting on and off for a while now." Cash shrugs nonchalantly. "You know how they are."

I can tell there's more to it, but he looks away, concentrating on the horse, and I know he's not planning on elaborating any further, despite my piqued curiosity.

"Do you know where he is?" I ask, trying so hard not to be obvious. "Colt, I mean."

Cash looks at me again, his lips twisting in thought as he considers my question. "He's gone to the auctions." He eyes me a moment longer, readjusting his hat once more. "Why?"

*Because I want to ask him why he walked out on me last night, half-naked and desperate.*

"I was just wondering if . . . if he was okay . . . after last night, and all," I stammer, cursing under my breath at my sudden inability to form a damn sentence.

Cash's gaze lingers unnecessarily long, and I quickly turn away. I've never been able to hide much from my big brother; I swear he was a special agent in his past life.

119

"I'm going into town. I need to pick up a few things." I step down off the fence rung, wiping my hands on the backs of my jeans. "You need me to pick you up anything?"

He shakes his head, but when he goes back to watching the wild horse buck and refuse to submit, I don't miss the faintest hint of a smile that curls his lips. He knows. I can't keep anything from him. But I ignore it, I ignore him, turning and crossing the yard, hurrying to my rental car before he can call me out right there by the stable yards.

The streets in town are relatively quiet, in stark contrast to the chaos of New York City that I've become accustomed to over the last ten years. But still, I keep my beanie pulled low, my head cast down as I amble along Main Street. I don't really know what I'm doing in town. I just couldn't sit around the house all day, not with the way in which my emotions are running amok in my mind.

That house feels tainted right now. What was once a place filled with good memories, love and family, is now nothing more than a reminder of my dead father, my brother who loathes me, and the love of my life who no longer wants anything to do with me.

I grab a to-go coffee from one of the many trendy cafés lining the promenade, and I continue wandering aimlessly, checking out the store windows, cowering from the wind as it barrels through the street, taking no prisoners on its way through the town.

It's all so weird. Black Canyon looks exactly the same as it always has from a distance, but the closer you get, the more you realize everything has changed. I mean, old Mrs. Schultz's bakery has been replaced by a vegan brownie bar. A vegan-anything in a cattle-ranching town is beyond absurd. And across the street is a vape store, for God's sake. It's like the place has been gentrified when there was nothing derelict about it in the first place; morphed into a hipster, upmarket layover for entitled tourists to stop in on their way to the ski resorts in the winter.

120

My eyes wander to the shop window of a surprisingly fashionable boutique. *Oh, red bottoms.* But just as I stop to look at the cute pair of Louboutin boots in the display, I'm almost knocked on my unsuspecting ass by a relentless force ramming into me like a damn Mack truck, causing me to spill my coffee all down the front of me for the second time this week.

"Shit!" I look down as coffee drenches the legs of my jeans, the cup falling from my gloved fingers, what's left of its contents spilling onto the sidewalk.

"Oh my God, I'm *so* sorry!"

"Mommy, the lady said shit!"

"Honey, don't say shit!"

Confused and totally out of sorts to say the least, I glance up from the mess down the front of me to see a little girl peering up at me, a small hand plastered over her gaping mouth, bright eyes smiling mischievously. And then I lift my chin, looking upward to see a somewhat familiar face blinking at me with a knowing smirk.

"Gucci gal?"

I smile. "Rylie, hey!"

She looks different today. A little less eyeliner, the nude eye contradicted by bright red lips. Her dark hair is piled on top of her head in a messy topknot I know I could never pull off. She wears leather tights, an oversized Def Leppard T-shirt with a vintage Eighties jean jacket over the top. She's so cool. Effortlessly and enviably so. Definitely not Canyon material. When I grow up, I want to be just like Rylie—though, I'm almost certain I'm at least a couple years older than she is.

"Oh, Lord, I'm so sorry, doll, I wasn't even paying attention to where I was going!" she apologizes, rifling through her purse before pulling out a handful of questionably scrunched-up Kleenex.

"Thanks." I take the tissue from her, assuming they're unused, mopping up the coffee trickling down over my leather jacket.

"And don't worry, it was totally my fault. I was too busy admiring these boots." I point to the window to my right.

"Cute," Rylie coos, peering through the glass.

I glance down at the little girl. She studies me curiously, holding on tight to Rylie's hand. She's beautiful. Blonde curls, wild and unruly. Big eyes full of curiosity and mischief. A smattering of freckles peppered over her nose. Chubby cheeks with dimples that pop when she smiles up at me, so shy, so cheeky, so adorable.

"Hi." I crouch down. "What's your name?"

"Emmy." Her cheeks blush a little and she looks down to her feet, cowering into Rylie's side.

"It's nice to meet you, Emmy." I hold a hand out. "I'm Quinn."

Emmy glances from my hand, up to her mom as if to check, and I try not to take offense that she clearly needs permission to shake my hand; I am a stranger after all. But when Rylie nods, when Emmy feels I'm trustworthy enough, she places her dainty little hand in mine, and I shake it gently, meeting her innocent and captivating gaze. She's adorable, and I'm momentarily taken aback by the little girl, wholeheartedly enamored of her.

I stand back up, smiling at Rylie. "She's beautiful."

She rolls her eyes indulgently. "And don't she know it."

I laugh, smiling fondly down at the little girl.

"Let me buy you lunch," Rylie offers. "It's the least I can do for . . . this whole situation . . ." She pauses, waving her hand in front of me, indicating the coffee staining my jeans.

I glance around, for what, I don't even know. I look from Rylie, down to Emmy who's still staring up at me with those curious eyes, and back again, managing a smile. "Sure." I nod. "But, first," I say, pointing to the boutique we're standing outside, "I'm just going to duck in here and see if they have a pair of jeans in my size."

With a fresh pair of jeans on, my coffee-stained pair in the carry bag provided by the boutique, I join Rylie and Emmy at a table inside a bistro on the other side of Main Street. It's just started raining again, the raindrops pelting against the window we sit by. Emmy sneakily blows a hot breath of steam onto the glass, drawing a smiling face with her index finger and giggling to herself as if it's the funniest thing ever. She is too adorable, and I can't help but smile as Rylie shakes her head at her daughter.

"I'm surprised to see you're still in town," Rylie says after we place an order with the server.

I glance down at my glass of water, swiping at the condensation as it drips down the side. "Yeah, I don't know how long I'll be staying for." I shrug a shoulder, meeting her eyes. "Maybe indefinitely. I don't know yet. Family stuff . . ." I explain.

She nods in understanding. "Your family is still here?"

"My brothers are here." Those words hurt surprisingly more than I thought they would, but I ignore the lump of emotion wedging its way into the back of my throat, taking a sip from my water in the hope that it will help wash it down.

I sense Rylie can tell there is more to my story. A sadness. But I'm so relieved when she decides to change the subject, smiling at me and narrowing one of her eyes as she studies me closely. "Let me guess," she begins. "You're back in town from . . . Los Angeles?"

I manage a smile, shaking my head.

Her brow furrows, her lips twisting ever so slightly with another guess: "Salt Lake?"

I laugh. "New York."

At that, Emmy gasps, her eyes wide as she looks at me from across the table.

"Oh God. Here we go." Rylie sighs dramatically.

"What?" I ask, looking between the two of them; they look so different, but their mannerisms are almost identical.

"She's *infatuated* with New York," Rylie explains, nodding to her daughter. Adding conspiratorially, "I blame Taylor Swift. I took her to the 1989 concert, and ever since then she's been obsessed with the damn city."

I laugh, meeting Emmy's wide-eyed gaze.

"Is it everything dreams are made of?" she asks, her sweet voice hopeful.

*I thought it was . . .* I think to myself.

Biting back my smile, I nod. "It's . . . pretty spectacular."

She sighs, a wistful smile playing on her lips. "Daddy said one day he'll take me. I want to go see the big Christmas tree all lit up."

Rylie smiles lovingly down at her daughter, brushing a wayward blonde curl away from her face. And I take the moment to glance at Rylie's hand, her fingers, noticing no wedding ring, no engagement ring, no rings at all, in fact. But I quickly avert my gaze, keeping my nosy curiosity to myself; it is the twenty-first century, after all.

"New York's great, and all," I continue, smiling at Emmy with a wink. "But being in a huge city like that, it really makes you appreciate your home."

My words and the hidden meaning behind them hang in the air, and they're not lost on Rylie. She casts me a meaningful glance, her smile genuine as something unexpected passes between us, but before she can question me, the server returns to the table with our food.

124

# Chapter 15

Rylie and I sit together on the bench seat outside Merle's Toy Emporium, watching Emmy through the window as she gazes at all the toys with excited wonderment, pure joy lighting up her face with everything she stumbles across in the poky little store. She's so beautiful, sweet and innocent, and a dull ache begins gnawing at me on the inside when my mind suddenly wanders back to the thought of Colt, and everything we could have if I'd stayed all those years ago.

"Thanks for lunch." I smile at Rylie, blowing on my to-go cup of coffee in an attempt to cool it down before I drink it, since I didn't get much of a chance to finish my earlier cup.

"Thanks for the coffee," Rylie retorts, humming in appreciation as she takes a sip.

We sit in a comfortable, companionable silence. That is until Rylie shifts on the seat beside me, and I can feel her curious gaze fix in my direction. I cast a sideways glance, finding her brow furrowed as she studies me closely.

"What did you mean before?" she asks.

I turn to her, quirking a brow.

"When you said a city like New York really makes you appreciate home?" she clarifies, answering my unspoken question before adding with a chuckle, "Because I know no one could miss a hole like the Canyon. Hell, I'm only here because my father wanted to retire in New Mexico and didn't trust no one else to run his damn bar."

I gape at her, my eyes bulging. "Wait! Duke's your dad?"

"You *know* Duke?" She answers my question with one asked with just as much surprise.

"Yeah." I laugh. "Duke is a legend in this town. He was really good friends with . . . with my father." My gaze inadvertently wavers, the mention of my father stinging like salt in a wound that just won't seem to heal.

"Who's your dad?" she asks casually.

I shift in my seat, her question hanging in the air. I clear the lump of emotion that has suddenly found its way into the back of my throat. "Royal Wagner."

Suddenly, her eyes go wide, her face falling. "Oh my God, Quinn. I'm– I'm so sorry."

I shake my head, dismissing her apology. "Thanks, but it's fine." I take a sip of my coffee to avoid having to offer any further awkwardly muttered words on the topic.

"That's why you're here!" she exclaims quietly as if just realizing, and I watch as she starts to make sense of everything. "You came back into town because your father died."

"Yeah . . ." I look down a moment, pressing my lips together.

"Dad spoke a lot about your father over the years," Rylie continues. "He was a good man."

"Yeah, he was." I smile at her through the burning tears that sting my eyes, but I blink them back, desperate to change the topic of conversation from my dead father. "So, Duke moved to New Mexico?"

At the mention of Duke, Rylie dramatically throws her head back with a groan. "Yeah. So, I grew up there with my mom. She and my father split when I was a kid. But then, a few years back he started coming down to visit more than he'd ever visited when

126

I was a kid . . ." She steadies me with a sardonic glance. "Turns out, they fell in love with one another twenty years after they ended their marriage because they couldn't stand the sight of each other."

I can't help but smile.

"So, he wanted to retire, and move down to be with Mom. But he didn't want to sell the bar," she continues. "I'd just broken up with asshole . . . number seventeen, I think," she says in mock considering before smirking. "So, I told Dad I'd come up here and look after the place for him," she deadpans, grabbing a hold of my forearm. "And here I am . . . seven years later."

I laugh because I know what she means. A place like the Canyon, the beautiful scenery, the kind people, the charming, effortless lifestyle, it can trick you into falling in love with it, trapping you without you even realizing until it's too late. By the time you realize it's probably time to move on, you're so deeply rooted here, it's impossible to leave.

Rylie smiles, regarding me for a long moment. "I knew I'd like you from the moment you stepped foot in the bar with a three-thousand-dollar handbag hanging from your shoulder."

I chuckle, meeting her eyes. "Likewise."

"So, tell me . . ." she presses, arching one of her perfect brows. "What's got you thinkin' you might stay indefinitely? Because I can tell, Quinn . . . It's more than just your daddy's passing."

"Am I that transparent?" I scoff, glancing down at my coffee.

"Not really," she answers truthfully. "But, doll, I saw a sadness in your eyes that first night in the bar; your heartbreak radiates from you. And I know whatever it is, you need someone to talk to."

She's right. I do need someone to talk to. I have no one. I can't talk to Cash; we've never had that kind of relationship. I certainly can't talk to Tripp; he hates me and can't seem to stand the sight of my face. Rylie may be a relative stranger, but I have a feeling she might be the only person to even come close to understanding what I'm going through right now. If I can't trust a girl like her with my jaded past, then who the hell can I trust?

I meet her kind eyes, and I release a heavy sigh. "I don't even know where to start, so I guess I'll just start from the beginning?" I cast her an uncertain glance.

She nods, her hand remaining on my forearm.

I take a deep, fortifying breath, considering my words. "Do you . . . do you know Colt Henry?"

My question hangs in the air for an unnervingly long few beats. Rylie's brows draw together slowly, her expression falling as she stares at me for a long, overwhelming moment, recognition flashing in her eyes and something else, something I can't quite decipher within her gaze before finally she nods. "So *you're* that girl?"

And there it is. The proverbial elephant of my life. My scarlet letter.

"Yep. I'm *that* girl . . ." My shoulders fall in resignation. I *was* that girl. I'm not anymore, though.

Rylie swallows hard, and she casts a furtive glance in through the window to check on Emmy before moving closer beside me, her hand squeezing my arm, reassuringly. "It's okay, Quinn. You can talk to me."

I look up to the gray sky, searching the clouds for what, I don't even know. Raking my teeth over my bottom lip, I continue. "I was in love with Colt before I even knew what love was." I smile through my emotion, glancing briefly at Rylie. "His mom took off when he was just a baby. His dad went to prison when Colt was only a child, and he never came out. Colt had a really horrible life as a kid. His grandmother looked after him as well as she could, but she was an old woman, and he was a handful. Always getting into trouble. He's been best friends with my brother for forever. Tripp?"

Rylie nods and gives a small smile. "I know Tripp."

"Colt practically lived with us, and he and I grew close. Then, when his grandmother passed away, Colt was only sixteen, and he had nowhere to go, no one to go to. So my dad kind of took him

128

in. He lived in a cabin on our ranch. He still does . . ." I pause a moment, racking my brain with the memories that consume me. "Colt and I started dating when we were just fifteen. But it moved so quickly, it didn't feel like a normal teenage relationship. I loved him. It was as if he was another part of me, if that even makes sense." I stop to shake my head, fearing I sound utterly ridiculous.

"It does." Rylie pats my arm, encouragingly.

"Colt had this crazy dream that he wanted to be a professional cowboy." I smile at the thought. "When he came to stay at the ranch, he started doing some work on the weekends and after school for my dad. One of the ranch hands took him under his wing and showed him the ropes, and Colt had this weird ability to stay on a bucking bronco for way longer than eight seconds. So, he decided that that was his calling. He was going to join the circuit and become a champion."

"That sounds like Colt." Rylie smiles, looking straight ahead, her gaze focusing on Emmy through the window as the little girl talks animatedly with Merle, the store owner.

"I'd always wanted to get the hell out of here. Away from the ranch. Away from Montana. Away from everything. New York was my dream ever since I was a kid . . . kind of like Emmy."

Rylie laughs quietly.

"I got accepted to NYU. But Colt wasn't going anywhere. Originally, we'd talked about leaving this place, together. But, when it came down to it, he realized this is where he belongs." I look around at the town surrounding me. "He wanted to stay here. I-I had to leave."

At that, Rylie questions me with a glance, and I know she wants to ask.

"My mother killed herself when I was kid . . ."

Her eyes widen at my confession.

"We don't really talk about it . . ." I shake my head, adding a nonchalant shrug. "She was just so sad. She loved my father more than anything. He was her one and only," I say with a sad smile.

"But she felt like she'd lost herself here. She gave up everything to stay here in the Canyon with my dad, and I guess that regret ate at her on the inside, so much, she couldn't handle it."

"Oh my God, Quinn." Rylie gasps. "I'm so sorry."

I avoid her apology, continuing, "I didn't want to leave Colt, but I couldn't stay. My mother made me promise that I would never give up on my dreams, and I owed it to her. I had to live my life because she didn't get to live hers. I had to go to New York. And I did. And I loved it. I had planned on going on to grad school. And staying in the city afterwards to start my dream career in business. But then, Colt flew out to see me, and . . . he proposed to me."

Rylie blinks at me, hanging on to every one of my words.

"He asked me to marry him, and of course I said yes. And I had all intentions of marrying that boy. He was the love of my life and I couldn't imagine living without him." I look down at my hands, as the reality of my past comes flooding back to me. "But the closer it got to the wedding, the more I started to question it. Did he really want to marry me? Or was it all just a big elaborate scheme to stop me from staying in New York? To bring me back home to the Canyon? Was this his way of forcing me to give up on my dreams? Could I really give up everything I'd worked so hard for, to marry Colt and wind up just another rancher's wife? Could I break the promise I made to my mother? It was all so much. Too much. I was terrified that I was going to end up like her."

"So . . . You didn't go through with it."

I meet her knowing gaze, her eyes sad. "I hate myself for what I did. I wish I could change it all. I wish I could go back and break up with him before I left for college. I wish I could go back and decline his marriage proposal. I wish I could go back and at least call off the wedding before he'd got dressed in a suit and stood at the altar with Reverend Jackson in front of all our friends and family. But I didn't do any of that because I knew it would hurt too much to lose him. Because I was too goddamn selfish, and I put my feelings before his."

"What happened . . . after you left?" Rylie asks, her voice soft and cautious.

I blink hard and a tear slips free, trailing down my cheek, but I quickly wipe it away with my gloved hand, sniffling back the rest of my tears as best I can. "I left. And I didn't think I would ever come back. I really thought when I was standing there in the airport saying goodbye to my father, that I was never going to come back to the Canyon. I knew I'd ruined everything. I'd broken Colt's heart. The look in his eyes when he came to find me after . . . It killed me. I'll never forget that look for as long as I live. So, like the coward I am, I ran away back to New York, and I pretended as if my past didn't exist.

"But a few months later, it slowly started to kill me from the inside out. I couldn't sleep. I barely ate. I wasn't focusing on school. And I knew it was because the guilt was eating at me. The guilt of breaking his heart. The guilt of breaking my promise to my mother. The guilt of cheating myself. I'd made a horrible mistake, and I wanted nothing more than to take it all back." I sigh heavily. "I booked a flight home for the coming weekend. And I wrote down this big long speech that I was planning on giving to Colt, to beg him for forgiveness, to plead for him to take me back. I was willing to give everything up for him, if he would just take me back."

I wipe my nose with the back of my hand. "But then I got a phone call in the middle of the night from my father. He told me that Colt had wrapped his truck around a tree. He'd been drinking a lot after the breakup. He wasn't handling it. And so one night, he got behind the wheel, and at eighty miles an hour, he drove head first into a big old fir tree on the side of Old Prairie Road, and left himself for dead in the middle of a cold January night."

"D-did-did he try to . . ." Rylie trails off, unable to finish her question.

"The road accident investigators deemed it an accident. Driving under the influence," I say with a shrug. "But Sheriff Dwight told my dad there were no skid marks, nothing to show that he swerved. He willingly got behind the wheel of his truck with a bottle of whiskey, and he did what he did."

"Jesus," Rylie hisses under her breath, looking down a moment. "I didn't know." She mutters something unintelligible, shaking her head.

"Colt doesn't know, but I came in on the next available flight. And I sat with him in the intensive care unit, right by his bedside, holding his hand, for . . . days, and nights. I refused to leave him because when he woke up, and I knew he would, despite what the doctors were trying to tell us, I wanted him to see me there. To know that I came back to him. That I would never leave his side again."

"What happened?"

I shake my head, dismissing Rylie's question. "It doesn't matter."

A silence sits between us, heavy with overwhelming emotion. And although the story of my past brings with it that same unbearable pain I've tried so hard to hide for ten years, it feels good to finally let it all out. It's almost as if a weight has been lifted off me. Like I can finally breathe again.

"He's the reason you're still here, huh?"

My gaze moves to Rylie, and I find a sad, yet knowing smile ghosting over her lips, the gleam of unshed tears sparkling in her red-rimmed eyes. "Colt," she says, even though it's obvious. "You still love him."

"More than anything." I nod. "I never stopped. I just tried to force myself to forget."

A few beats pass, and I meet her gaze as she studies me so closely.

"You know what I said the other day?" she continues. "About redeeming yourself?"

I nod again, smiling at the thought of her strangely accurate words.

"I meant it, Quinn. Yeah, sure"—she shrugs a casual shoulder—"you've made some mistakes in your life. I mean, who the hell hasn't? But you're not a bad person. You're definitely not an asshole. Trust me. I can spot 'em a mile away. For some reason, I attract them. It's like a sixth sense, or *the force*, without the cool lightsaber. I attract assholes. It's my God-given gift."

I laugh as fresh tears fall from my eyes, and she smiles at me.

"I can see it in your eyes. What you feel for Colt is true and honest, and so incredibly real. And love like that doesn't come around too often." Her voice is strained, and I can hear her own emotion in every one of her words. It's difficult for her to say them. She's been hurt before. "Don't let it get away, Quinn." She offers a sad smile, squeezing my hand.

"You're right."

"Of course I'm right." She gives me a smug wink.

My gaze drifts over her. Taking her in from her lipstick, to her nail polish, to the tattoos inked into her fingers. She's enviably confident and strong. But beneath her facade I can sense an almost debilitating sadness. She may keep it hidden behind her tough exterior, but she's not as strong as she makes herself out to be, as she wants people to believe. I can tell.

"If you ever wanna talk . . ." I say, looking into her eyes, and when I do, I know I don't have to finish offering.

She simply smiles, nodding once, but before any more can be said, Emmy comes tearing out of the toy store with a box clutched under her arm, an infectious smile beaming from ear to ear.

"Mommy, look what Mr. Merle gave me!" she squeals, holding the box up in the air.

"A five-hundred-piece Empire State jigsaw puzzle," Rylie reads the box out loud, casting me a deadpan glance. "How fun."

I chuckle to myself.

"I told him how much I love New York, and he said I can have it. No foolin'!"

"Lucky girl." Rylie glances over her daughter's head, to Merle standing in the window, the elderly man smiling with a wave. She waves back.

"I'm gonna see if Daddy wants to help me put it together!" Emmy starts jumping up and down on the spot, giggling.

"We should go." Rylie quickly turns to me, her lips pressed together in a tight smile. "*Someone* needs to go home and sleep off the sugar rush she's about to start coming down from."

I stand with Rylie, and I look down at Emmy, crouching to her height. "It was so nice to meet you, Emmy."

Emmy regards me a moment, piercing green eyes searching mine. And, before I can even prepare myself, she launches at me, wrapping her arms around my shoulders and embracing me with a hug that almost knocks the wind right out of me.

"Come on, Emmy." Rylie takes her daughter's hand, pulling her away from me.

I stand, returning Rylie's wave and watching as the two of them hurry up Main Street, toward Duke's Saloon. Emmy glances back over her shoulder, one last gentle smile playing on her perfect little lips as her gaze meets mine, her small hand waving goodbye to me, and I wave back with a smile, still completely enamored of that little girl.

Pulling into the parking lot of the Livestock Auction House, my mind is racing with everything I've been trying to talk myself into during the half-hour drive here from town. My hands are clammy, my heart racing. Hesitation and self-doubt rear their ugly heads, but I just keep hearing Rylie's words on repeat. A love like the one I feel for Colt doesn't come around very often. I can't let it get away. Sure, I could have waited until tonight, after he was done with the auctions, but I worried I might have convinced myself otherwise. I need to see him now before it's too late.

"Can I help you, girlie?"

I startle at the man looking down at me at the entrance, holding a clipboard in his hand.

*Girlie?* I'll have you know I'm a twenty-nine-year-old woman, mister.

"Um, y-yes, sir," I stammer shamefully, clearing my throat in the hope it will provide some kind of confidence. "I . . . um . . . I was looking for Colt. Colt Henry?"

The man's bushy brows knit together. "He's up in the members' only section."

I nod with a smile. "Thank you," I say, stepping around him.

"Where do you think you're going?" He stops me, his clipboard held in my face.

I gawp up at him.

"What part of members' only don't you understand, girlie?"

Wow. Okay. I steady him with as polite a look as I can manage, when all I really want to do is take his clipboard and slap it upside the back of his head. Placing a hand on my hip, I quirk a brow. "You mean the *Royal Wagner* members' only section, don't you?"

He nods.

"I'm Quinn. Royal's daughter."

I swear, the man almost swallows his tongue. His eyes widen, his hands fumbling with his board as he clears his throat excessively, scanning the paperwork in front of him as if it holds whatever answers he's looking for.

"Oh, I'm–I'm s-sorry, Miss . . . erm . . . Wagner," he stammers through his apology, quickly moving aside and removing his hat. "And I'm terribly sorry to hear about your pops. He was a good man." He bows his head.

I press my lips together in a forced smile, nodding at him on my way past as I step inside the big arena.

The place is huge. I remember coming here with Dad when I was younger. I loved seeing the giant bulls being paraded around the yard, men furiously bidding on each and every one. Adrenaline and competition thick and heavy in the air. It was all so exciting. Of course, back then I didn't really understand, but it still gave me a rush.

135

I continue up the stairs to the members' only viewing deck, the place crowded with wealthy landowners too busy drinking at the bar to bother with the current showing of heiferettes. I snake my way through to the mezzanine, which is when I spot Colt standing looking down at the yard, an auction catalogue tucked under his arm, a paddle in one hand, a bottle of water in the other, trying to appear interested in whatever it is the older man beside him is talking to him about.

He looks every bit the rancher, in his checkered shirt, snug Wranglers, leather boots, and Stetson perched on his head. And I can't help but smile at the sight of him, my heart skipping a few beats. But then I remember why I'm here. I remember last night. And that smile falls at precisely the same time he glances causally over his shoulder, as if he can sense me. Confusion, shock, and something else flashes in his eyes as he regards me, and his jaw clenches before he excuses himself from the man beside him, beginning toward me through the crowd, his eyes not once leaving mine.

"Hey, I . . ." I begin.

But he just steps around me, his hard chest brushing against my arm, stopping only to wait for me to follow. And I do. He leads the way through the crowd, down the stairs and out of the arena, all the way back out to the parking lot.

"What are you doing here, Quinn?" Colt asks, folding his arms over his chest as he steadies me with a hard look.

I stare up at him a moment, taking in every part of him. "Are you okay?" I ask, indicating the swollen black eye my brother gifted him last night during their fight outside the sheriff's office.

"I'm fine," he mutters dismissively before asking again. "What are you doing here?"

I swallow hard. "I-I want to talk about . . . about last night."

Colt shakes his head, his teeth gritting together. "There's nothing to talk about."

"Colt—" I begin, imploring him with my gaze. There is a lot to talk about and he knows it.

136

"I'm at work!" he exclaims, cutting off whatever it was I was about to say. "This is my damn *job*! My *life*!"

"I know, I just . . ." I trail off, searching frantically for whatever it is I need to say, and panic begins to set in as Rylie's words reply in my head. My love for him is true and real and everything in between. I can't let this go. I can't let *him* go. "I just– I need to talk to you."

Colt stares at me, his eyes moving between mine, momentarily dipping down to my lips before quickly reverting back as if to catch his own wayward thought. Meeting my gaze with a slightly less threatening look, he swallows hard, his Adam's apple bobbing in his throat. He glances at our surroundings a moment. I can tell he's battling to find the right words just as much as I am.

"Fine," he finally relents, his voice low and deep. "I'll be back at my cabin later tonight."

Part of me wants to ask him why later tonight. What is he doing between now and then? It's a Friday night. Is he going out? Is he seeing a woman? But I keep my mouth shut, exhaling a trembling sigh, so thankful, so relieved, but instead of showing any sliver of emotion, careful not to give himself away, Colt simply steps around me and disappears back into the auction house, leaving me there in the parking lot with a small glimmer of hope in my heart.

## Chapter 16

I slept away most of the afternoon.

Tripp was still on the road, Cash was elbow-deep in muck, busy helping one of the ranch hands with a heifer in breech, or something equally as gross, and the house was quiet. I needed sleep. I slept a total of three hours last night, and not much more than that since I've been back in Montana. I needed sleep because I needed to clear my head in preparation for my impending conversation with Colt.

I only intended on lying down, maybe napping for an hour or so, but somehow, I managed to fall into a deep sleep, and when I woke night had fallen outside my bedroom window, and the small clock on my bedside table told me it was almost eight-thirty.

I fly bolt upright.

Surely he'll be home by now, right?

Unless my suspicions were correct and he is out. What if he's on a date? What if his date wants to carry on their night together? Oh God, what if I show up at the cabin and he has someone there? Surely not. He knows I'm coming to speak to him.

A quick shower, a fresh change of clothes, and half a grilled cheese sandwich later, I'm now sitting in the great room with the crackling fire warming me from across the room, staring at the clock on the mantel, trying to muster the courage I need to get the hell out of here, get in my car, and drive across the ranch to the cabin.

My heart races at the thought of seeing Colt. I'm so nervous. I've never been this nervous. I know I need to open up to him, to tell him the truth, that I never stopped loving him, and that being back has made me realize that I never will stop loving him, but I'm so frightened he's going to shut me down again, and I'm not sure my heart can handle it. I consider myself a reasonably strong woman. Not a lot gets to me. I'm this way because my father raised me this way; he raised me in a way to be nothing like my mother. But Colt, he's that one person who could end it all for me. He has the power to take away my strength, to leave me a depleted mess on the floor without effort or reason. He doesn't realize it but he holds my heart in the palm of his hand, and with just one look of unaffected indifference, he can crush it to within an inch of its last beat.

The clock chimes, and I sit up a little straighter counting the gongs.

It's ten o'clock.

Surely he has to be home by now.

But what if I'm too late? What if he's in bed?

*Get a goddamn grip, Quinn.*

I swallow the anxiety lingering at the back of my throat, and I stand, smoothing down the front of my jean shirt, nervously tucking my hair behind my ear. I need to leave now before I can manage to somehow talk myself out of it. I stop in the foyer on my way out, grabbing the keys to my rental car, my leather jacket from the coat hook, shrugging it on as I walk outside into the cold night air. But, of course, just as I walk out onto the porch, I come face-to-face with Tripp finally arriving home from his day trip to Wyoming.

It's the first time I've seen him all day. The last time I saw him was last night, when he was completely wasted and out of his damn mind, on the ground, fighting his best friend in the whole world, right outside the sheriff's station.

I glance up at him, taking him in. His face is just as bruised and as swollen as Colt's, but unlike Colt, Tripp doesn't look like he's going to be okay once the bruises fade. Dressed in a sweater at least a size too big, the hood pulled up over his head, his eyes are dark and cold and empty. His normally imposing demeanor suddenly appears weak and frail. He's the shadow of his former self, and the sheer sight of him makes my heart hurt like hell.

"You look like shit," is all I can manage to say, and I don't even know why, but the words are out of my mouth before I can stop them.

Tripp doesn't say anything, he just glances down at the Wendy's bag in his hand, and I watch as his Adam's apple bobs in his throat with a hard swallow. I want to reach out, wrap an arm around him and pull him close, just hold him for a minute. But I don't. And I don't even know why. It's evidently clear that he needs someone right now, but I guess I'm just scared of him fighting me again. Because as angry as I am with him right now, I need him just as much as he needs me.

"You okay?"

He nods once, his eyes still cast on the fast food in his hands.

"I'm heading out for a bit," I say, looking him up and down. "But I can stay . . . if–if you want me to?"

Tripp glances at me, studying my face, a sliver of hope gleaming in his glassy eyes. But, almost immediately that hopeful gaze is replaced by the same disdain I've seen in him since I've been back. His jaw tightens as he averts his eyes out into the night. "I'm fine," he mutters with a shake of his head. "Just gonna eat this and hit the sack."

My shoulders fall.

God, I just want him to talk to me.

*Talk to me, you insolent fool!*

I'm his twin sister, for Christ's sake.

"Okay." I force myself to back down, stepping out of his way of the door. "Call me on my cell if you need me."

Tripp doesn't acknowledge me any further. It's as if I'm not even standing there as he steps around me, his head bowed, body guarded. And I watch as he moves inside the house, the front door closing in my face. As I stand on the step, in the unforgiving glare of the porch light, I can't help but wonder exactly how we even came to be in a place this bad.

Colt lives in the cabin, on the other side of the bluff, the further-most residence on the ranch, about ten or so miles from the main house. He's been staying here since he was sixteen, after his grandmother died and he had nowhere else to go. Dad didn't want him in the house under the same roof as me for obvious reasons—what father would want his teenage daughter living under the same roof as her boyfriend—so, he moved him into the cabin that had been empty since my grandfather passed away.

My grandfather originally had the cabin built for my mom and dad to move into when they married. But, Grandpa was on his own, and he liked the view of the sunrise in the morning, so not long after my parents' wedding, he moved himself out, my parents took over the main house, which is where Cash was born not long after, right there on the floor in the great room when he came six weeks earlier than expected.

Before I know it, my headlights illuminate the small rocky drive that leads up to the cabin, and I pull up next to Colt's truck parked outside. I release a hard breath, my hands still gripping the steering wheel as I peer up through the windshield to see the lights on inside. He's in there. And despite my reservations, I know I can't just sit in my car all night, so I force myself out, albeit reluctantly, wiping my clammy palms on the back of my jeans as I walk up the steep steps to the verandah.

I'd like to say that the reason I'm shaking is due to the eleven-degree night air, but that's not it. I'm nervous as sin. I might actually be sick. But I continue to the front door, and for a moment I just stand there, staring at the stained-glass panel, preparing myself, considering what the hell I'm even going to say when he answers. I have so much I need to say, want to say, but how? I shake my head at myself, looking down at my boots. Maybe I shouldn't have come here. Maybe he's better off without me. Maybe we're both better off apart. But I love him.

*Jesus Christ, Quinn. Get it together.*

With a deep breath, I smooth my hair back from my face with trembling hands before knocking once, waiting with bated breath and a racing heart that feels as if it's about to burst right out of my chest.

"Hey."

I let out a high-pitched yelp, almost jumping out of my skin, clutching at my chest as I swing around, finding Colt watching me from the porch swing, his silhouette shrouded in darkness, hiding him from view.

"Jesus, you scared the shit out of me!"

He chuckles lightly, standing to his feet, the chains of the swing clunking and rattling in objection as it moves back and forth in his wake. And as he comes closer into the glow of the light shining out from inside the house, I get a better look at him. His Stetson has been replaced by a backwards ball cap. He's still wearing those same jeans that look as if they've been made just for him. And, a Broncos sweatshirt shields him from the cold, paired with a pair of tattered old moccasins on his feet.

He looks cozy, and all I want is for him to wrap his arms around me, hold me against him so I can bury my face into his chest and bask in his warmth. But he doesn't hold me. In fact, he barely even brushes against my arm on his way past, briefly glancing down at me as he opens the door. He does, however, step aside to allow me in first, as he always does, so you can't say chivalry is completely dead. But I don't want chivalry. I just want him.

I know this cabin so well. I spent a lot of my childhood here. I would come almost every day after school to visit my grandpa when he was still alive. I even had my own room here, at the end of the hallway. I was Grandpa's little angel almost more than I was my dad's. I loved this place then and I love it now because it reminds me of him.

I remove my jacket, hanging it on the rack by the door, lingering awkwardly in the entry, watching as Colt continues inside. I take the opportunity to look around. A big flat-screen hangs on the wall, looming over the entire living room, displaying a muted football game. An old record player in the corner of the room that I'm certain was once my grandfather's, plays some old bluegrass song. Colt's rodeo trophies and medals and shiny belt buckles line the mantel in a proud display. Dusty old first editions of books I've never heard of are stacked on almost every surface. It's all very Colt, and I can't help but smile as I nervously wring my hands together behind my back.

The shutter slides open and Colt appears in the cutout wall that separates the living room and the kitchen. "You want a beer? Or whiskey? Bourbon?"

"Um . . ." I take another tentative step inside, tucking an imaginary strand of hair behind my ear. "Whatever you're having is fine."

He returns soon after, walking toward me with a couple of PBRs, handing one bottle to me, and I offer an appreciative smile, taking a big gulp from it in the hope that it will help to ease my infuriating nerves. I hate this energy. I know Colt better than I know anyone. But we're almost like strangers. It doesn't sit right with me.

Colt glances at me, his intimidating gaze unwavering. "You . . . wanna sit?" He points to the sofa, and I nod, quickly ducking past him and taking a seat on the sectional. He follows suit, sitting down at the other end, gulping a long swig from his beer.

"How was your . . . night?" I ask, breaking the awkward silence and hopefully the ice. "Did you do anything fun?" I don't mean to pry, but I also do. And of course he gives me nothing.

"No." He shakes his head, doing all he can to avoid my eyes, choosing to watch a slow-motion replay of the game playing on the television screen instead.

I twist my lips to the side, looking down at my beer bottle. I begin picking at the label as I rack my brain, trying desperately to think of something, anything to say, but I have nothing. This is more difficult than I had anticipated. He's giving me less than nothing. I mean, hell, he's barely even looking at me, and I'm supposed to tell him how I feel. Unlikely.

When the game on the TV cuts to a commercial break, Colt finally obliges me with a casual, fleeting glance in my general direction, and I meet his eyes with my own before he awkwardly looks away. I know he can sense how terrified I am, and despite his demeanor, I can see he's just as scared. It's written all over his otherwise stoic face. I think he forgets how well I know him, even after all the years we've spent apart. And I find some solace in the fact that he's feeling this too; he's just a little better at masking it than I am.

"So?" He shrugs, shaking his head at me. "What did you need so badly to come and talk to me about?"

I dampen my suddenly dry lips with the tip of my tongue, stalling. My heart thumps wildly in my chest. I wouldn't be surprised if he can hear it. But I don't care. I swallow my own nausea, blinking once. I know it's now or never. And, despite my reservations, I think back to what Rylie said. A love like this doesn't come around very often. She's right. There's no way that I can let it go without a fight.

I steady him with an imploring gaze, gauging him while I take a deep, fortifying breath. And then I throw all semblance of caution to the wind. "I still love you, Colt."

# Chapter 17

Colt's brows knit together in confusion, in anger, I can't tell. He blinks once, then once more, his intimidating and infuriatingly aloof, slightly callous gaze fixed on me from across the other side of the sofa as my words continue reverberating through the room like a broken record. And, the longer he goes without saying anything at all, the more I wish I could go back in time, just thirty seconds ago, and never say what I just said.

I mean, *I still love you*?

I shake my head at myself. What an idiot.

I shift in my seat, gripping the bottle of beer in my hand like it's all I've got, while I consider my own words. I clear my throat in the hope that it will help to provide some courage to say what I desperately need to say. "Last night, you asked me why I couldn't love you enough back then."

He blinks again, his face blank, impassive. No furrowed brow. No emotion whatsoever, Just nothing.

"Well . . ." I continue, staring down at my beer, its label in shreds. "The thing is, Colt . . . I-I did love you enough back then. But that was just it."

I glance up again in time to see him take another long drink from his beer, still stoic, still silent. I know he's waiting for me to finish saying whatever it is I have to say, but one grunt of recognition wouldn't go astray.

"I was scared. We were so young. All I kept thinking was that I was giving up everything to marry you. Everything I'd worked so hard at. All my hopes and dreams. And I was terrified of losing who I was, who I was meant to become. I kept thinking that we'd get married young, and then sooner or later we'd wind up resenting each other. I was confused, because I loved you more than anything—I truly did—but I just . . ."

I realize my explanation is poor and confusing. And trite. It wasn't you, it was me. I can't help but roll my eyes at myself as my own shoulders fall with a heavy sigh when I meet his eyes again. "The truth is, Colt . . . what I never told you back then was that . . . I was terrified that I was going to end up like my mother. She gave up everything for my dad. She had dreams of moving away from here, but she didn't. She stayed and became the perfect little housewife . . . and she ended up so sad." Tears cause my eyes to sting, but I continue. "I know what I did to you was wrong. *I* was wrong. I've regretted it every single day of my life ever since.

"I wish I could go back and change what I did. But I can't. I did what I did, and nothing I say will ever change that. So I have to own it. But I'll never forgive myself. I ruined everything. I lost everything with that one stupid decision. But most importantly, I lost the love of my life with one unforgivable, irrevocable mistake that still, to this day, makes me so angry with myself."

Colt shifts, causing me to pause. I think he's going to say something, but he doesn't. He leans over to place his empty bottle onto the makeshift coffee table, which is just a couple old pine crates stacked on top of one another. With a heavy sigh, he rests his elbows on his knees, removing his baseball cap, his head bowed as he ruffles a hand through his hair, replacing the hat again. But he doesn't look at me. He just rests his chin on his clasped hands, staring down at the old Navajo rug that originally belonged to my grandpa; a gift he'd been given by the chieftain from the nearby reservation.

He's still silent.

I continue. "I love you, Colt. I know it's been ten years, but I never stopped loving you. It's only ever been you, and you know what? It's probably going to be you until the day that I die. So please, don't ever think for one minute that I didn't love you enough back then. Because I did. It was my love for you that made me do what I did. And I'll never forgive myself for letting you go." My throat closes up with emotion, and for a moment I can't continue. I can barely even breathe.

Tears sting my eyes.

I promised myself I wasn't going to cry, not in front of Colt. Afterwards, yes. I could go back to the house and cry into my pillow until I had no tears left. But not now. I grasp on to the last stitch of composure I have, clearing the swelling lump from my throat. "I need to tell you something . . ."

I watch Colt as he stares into the fire, his face stark, wide eyes unblinking.

"I came back for you."

He flashes me a confused sideways glance, his throat bobbing with a hard swallow. "You . . . you what?"

I nod, sniffling once again. "I'd booked a flight to come home the weekend after midterms. To tell you I'd made a mistake. To plead with you to forgive me. To beg you to take me back. All I wanted was you, and I couldn't live with the mistake that I'd made." I release a stammering breath. "But then . . . the accident happened." I sniffle, biting down hard on my trembling bottom lip. "I dropped everything, forfeited my midterms and I came straight home and I stayed with you by your side, holding your hand, reading to you, playing you some of your favorite songs."

"But you weren't . . ." His brow furrows as he stares straight ahead, trying to process my words. "You weren't there when I woke up."

147

I bury my face in my hands, nodding. Sure. I could tell him the truth. The real reason I left again. But I just can't bring myself to say those words, in case he cements the fear and the doubt that's crippled me for ten years. "Why would you want me there when you woke up? I was the reason you were lying in that hospital bed. It should have been *me*! It was all *my* fault!" I cry through a racking sob, swiping at the traitorous tears trailing down my cheeks.

"It wasn't your fault, Quinn," Colt suddenly says, his raspy voice gruff like gravel as it cuts through the air. He finally glances at me, a deep crease pulling between his brows. "I'm the one who drank a fifth of whiskey. I'm the one who got behind the wheel on my damn truck when I couldn't even see straight. *I* did that. That's on *me*." He turns back to the fireplace, staring at the dancing flames.

His words don't make me feel any better.

"Colt, I've spent the last ten years of my life trying to move on from what I did, from losing you. Placing a Band-Aid over the wound of my past. Ten years pretending to be someone I'm not, forging a whole other life for myself just so I could forget who I was and what I did, what I lost. And it worked. For a while. But that's the thing about Band-Aids; they don't stay stuck forever."

Colt clamps his bottom lip between his teeth, chewing almost painfully on the flesh as the flames of the fire reflect in his glassy eyes.

"My mom made me promise that I would never stop chasing my dreams, but dreams weren't real. What I had was real. I left my heart behind when I ran away all those years ago. And I can't live without my heart, Colt . . ."

He looks at me then, his head turning slowly, a heavy gaze fixed on me.

"It's you. You're my heart." I implore him with a look of earnestness, and I've never allowed myself to open up as much as I am right now. "It's always been you. And, no matter what,

148

no matter how much it continues to kill me inside, it's only ever going to be you."

My words leave an overwrought silence hanging in their wake, the record that had been playing now long finished. Nothing but the occasional crackle of the fire fills the silent, heavy void in the air between us. I stare at Colt, study him. From the obvious tension in his tight shoulders, the tension he's trying so hard not to let show through his stoic facade, to the way his left knee jumps ever so slightly with every bounce of his feet. His face remains stark, unaffected, his furrowed brow the only thing giving away the fact that maybe he isn't as unperturbed as he'd like me to believe. But that's all I've got. Sometimes I can read him, other times it's almost impossible. But God, I wish I could tell exactly what he's thinking right now.

I look down at the redundant bottle of beer in my hand, placing it onto the coffee table as steadily as my shaking hand can manage. My gaze flashes to Colt, and I eye him warily.

"Do you . . . do you have anything you want to say?" I ask, my voice soft, quiet and blatantly full of the kind of hope I'm certain makes me sound pathetic.

Of course he says nothing, and his intense gaze falls from me to the floor at my feet, and he seems set on staring at nothing, his eyes empty and hollow. I've just opened my heart and given him all I have to give, and he's got nothing, and desperation suddenly begins to rear her ugly head from deep down inside of me.

"You told me you didn't care enough about me to hate me anymore." My voice is a little rough, but I'm reaching now, for anything I can grab to get some semblance of a reaction from him. "But you were lying, Colt. I know you were!"

Still nothing.

"When you kissed me last night, I could feel it on your lips, your tongue, in the way your hands were holding me with such need and desperation it was as if you'd found me after years of searching, and you couldn't bear to let me go in case you lost me again." I'm almost incredulous now. Angry that he isn't giving me anything, not one single emotion. I'd rather he fight me, curse me out, anything. I can't stand his silence. "You still love me, Colt. I know you do. It's in the way you look at me, in the words you don't say . . . It's tattooed right over your damn heart!"

And still, nothing.

A sudden and unexpected anger erupts inside of me, exploding deep in my belly, and I can't take it anymore. I can't sit here and give him every single part of me without receiving anything in return. And, maybe this is his way of getting back at me. Maybe this is what he wanted all along. Maybe this was closure for him, to know that I have always loved him, that I will always love him. Maybe now he can finally move on, knowing I'll hate myself for the rest of my life for losing him, loving him until the day I die.

My heart aches more than it's ever ached before, tears hot as they sting my cheeks.

Colt remains seated, hunched over, staring at nothing, completely immune to the emotion pouring out of me as I stand with a sob, silently cursing myself. I begin toward the door as fast as I can, stepping around him, but right then I feel a hand grab hold of my wrist, stopping me, shocking me so I almost stumble.

I close my eyes tight for a moment as relief floods through me. I take a deep, trembling breath in the hope that it will calm me, prepare me for what, I don't even know. I chance a risk, glancing down at him, finding his head bowed before he slowly looks up at me with eyes so full of fear and trepidation, so careful and tentative. So scared. But then I see it. I see it in his stare. The fear. The trepidation. The want. He's just as desperate as I am.

He grips my wrist so tight, lifting his other hand and grabbing my hip, slowly yet forcefully pulling me closer until I've got nowhere to go but between his knees. His hand remains on my hip, the pad of his thumb finding the sensitive skin beneath the hem of my shirt, stroking me, his touch featherlight, his eyes intense, never once leaving mine. He lets go of my wrist, and I hesitate a moment before carefully reaching out, removing his baseball cap. I push his hair back from his face, my nails gently scratching his scalp, and momentarily his thick lashes flutter closed, a heavy yet trembling breath exhaling from within him as he rests his forehead against my stomach, taking the moment he needs. But that moment is fleeting, and he's quick to look back up at me through his lashes, both hands on my hips now, urging me down onto his lap.

I stare into his eyes, my gaze dipping down to his lips, watching as the tip of his tongue coats them, causing them to glisten beneath the muted glow of the fire. And never before have I ever wanted for anything, the way I want, need, to kiss him. I'm shaking with that need, my entire body trembling beneath the weight of his heavy stare. He holds me so close, so tight, like he can't let me go, and there's something in his eyes I wasn't expecting, something that causes my heart to skip at least a few of its mandatory beats. Confirmation. He still loves me. It's blatantly obvious within that heavy, penetrating stare. He never stopped loving me. He loves me, wholeheartedly and irrevocably.

I wrap my arms around his neck, inching closer and closer until there's nothing more than a hairsbreadth left between us. His breath is warm as it fans against my lips. His eyes are blazing, wild and untamed as they regard me, imploring me, silently pleading for the permission he needs. I gently nudge his nose with my own, nestling closer, melding into him. And that's all the consent he requires before he captures my bottom lip between his, sucking it slowly, his teeth grazing it until I allow him the access he so obviously wants. His tongue glides into my mouth, our kiss unhurried, deliberate, and easy, before heating with every soft breath, every hushed moan, every whimper falling between us.

Colt kisses me as if I'm his everything. I feel every one of his emotions: desire, desperation, relief, fear, and foreboding. This is a kiss like nothing else. Like nothing I've ever felt before. I'm entirely lost within the feel of his lips and tongue, his hands gripping my waist like he's so happy to have me, but so terrified of losing me again that he can't possibly risk letting go.

I missed his scent. A heady combination of mint, vanilla, pine, and the lingering hint of a long-forgotten whiskey. It's a scent I would bottle if I could, just so I could keep him close at all times. Spray it on my pillows, my clothes, all over, just to remind me of everything Colt. I rake my fingers through his mess of chestnut waves, pulling and tugging on the longer lengths ever so slightly, my nails scratching his scalp, causing him to groan into our kiss.

Momentarily he breaks away from my lips, peppering kisses down over my jaw, my neck, coming to stop at the base of my throat. His mouth lingers there, blowing warm breath on my already heated skin, nipping lightly with his teeth. I drop my head to the side and I hear the faintest of chuckles before he attaches his lips to my favorite spot. The one spot that only he seems to know about. No one else. His spot. And I can't contain my own sounds as they slip from my lips with every glide of his tongue, every nip, every slow and steady suck, as warmth pools in the pit of my belly.

"Are you s-sure about this?" he murmurs against my skin, his voice barely the ghost of a whisper with every stammer.

"Yes," I say with a breathless sigh, my throat raw and hoarse as emotion and desire claim me.

I wrap my arms around his neck even tighter, holding him right there. My stomach pulls tight, clenching. The sound of my gasping breaths seems to drown out the silence around us. My racing heart beats hard against my chest, so hard I'm sure he can feel it.

Suddenly, and without warning, I'm moving. Colt shifts beneath me, his hands moving to my butt, holding me steady as he finds his feet without effort or struggle. I hold on tight, wrapping my legs around his waist, anticipation coursing through me as he carries me down the darkened hallway, his gaze fixed intently on mine as we enter the master suite.

Colt places me down on the foot of the bed, standing above

152

me, looking down at me in a way I don't think I've ever been looked at before. In fact, I don't even know how to describe it. Wonderment? Awe? Adoration? Myriad emotions flash within that one piercing stare. It's almost as if he can't even begin to believe that I'm here. But I am here. I'm not going anywhere. And, if he'll have me, I'll happily stay forever.

I watch as he lifts the hem of his sweater, pulling it off, leaving him in a thin cotton undershirt that's climbed halfway up his smooth, taut torso. But in one swift move, he reaches over his shoulder and tugs it over his head with one hand in a move that makes me openly swoon. His hair stands up in almost every direction, adorably contradicting the feral look of pure want and need in his eyes as he continues staring down at me, his lips parted just enough to allow for his shallow, hurried breaths.

My eyes roam his body, unabashed, my hands following suit, reaching up and gliding over skin as it pulls tight over strong muscle. I find my name again, right there, intricately inked over the jagged scar, the violent memory of his past. His lashes flutter and his eyes close tight, and when he grabs my hand, I think he's going to pull it away, but he does the opposite. He presses it firmer against his chest, covering it with his own, his eyes opening to fix on me.

"You said I was your heart?" he rasps, his voice almost breaking mid-sentence.

I nod.

"You *own* my heart, Quinny," he rasps. "You always have."

"W-what?" I stammer, my voice so soft, I'm not sure he heard.

Colt crouches down, still holding my palm against his heart with one hand, cupping my face with his other. He stares into my eyes, in a look so all-consuming it's almost my undoing.

"It's always been you," he whispers.

I gape at him, blinking once. His words, and the sentiment behind them, have just about ended me. I could die right now, and everything would be okay.

I study him, every single part of him, my eyes flitting between his, finding nothing but a heart-wrenching sincerity within them. I reach my free hand around, cradling the back of his head, urging him closer and closer until his lips barely graze against mine. Our eyes are still firmly set on one another's in a closeness I know neither of us have ever felt. I hold my breath as anticipation stirs between us. And, in a burst of unbridled passion, our lips crash together, and in that moment and I am his and he is mine, and together, nothing else matters.

# Chapter 18

I trace the tattoo of a wilting rose inked over Colt's shoulder as I lie against his chest, resting my chin upon him, feeling the rhythmic lull of his beating heart. The heart I own. The heart that beats only for me. Nobody else. I can't help but smile. At everything. At how perfect and effortless our reunion was. At how right this feels. I know it seems strange, but having Colt back in my arms makes the thought of losing my father feel slightly less painful. Colt is home. Everything feels exactly how it should have felt all this time.

"What are you grinning at?" Colt asks, his voice deep and low, reverberating up through his strong chest.

"What do you *think*?" I quirk a brow, offering him a wry glance.

He chuckles, and it's a delightful sound, one that warms me from the inside. His hand smooths over my bare back, his calloused fingers kneading my skin, and it is at that moment that I realize just how much I missed his touch. He can ignite the fire deep inside of me with the gentlest graze of his hands and fingers, provoking goose bumps to erupt all over me. I shudder against his touch, and he notices. A knowing smirk ghosts over his lips as he takes my hand in his, lifting it to press a kiss to the backs of my fingers.

155

"Why weren't you there when I woke up?"

I'm caught off-guard by Colt's question left hanging stagnant in the air. My brows knit together as I lift my chin, watching him. But he doesn't meet my eyes. Instead, he just stares down at our intertwined fingers.

"You said you came back for me . . ." He says it so nervously, so unlike him, it's heartbreaking. "But when I woke up from the coma . . . you-you weren't there."

I knew telling him the truth—that I came back for him—would result in questions being raised. But that doesn't mean I am in any way prepared to give him answers. For ten years it has stayed with me and only me. And Tripp. But Colt deserves to know the truth. It doesn't excuse my absence, but maybe it might help him to understand why I never came back.

"I stayed . . . for six days. And nights." I meet his hesitant gaze. "I never left."

His brows pull together as he listens to my words, and I can see so many questions reeling in his mind as he rakes his teeth painfully over his plump bottom lip.

"I needed to come home to tell you that I'd made a mistake. That I loved you, and that I would always love you. That I would give everything up if you would just take me back." I focus on the ink covering much of his chest, remembering back to that moment in my life, the catalyst for every reason I stayed away for so long. "I booked my ticket and everything. I didn't know how you would take it, and I was so nervous. So scared. I was sick to my stomach with the thought that you wouldn't accept my apology. That you would never forgive me for what I did. But I had to do it. I had to try anything and everything I could, because being without you was slowly killing me." I close my eyes for a moment. "And then Dad called me to tell me about the . . . accident." At that, I open my eyes, my gaze moving to Colt, and in a flash so fast I almost miss it, I find a sliver of guilt in his eyes. But I don't question it. I continue, "I came back straight away. I was so scared I was going to lose you for good, and my last memory of you would be that obliterating look in your eyes when I told you that I couldn't marry you."

Colt sighs a heavy breath, his hand still holding mine so tight, and that's all the encouragement I need to go on.

"I stayed with you. By your side every day, holding your hand. At night I curled up in the chair in the corner, and I just sat there staring at you, thinking of all the things I wish I could go back and change. Thinking of everything I would do differently if you'd only wake up." I swallow hard. "After almost a week, your doctor forced me to go outside, to get some fresh air, to see the sunshine. I didn't want to leave you, because I was so worried you were going to wake up when I wasn't there, and I needed to be there when you did. I needed to see your eyes, and I needed you to see me, to see that, not only did I come back, but I stayed as well, and that I would stay, forever. But, I did as I was told, what the doctor told me to do, and I allowed myself a three-minute breather to step outside, which is when I ran into Tripp . . ."

At the mention of my brother, Colt's furrowed brow deepens, his eyes watching me intently.

I find it difficult to continue. I don't know if I can. Tripp is Colt's best friend. His brother.

"W-what happened?" he presses, cutting through my doubts.

I stare at him a moment, studying him closely from the jagged scar that trails from his clavicle, all the way down to the top of his abdomen. It brings back so many haunting memories from that time. He suffered a clean break to his femur, a shattered pelvis, a fractured skull, which caused a bleed on his brain, four broken ribs, one of which narrowly missed his heart, puncturing his lung. He almost died. In fact, he did die. Colt's heart stopped while he was on the operating table. For at least a few minutes, he was gone. Lord knows how he survived that. But he did. He survived, and I wasn't there when he woke up.

I take a deep breath, meeting his unwavering gaze. "Tripp told me to leave. To get the hell out of here, away from you." I witness the hurt flash in Colt's eyes, the betrayal, but I continue, "He told me you hated me, and that I was the reason you . . . the reason you got behind the wheel that night. He told me that it was all my fault, and that if I stayed, I'd be your ruin."

Tears fall, sliding down over my cheeks, dropping down onto Colt's chest. But I make no effort to wipe them away. I cry. I sniffle back the rest of my emotion, staring down at my name on his chest, finding some comfort in those letters, realizing just how wrong Tripp was. I wasn't Colt's ruin. Maybe, just maybe, if that tattoo has anything to do with it, maybe I was the reason he woke up.

Colt says nothing. His face remains blank, save for the furrowed brow, which gives away the emotion swirling around in his head. But he stays silent, staring down at our hands clasped together.

"Tripp had no right in saying that shit to you. It wasn't your fault," he finally says after a few long beats, his raspy voice almost a whisper, and full of pain. "I was in a dark place after you left me. I was drinking every damn day. Drugs, too."

My eyes widen at that admission. Drugs. It sits like lead in my belly.

He sighs, shaking his head, casting me a tentative look. "I pushed everyone away. Tripp. Your dad. Everyone tried to pull me out of it, but I just let the pain of losing you eat at me until there was nothing left. I let everyone down. Hell, your dad had to bail me out when I got in too deep with a dealer from Bozeman." He shakes his head and gives a heavy sigh. "I let him down so many times, and that's what I hate the most. Disappointing your pops. But he never gave up on me."

I smile through my tears at the mention of my father. Because the truth is, as hard-ass and abrupt, and stone-cold as he came across on the outside, he was the kindest, most selfless person I've ever had the fortunate experience of knowing and loving. And I don't doubt one bit that he would have made it his mission to help Colt. I'm so thankful he was my father, and I am so proud to be able to call myself his daughter.

"I did some real stupid shit after the accident. For a long time I wasn't in a good place. That's the thing about pain medication. They dose you up on it in the hospital, but then when you get out, you can't go on without it. I was high on shit, I didn't even know what, every damn day. I was a fucking mess. Your dad literally came and grabbed me by the scruff of my neck and shook some damn sense back into me."

Silence follows Colt's words, my mind wandering back to the day of the accident. There's something I've always wanted to ask, but I couldn't ever bring myself to dig into it because I was terrified of the truth. I knew Dad knew, but I couldn't ask him because, over the years, Colt and what had happened had become a moot point between me and my father. I didn't ask. He didn't tell. There was a mutual understanding there.

"Can I ask you something?"

Colt hesitates before nodding once, and I shift a little, turning so I can really see him. Because, the truth is, I just really need to know. I don't know why. I guess I kind of already know. But I need to ask. I need to see it in his eyes when he tells me.

"There was no . . ." I trail off, biting nervously on my fingernail, staring down at the tattoos on his arm.

"What is it?" he asks, gently pulling my finger away from my mouth.

"There were no tire marks . . . on the road at the crash site. They deemed it an accident. Alcohol-related. But . . . was it . . . Did you—" I can't do it. As much as I want to, need to ask him, I just can't bring myself to do it. The words simply won't come out. I force myself to meet his eyes, although I'm scared of what I might find, but I need to. And when I do, it's terrifying and heartbreaking and everything in between. That single revelation alone brings a shiver to run down my spine, tears pricking my eyes.

Colt takes a deep breath, his nostrils flaring from his emotion, his jaw clenching as he stares down at my hand in his. "I don't really know what the hell was going through my head that night." His eyes flash to mine. "I was doped up, drunk out of my damn mind. I even knocked your brother on his ass with one punch when he tried to take my keys away from me."

I stare at him for a long moment, the weight of his confession crushing my heart.

"Why?" is all I can ask, shaking my head in confusion, my brow furrowing of its own accord. "You had the whole world at your feet, Colt. You wanted to be a champion. You were almost there. You could've had it all. Why would you give up everything to just . . ." Again, I stop short of finishing, because, again, I see it in his eyes, and the stark realization is like a slap to the face.

"That's the thing, Quinny . . ." He sighs, a racking, trembling breath. "None of it meant anything if I didn't have you."

A sob falls from my lips as an overwhelming sadness consumes me. Ten years. Ten years wasted, full of so much unnecessary heartache. Lives ruined. And to think it could have all been avoided if I'd just stayed. If I'd never left. If I'd never made that promise to my mother all those years ago. She was sick. It was her illness that drove her to do what she did. I could have stayed, and I could have been happy. I could have lived the life she should have lived; a happily ever after with the man I loved.

"I wish I could take it all back, Quinny. Everything," he rasps, reaching out, the pad of his thumb gently wiping away one of my tears. He cups my cheek and I lean into his touch, closing my eyes.

"I'm here now," I whisper, basking in the warmth, the strength and the familiarity that his touch alone provides.

"When are you going back?"

My eyes open to find him watching me, gauging me.

"To New York?" He clamps his bottom lip between his teeth as he waits for an answer, and I can't be sure he's not holding his breath.

I swallow hard, my heart thumping hard in my chest as I shake my head, shrugging. "I don't know if I am. As much as he won't admit it, I can tell that Tripp needs me. Cash . . . he needs me, too."

His fingers toy with the longer lengths of my hair, but he remains silent.

*Say you need me, Colt. Say you need me, too. Please!*

"What about your job?" he finally asks, his eyes flitting to me before going back to my hair.

Not the question I was expecting, or hoping for, but I think I know why he's asking. He wants to know if I mean what I say about staying.

"I got *fired*." Despite my tears I can't stop the laugh that bubbles up from the back of my throat.

"What?" He guffaws, the hint of an incredulous smile curling his lips. "*Fired?*"

I nod, sheepishly. "I lost out on a huge deal. My boss wasn't happy. Hell, not even the untimely death of my father could save my ass from that tyrant."

He seems to consider what I've told him. "Who the hell fires someone at the same time their dad passes away?"

I laugh again, derisively. "Edward Hawkins, that's who."

"Your boss?"

I nod, sighing heavily.

"What about the rest of your life back there? Your friends?" Colt presses.

I laugh once again, but this time there's little humor to the sound. "Well, actually . . . I don't have a lot of friends back in New York. I spent so long working my way up in the company, by the time I made it as far as I was going to go, I didn't have time for friends. I know it sounds pathetic, but my weekends were spent working. Nights, too. My only real friend is Oliver, my assistant—well, my ex-assistant, now, I guess."

"Oliver?" Colt presses, and I don't miss the clipped tone in his voice.

"Yes, *Oliver*." I bite back my smile, offering a sardonic quirk

161

of my brow. "He's twenty-four years old and he's as gay as a man can be."

"Oh . . . okay." His cheeks flush, complementing the contrite smirk pulling at his lips. "So, you really spent the last ten years of your life alone?"

*Oh, he's still fixated on that?*

I nod. "Grad school was spent studying. Then I worked sometimes eighty hours a week while I was interning. Any free time I got I usually just spent it at home, researching the market and memorizing local comparisons, square-footage calculations. All that *fun* stuff . . ." I can't help but scoff at myself. "But then, when I was alone, that's when the memories of the past would get the better of me. So, I worked. Even when I didn't have to. Work kept my mind busy. And so, friends and a social life took the back burner for a long time."

He regards me, clearly thinking hard about what I've told him.

I flash him a knowing smile. "But, if what you're really asking is whether there was anyone else, well, there wasn't. Nothing serious, anyway. But, I mean, it's been ten years, Colt. Of course there have been others. For you, too, I bet."

At the mention of others, he glances away, his jaw clenching. "Yeah, I guess."

*Who?* I want to ask. I need to ask. I desperately want to know. But I don't ask. It already hurts knowing he's been with other women; I don't think I could deal with hearing all the gory details. I know there's a lot that must have happened in the past. Hell, there's ten years' worth. But I'm not going to press him. I can tell it hurts him to talk about it, and I don't want to hurt him by bringing up the worst memories from his past.

"Are you just planning on staying here at the ranch, forever? With Tripp and Cash?"

He shrugs, swallowing hard. "Actually, there's this spot for sale. On the other side of Black Mountain. It's not a lot. A couple hundred acres. I've been saving up for a few years, for a down payment, but with what your pops left me . . ." He shakes his head a moment, still clearly so taken aback by his ten percent share in Wagner Ranch. "I'm thinking maybe I'll buy it. Something to go home to every day. A place to call my own, y'know?"

I smile. "Colt Henry; landowner."

He chuckles. "Your dad taught me a lot. I wanna do something with that."

I smile at him. My dad would be so proud. Of course he loved Tripp and Cash more than life itself, but he loved Colt, too. He saved him. Maybe he saved him for me, knowing that one day I would come to my senses and come back for my heart.

"What are you thinking?" Colt asks, his eyes studying me.

"Nothing," I lie, shaking my head. "Hey, if you want me to represent you with the land purchase, price negotiations and all that sort of stuff, I can. I've been told I can be pretty ruthless when it comes to real estate. They don't call me Killer Quinn for nothing." I offer a devious smile.

"Who calls you Killer Quinn?" He laughs under his breath.

"Well, no one," I relent. "I did try put it on my business cards, but our marketing team wouldn't approve it."

He chuckles again, and I love that we've gone from heavy and heartbreaking, to light and fun within a matter of seconds, so seamlessly. But that's always been us. I missed that about our relationship, and I stare at Colt, studying his perfectly pouted lips, the tiny freckle just to the corner of his mouth. His dimples. The shimmer of mischief that dances in his eyes. I missed everything about him; every last tiny, little detail.

"I need to thank Rylie," I muse.

"Rylie?" His brows pull together, his gaze regarding me carefully.

"From Duke's. Do you know her? Did you know she's Duke's daughter?"

"Yeah, I know Rylie." He nods once, offering a casual shrug. "What's she got to do with it?"

"I met her the other night. The night you *rescued* me before you almost pummeled that cocky little cowboy to death," I say with dramatic flair. "And I had lunch with her and her daughter Emmy today." I continue with a smile, "I told her about you. About our past. Of course she'd heard stories about me. But she didn't judge me. She listened. And she gave me some advice. She was the one who suggested I come talk to you, and so I came straight to the auctions after I left her."

"I'll send her a thank-you card . . ." Colt mutters, shifting beneath me, and I watch as a small, playful grin lights up his face, his dimples popping, only adding to the sudden glint of mischief in his eyes as he comes over me, flanking me. "Why the hell are we talking about Rylie, anyway?" His eyes burn as they bore into mine.

"I have no idea . . ." I manage, words failing me as I stare up at him, suddenly breathless with just one look.

From here, he's even more beautiful. The soft glow of the bedside lamp illuminates his skin, casting him in an ethereal glow. The grin pulling at his lips causes the sparkle in his eyes to dance. His hair is, once again, sticking up in almost every direction. Hands planted on either side of my head, his biceps tight and chest strong as he hovers just above me, my name over his heart right there, glaring down at me, reminding me that this beautiful, slightly broken, painfully scarred, yet flawlessly contradicting and perfect in almost every way man, is all mine.

Colt lowers himself, his lips attaching to the side of my jaw, trailing down over my neck. His hand skims my side, eliciting goose bumps from my head, all the way down to my toes. I *need* him, in every sense of the word, I need this man more than the air I breathe. I rake my fingers through his hair, gently holding him and urging him closer until his lips claim mine in a kiss so all-consuming, the rest of world just slips away.

# Chapter 19

I wake with a smile, a familiar warmth flooding through every single fiber of my being, accompanied by that painful yet satisfying ache between my legs, reminding me exactly what I spent most of last night doing. Opening my eyes, I see the room is shrouded in that early morning darkness, nothing but the tiniest sliver of light illuminates the dust particles fluttering aimlessly through the air as a single ray of the dawning sun manages to break its way through a crack in the shutters.

I roll over, reaching for Colt, but the bed is empty, and the place in which he'd lain all night with his arms wrapped protectively around me is now cold. Sitting up, I clutch the bedsheet to my naked body, hazy eyes narrowed as I search the bedroom to find it empty, nothing but the long-forgotten hint of his scent lingering in the air around me.

Through the dim light, I locate my discarded underwear on the floor. Colt's sweater is lying on the back of the armchair in the corner. I pull it on, covering myself, the hem falling to my mid-thigh, and I tuck my bare feet into the moccasins he'd kicked off and left by the door last night, before I walk out into the silence of the corridor, continuing out to the living area.

Silence.

The dwindling fire in the living room crackles and hisses with one lone flame flickering with everything it has, doing its best to warm through the bones of the cabin. But Colt isn't here. I wrap my arms around myself, staring at the fireplace, hoping like hell he hasn't woken up with second thoughts or a dreaded case of the morning-after regrets. Last night meant more to me than anything that has ever mattered to me before. I can only hope it meant just as much to him.

Braving the early morning cold, I walk out through the front door, shivering immediately from the blast of icy air as it hits me square in the face. Turning, I follow the verandah, stopping short when I find him there, his back to me as he stands at the railing, looking out over the sun trying desperately to break through the clouds as it rises over the mountains in the east. And I can't help breathing a sigh of relief at the sight of him, smiling to myself like the cat that got the canary. He's stunning. And the thing about Colt is he doesn't even realize the effect he has on me.

"I thought you'd left?"

Colt turns, sunlit from the back, illuminating his outline with a golden aura and my breath is stolen from me. With a steaming mug of coffee in his hand, he looks me up and down, his eyes widening momentarily as they linger at my exposed thighs.

"Jesus," he murmurs under his breath, slowly licking his bottom lip, and an involuntary shiver runs through me at *that* involuntary action.

Your body changes a lot in the ten years between twenty and thirty. Cellulite dimples begins to appear in places you never even imagined. Stretch marks line your skin from the constant and never-ending battle of gaining and losing weight. Things just don't sit quite as high as they once did. Normally, with any other man, I might be self-conscious. But with the way Colt is watching me, looking at me like I'm the only woman in the whole damn world, I've never felt more beguiling.

"You're gonna freeze your ass off," he says in a low, gravelly voice that sparks that fire deep inside me.

I smile, rolling my eyes at him when he flashes me that smart-ass smirk, and I tug only slightly at the hem of his sweater I'm wearing as I cross the verandah, closing the distance between us. He holds one arm out and I gladly nestle into his side, looking up at him as he glances out over the breaking dawn. And in that moment, I am wholeheartedly captivated by the way the dull light of the sun illuminates his face, reflecting in his eyes, shadowing the scruff lining his jaw and top lip. His is a beauty like no other. I could get used to this. I hate that I missed ten years of waking up to him looking like this.

I reach out for his hand, taking hold of the mug, and I pull it close, helping myself to a sip of his coffee, humming as it warms me through.

"You good?" he asks, a chuckle shuddering through him.

"Yep." I nod, smiling up at him with an innocent battering of my lashes.

He places the mug onto the timber railing, bringing both hands to my waist, pulling me flush against him, and I meet his eyes, finding a sincerity within them as they smile down at me. And, before I can prepare myself, he takes my breath away once again with a gentle yet urgent kiss, his tongue tentatively trailing the seam of my lips before invading my mouth, causing me to hold on tight, wrapping my arms around him for leverage. After a moment almost too quick, he pulls away, just enough for his lips to place a soft, lingering kiss to the very tip of my nose before he rests his forehead against mine, his gaze penetrating as his eyes implore mine.

It all feels so right. His eyes. His lips. His hands resting on my hips. His heart. His minty morning breath gently fanning against my skin. Nothing has ever felt so right. And I know, without doubt or reason, that I am exactly where I need to be. And the fact that it took me so damn long to find this kind of perfect, makes me sick to my stomach. So much time wasted, and for what? I swear, it takes all I have not to cry over the moments we've missed, what we lost over the years. I force myself to close my eyes, breathing steadily in through my nose in an attempt to hide the emotion as it overwhelms every part of my soul.

"I have to get to work," Colt says gruffly, pressing a kiss to my forehead.

I roll my eyes, mocking. "The ranch life."

"Hey, I didn't choose the ranch life." He grins, his dimples popping. "The ranch life chose me."

"They always say a woman will wind up with a man just like her daddy . . ." I muse.

But at that, the air between us shifts as Colt's demeanor seems to change right before my eyes. His gaze drops down to my lips before reluctantly meeting my eyes once again. With a hard breath he takes a step back from me, looking out over the morning as he finishes what's left of his coffee. And I'm left standing here wondering what the hell just happened in the point-four seconds since that kiss that literally left me breathless.

"D-did I say something wrong?"

He meets my eyes again, a small crease pulling between his brows. I can see his inner turmoil; it's written all over his face. Slowly, almost reluctantly, he closes the distance between us once again, his hands returning to my waist, gripping me tight as he considers whatever it is he's trying to tell me.

"Do you . . . r-regret last night?" I search his face, hoping like hell that's not what this sudden shift in moods is about.

"What?" He balks, pulling back a little to regard me incredulously. "Of course not!"

"Then what's wrong?" I shake my head once, my eyes beseeching his own for even a hint of the truth.

He looks down between us, to his Broncos sweatshirt that I'm wearing, raking his teeth painfully over his bottom lip once more, stalling again.

168

"Colt," I press, urging him to tell me whatever it is.

"Are we really gonna do this?" he asks, his voice so hushed I almost miss his words with the morning breeze as it rustles through the birch trees surrounding the cabin. He chances a look at me, and I find nothing but angst in his tentative stare. "I want it. I do. More than anything . . . but . . ."

*But?* My heart sinks. There's something wrong. I can see it in his eyes. I can feel it within the desperation of his touch. I can almost hear it with every thrum of his pulse in the vein in his neck.

"I need time." He steadies me with an uncertain look.

"Time?" My brows knit together as I watch him, hoping like hell he's going to elaborate on that because I've never been more confused.

"Quinn . . ." He stalls once again, this time clamping his bottom lip between his teeth so hard, I'm surprised it hasn't reopened the split he received during his fight with Tripp.

"What?" I ask, silently pleading for him to tell me whatever it is he's not telling me.

He shakes his head to himself, looking down again, taking a moment. "Ten years . . . It's a long time. I just need some time to get my head around everything." He's conflicted. I can see it in his eyes. "I'm scared." His jaw clenches as he looks down at me.

My teeth grit together of their own accord, but I get it. I hurt him. Of course he's going to be apprehensive, and I understand his hesitation. But I'm also not an idiot. I never have been. Something is wrong, and whatever it is, he's keeping it from me. But I have no right to question him. I have to trust him. I have to believe that he will trust me again, enough to confide in me once he knows that I am wholeheartedly here for him.

"Okay." I nod. "I understand."

His shoulders sag as his tension dissipates. He rests his forehead against mine, his eyes flitting between my own. "I lied to you," he whispers.

My heart stops dead in my chest. "You . . . y-you what?"

169

"I lied." He nods. "I missed you like hell. And I *never* stopped loving you."

I release the breath I've been holding, staring into his eyes, and I find an earnestness within them. He means it. He loves me.

"I love you," I say quietly. "More than anything."

Colt fixes his eyes on mine, his hands gripping even tighter to my waist as he pulls me flush against him, pressing a chaste yet meaningful kiss to the top of my head. I bury my face into his chest, breathing him in and becoming lost with everything Colt. And I know in that instant, no matter what, we'll be okay.

# Chapter 20

I can barely wipe the smile from my face as I pull up to the main house, still smelling Colt's intoxicating scent on me, still feeling his lips and fingertips grazing over my skin. Last night is a memory I hope will stay with me forever, and I sigh contentedly, but I quickly force myself to stop thinking about Colt and what we did together, reminding myself of where I am and my current morning-after state. I scan the grounds outside, for what, I don't even know. But, with my nested hair pulled into a knot on top of my head, dressed in last night's clothes, the last thing I want is to be caught sneaking home like some wayward teenager. I'm almost thirty, for God's sake.

I jump down from the Land Rover, casting a furtive glance out over the ranch, in the direction of the stables as I hurry across the front yard. The last thing I want is to be caught by either of my brothers. I may be almost thirty, but that's just a situation I don't want to deal with while smelling of Colt and sex. Taking the front steps I keep my head down as I cross the porch to the front door.

"Where have you been all night?"

"Holy shit!" I stifle a scream, stumbling over my own two feet before coming to a skidding halt.

I turn on my heel, looking at the back of the chair my father used to sit in every morning, and for a moment, I can't be sure it isn't his ghost, having stayed up all night in the cold, waiting for me. He used to sit there at the crack of dawn with a mug of coffee perched on his knee, silently assessing the morning sky in an attempt to try and predict the weather. He didn't trust the news. He always said weather forecasters were the only people whose job actually allowed them to fail ninety-five percent of the time without consequence. So, it was here, looking out over the fields and the valleys, that he would plan his day dependent on the color of the sky, the density of the clouds and whatever direction the wind was blowing.

But when I notice a familiar head of sandy blond hair sticking up over the back of the chair, I realize it isn't the ghost of my over-protective father, and my heart drops into the pit of my stomach.

"Jesus, Tripp," I manage through a gasp, clutching a hand to my heaving chest. "You scared me half to death."

The old chair creaks as Tripp pushes up to stand, and he turns slowly, his eyes finding mine, his face blank and emotionless as he looks down at me. Coffee mug in one hand, he runs his other hand through his hair, his gaze raking over my form. Then, with one brow quirked, he repeats himself. This time, his question almost threatening. "Where have you been?"

Sure, I could play dumb. Pretend I don't know what he's talking about. *What do you mean where have I been?* But I don't want to insult him. And I can tell by the steely look in his eyes that he's not up for games. So, I say nothing. It's none of his business where I was, or who I was with. I simply lift my chin a little higher, meeting his gaze with one just as unwavering, folding my arms over my chest in a sudden show of defiance. And for a moment we just stand there, staring into one another's eyes, and it's almost like the game we would play as kids. Whoever blinks, whoever smiles, whoever looks away first, loses. I will not lose.

He opens his mouth to say something, but then it's as if he decides against it, pressing his lips together in a firm line, his eyes remaining on me with what looks to be a million conflicting thoughts racing through his mind at once.

I watch as he lifts his hand, raking his fingers through his hair, glancing away a moment. A deep crease pulls between his brows as he seems to consider himself. When his gaze meets mine once again, I feel my resolve shrink beneath the weight of his stare. But then, when he finally says something, I'm rendered shocked.

"I'm sorry."

I blink once, twice, my own brows pulling together in confusion.

Tripp heaves an almighty sigh, walking over to the railing. He places his empty coffee mug onto the balustrade, resting beside it, his big calloused hands wringing together in front of him. I've never seen him like this. Tripp has never been one for apologies. He's never taken the high road, or been the bigger man. He holds grudges and fights hard. But right now, he's actually contrite.

"I've been horrible since you've been home," he continues, his gaze fixed on the wooden decking. But then he furtively meets my eyes with his own, offering the slightest hint of a wry smile. "Actually . . . for the last ten years."

I shake my head. I have so many questions. But all I can think to voice is one. "Why?"

He glances out over the ranch, a faraway look in his eyes, and I watch as he considers his words a moment. "You know I met the girl I thought I was gonna marry?"

My eyes bulge. "What? When?" I gawp at him.

Don't get me wrong; the notion of Tripp being in love isn't completely absurd. Despite his often impossible mood swings, stubborn and gruff exterior, he's an attractive man. He always has been. Both he and Colt were idolized by the girls in my grade at school. But Tripp was never really interested in any of that stuff. He always said women were complicated, more trouble than they were worth. At one point when we were growing up, I even questioned whether maybe he was interested in men. But it wasn't that. He just wasn't in a rush.

173

He nods. "Her name was Meg. She was a college girl from Arizona, in town with her girlfriends for winter break, skiing up on Black Mountain. The January before you and Colt were supposed to be getting married."

"Why didn't you tell me?" I ask with a soft gasp. Granted, our relationship was strained while I was off at college, but we were still close back then.

He looks down a moment, shaking his head. "I was scared of screwing everything up. So I didn't wanna tell no one about it 'til I had a damn ring on her finger," he mutters with a derisive chuckle void of any humor whatsoever.

I feel a pinch in my heart from his words. But I remain silent, my brows knitting together in confusion as I try to make sense of his words, watching him, completely rapt in the way his eyes are sparkling like I've never seen them sparkle before.

"We spent the whole week together. She ended up ditching her friends, and it was just me and her every minute of the day and night . . ." He sighs, staring out over the fields. "God, she was beautiful. Silky black hair. Ocean blue eyes. She had the laugh of an angel. It reminded me of Momma's laugh." The hint of a wistful smile plays on his lips.

"What happened?" I ask, tentatively, knowing it obviously didn't end well.

Tripp hesitates, that smile disappearing, replaced by his brows knitting together in anger, and I can see the memory still hurts him. "We stayed in touch. I went down to visit her a few times. But she didn't want the long-distance thing. She wanted me to move there to be closer, until she finished school. But . . ." He scoffs to himself, shaking his head again. "Then . . . *that* summer happened."

I bow my head at the memory.

"You left. Colt was a damn mess. A few months later he had the accident. There was no way I could leave this place. I *wanted* to. And, I would've, but . . . I just . . . I couldn't do it. I knew Dad needed me. He never said as much, but I could tell."

174

My heart breaks for my brother. He's the way he is because of what I did.

"So, you just . . . broke up with her?" I ask.

He nods. "Yeah. Hurt like a bitch, too." He meets my eyes, laughing once under his breath. Although it's a laugh void of humor. A laugh that actually sends a shiver down my spine. "Hell, I'd already bought a goddamn diamond ring. She was planning on coming up for the summer, and I was going to propose to her."

I feel sick to my stomach as I glance down at my hands resting on the balustrade, my mind fraught with so many conflicting thoughts and emotions. I didn't know any of this. And now, I can't help but feel a little responsible for my brother's broken heart.

"When I said what I said to you outside the hospital that day," he continues, and I glance up from my hands. He steadies me with a serious look of remorse. "That came from a place of pain and resentment—deep, deep down. I didn't mean none of it. I said it out of spite because . . . well, because I knew no matter what, you and Colt would eventually find one another again. But me? I lost what you and Colt were always destined to have. I was jealous, I was spiteful, I was hurt, I was sad, and I was pissed off." He shakes his head. "But I didn't mean it. And for that, I am so sorry, Quinny. I never should have said that shit to you." He shakes his head. "I shouldn't have done half the shit I've done to you. You don't deserve my resentment. You never have. I'm just . . . I'm so damn angry with Dad, and I hate myself for it!" Sadness and pain cause his voice to break, but he just looks down a moment, closing his eyes tight and pinching the bridge of his nose.

I try so hard to swallow the ball of emotion that sits in the back of my throat making it hard to breathe, but I just can't. And that emotion stings at my eyes. But I won't cry. I can't. My shoulders fall and I turn so that I can face him, reaching out a tentative hand and placing it onto his arm. With a heavy sigh, I stare at him for a long moment, his heart and every single one of his emotions laid out bare in the air between us, and my mind is an utter wreck of thoughts, of what could have been, what should have been, and what wasn't. So many years wasted. So much time taken away. So much energy spent worrying about things that just don't even remotely matter in the end.

I release a trembling breath, shaking my head. What's the use in fighting and arguing over what was said, and what was done as a result? It's done, now. And now yesterday no longer matters. All we have are our tomorrows.

"Dad didn't know about Meg. I never told him. I was going to wait until she said yes, 'til she was my fiancée. And then, that didn't happen," Tripp continues with a shrug. "But this one time I got so damn angry with him for something . . . hell, I can't even remember what, now . . . and I told him I gave up the love of my damn life for him, for this place. I stayed. Me! You were at college. Cash was off starting his family. After the way he treated me all my life, it was me who stayed and gave up *everything*. And you wanna know what he said to me when I told him about Meg?" he asks me with a derisive scoff.

I nod, although to be honest, from the gleam of unshed tears glossy over his eyes, I'm not really sure I do want to know.

He continues regardless. "He said, don't worry about it, son. You're better off. You probably just would've gone and screwed it all up, anyway."

My jaw actually drops. I can't even believe it. I knew my father looked at me differently than my brothers. He loved me differently. I was his little girl. And I loved my father, with everything I had. He was the one true love of my life. My hero. My constant. But to hear this of him now, after he's gone, to see the unimaginable pain he's caused Tripp, it hurts like hell and it makes me so damn angry.

*Dad, what've you done?* I shake my head to myself.

Tripp shrugs after a beat, a heavy, defeated sigh following. "You know, he was probably right . . . I would've screwed everything up with Meg, eventually. I always do."

My shoulders fall and I turn so that I can face him, reaching out a tentative hand and placing it on his arm. "Tripp, no, don't say that."

He laughs another humorless laugh, shrugging a shoulder. "Why not? It's true."

I hesitate as I consider my words. I don't know if they're the right words to say right now, but I need to say them. "I know it's no excuse, and it probably means nothing, and you have every right to be upset at Dad for what he did to you, for what he said, for how he treated you over the years," I begin, squeezing his arm a moment until he forces himself to meet my eyes. "Dad was *always* hard on you. More than Cash. Obviously more than me. But . . ." I pause, biting down on my bottom lip, carefully choosing my words, ever cautious. "But it wasn't vindictive, or malicious. It didn't come from a bad place. And despite what you think, he didn't *hate* you, Tripp. He once told me that you reminded him so much of himself. So, I think he was hard on you, the way Grandpa was hard on him, because that's what he was used to. And I know that isn't an explanation or an excuse, and what he said and did to you is *not* fair, but in his own messed-up way of thinking, I think it was his way of loving you."

Tripp looks at me. Really looks at me. And within his heavy gaze I can't help but feel a little nervous. Maybe I've said the wrong thing. But then the smallest hint of a smile begins to tug at his lips, and I allow myself to breathe again.

"What?" I ask, my brows knitting together in confusion the longer he continues staring and smiling at me.

"You always said it was Dad who was the glue that held this dysfunctional family together." He muses a moment, regarding me carefully, his gaze studying every inch of my face. "But it was never Dad, Quinny. This place fell apart without you, the day you left. You're the glue. You always have been. And I'm sorry I held that against you for so long."

And, with that, with my heart swelling to at least eight times its size, it actually feels as if it's about to burst right out of me. Tripp throws an arm around my shoulders, pulling me into his side. He places a rough kiss on the top of my head as we stand there staring out at Wagner Ranch, our differences and the pain from our past set aside, quashed once and for all.

But then our moment comes to an abrupt end when he suddenly asks, "So, you gonna tell me where you were last night?"

My smile falters, and I close my eyes, that painfully swollen heart coming to a jolting stop as flames heat my cheeks.

"Um, I-I didn't . . ." I pull myself out of his one-arm embrace, regarding my brother as he watches me. I nervously tuck my hair behind my ear, searching for an answer, but, instead, I change the subject and hope he doesn't notice. "Hey, what are you doing tonight? We should go out. Just you and me. Grab a drink at Duke's. For old times' sake." I smile, praying my change of topic doesn't seem like the blatant admission of guilt it sure as hell feels like.

"Yeah, sounds good." Tripp nods. "I should get to work." He pushes off from the railing, collecting his empty coffee mug. "I gotta go check out one of the west fences. Damn wolves keep getting in and spooking the cattle."

I breathe easy at having dodged his bullet of suspicion, following Tripp toward the front door. But then he stops, and I glance up at my brother to find him gauging me with an uncertain look of trepidation in his steely gray eyes.

"What is it?" I ask.

"I'm sorry, Quinn." He pressed his lips together, a sheepish smile as he bows his head a moment. "The way I've treated you, it's been totally unacceptable. I'm an asshole, and . . . I'm so sorry."

I press my lips together with a smile. "Apology accepted."

"God, I missed you," he mutters under his breath as he ducks down, pulling me into another hug, and I breathe him in, smiling to myself, closing my eyes and realizing that finally, after ten long years, it actually feels as if I finally have my brother back. But then, another spanner is thrown in the works with his words. "Promise me you'll be careful with Colt?"

I still, my eyes flying open.

*Oh no.*

He knows.

"Whatever the two of you are doing, just . . . take it slow," he continues into my hair. "A lot of shit's happened since you left. I don't wanna see *either* of you two gettin' hurt again."

I swallow hard, reluctantly pulling back and meeting his knowing gaze. I bite down on the inside of my cheek, just waiting, but he says no more. And with one last knowing look, a tight-lipped smile, he drops his arm from around me and turns, heading inside the house and leaving me there with my stomach in sudden knots and wondering what the hell that was about.

# Chapter 21

I somehow convinced Tripp to come to Duke's. He was vehemently against it at first, telling me he didn't want to deal with the drunk, rowdy cowboys that frequent the saloon on a Saturday night, looking for trouble. He was already in it enough, with Robbie Shepherd; he didn't need to risk violating the conditions of his bail. He suggested a honkytonk truck stop on the other side of town, out by the interstate. But I wasn't having it. Duke's was our stomping ground back in the day, and this is like our sequel. The Wagner twins, back together again for round two; ten years later.

Of course, I won the argument. I can be very convincing. And so now, Tripp leads me in through the saloon doors, albeit reluctantly, glancing over his shoulder every so often to check on me. I smile as I follow closely, clutching the back of his shirt so as not to lose him in the crowd.

Inside, the lights are low, drinks are flowing, and the whole place is vibrating with the beat of the live band as they play a pumping country-rock tune to an enthusiastic crowd. We stop at the bar, waiting in a line six-deep, and I take the opportunity to look around, my eyes narrowing to see through the muted light. But when I spot a familiar face, finding Rylie ducking behind the far end of the bar, I can't help but smile.

And then in that moment a thought suddenly pops into my head, and my smile grows when I glance at my oblivious brother. He looks good tonight. Black jeans, a plain white T-shirt beneath an open blue jean shirt, tan boots, scuffed to perfection. With his Stetson left at home, his sandy blond hair is on display, swept back from his cleanly shaven face. Despite the one fading black eye, and the bandages covering the swollen knuckles he'd received in the battle of idiots outside the sheriff's station the night before last, he looks like a handsome, relatively sweet, twenty-nine-year-old off-duty wrangler, and the Cupid inside of me rears his mischievous head.

"Hey, do you know Rylie?" I ask as casually as I can manage, casually throwing my thumb in the direction of my newfound friend as she serves a customer from the other end of the bar.

Tripp follows the direction of my thumb, his brows pulling together as his gaze lands on the curvy brunette, and I don't miss the blatant look of familiarity in his eyes. Oh, he knows her all right.

"Yeah," he says with a grunt, his jaw clenching as he fixes his gaze on the back of the head of the person waiting in front of him. He offers a nonchalant shrug of his shoulders. "Everyone knows Rylie . . ."

As if she knows we were just talking about her, Rylie glances over her shoulder, zeroing in on me through the muted light, her eyes widening with surprise. She looks from me, to Tripp and back again, and momentarily she hesitates before finishing with her customer. And I don't miss the flash of something in her eyes. But, whatever it was, it's quickly replaced by a wide smile as she begins to move in my direction.

"Hey, doll," Rylie yells over the music, waving me toward the counter.

I pull Tripp with me by his shirtsleeve, abandoning his post in line, and I smile innocently as I approach the bar. "Hey, Rylie." I glance over my shoulder. "You know Tripp, right?"

Her smile falters momentarily, her gaze landing on my brother, her eyes raking him up and down. "Yeah, of course." She smiles again, a little tighter this time. "Hey, Tripp."

"Rylie." Tripp lifts his chin, pressing his lips together in a tight, forced smile of his own.

I'm not sure why, but the air between the two of them is stifling and awkward as hell, and I watch on as they avoid one another's gaze; Tripp glancing out over the crowded dance floor, Rylie looking down at her hands. My suspicious gaze darts between them, my brows pulling together. And I'm not sure why, but I have a sneaking suspicion that perhaps Rylie and Tripp don't just know one another. It almost feels as if there's something serious between two of them.

Did they date? There's definitely a past there—I can sense it between them. It's in the air hanging heavily between them. In the way they barely even acknowledge one another. In the words they refuse to speak. There's definitely something going on there.

But I sweep whatever it is aside, choosing instead to avert the awkwardness. "Rylie, can I grab two whiskeys? Straight up. And a couple beer chasers." I grin, nudging Tripp with my elbow. "My brother and I are gonna get shitfaced for old times' sake."

Tripp groans through a light chuckle, shaking his head.

Rylie smirks, the trepidation in her eyes dissipating with a genuine smile. She winks at me. "Coming right up, doll."

Tripp and I have been laughing and drinking, talking about all the stupid things we did when we were kids. And this night, laughing with my brother for the first time in what feels like forever, is one of the best nights I've had in a long time.

"Remember when we went cow tipping at Jenson's ranch?" Tripp quirks a brow, a knowing grin flashing at me from across the table.

"You got chased by a bull!" I laugh out loud, slapping the tabletop with my hand. "You screamed so loud you woke up Jenson."

"That guy was such a dick. He had it in for me since the first day of term, freshman year." Tripp throws his head back with a groan, remembering back to our biology teacher. "He came running down from his house, dressed only in his Y-fronts." He laughs at the memory. "Pulled a damn shotgun on my ass. I almost pissed my damn pants."

"The next day Dad went over there," I continue, and Tripp flashes me a knowing smile. "He ripped Jenson's stogie right from his mouth, tossed it to the ground and said, *Pull that shotgun on my kid ever again and so help me God, I'll shove that barrel so far up your ass, all you'll be smoking for the rest of your life is gunpowder, you damn inbred hick.*"

"He really was a badass, huh," Tripp muses, smiling down at the empty glass in his hands.

For the moment we fall silent, sharing a fleeting smile at one another across the table as we remember our father. And my shoulders sag in some semblance of relief, because for the first time since being home, I can see Tripp is maybe finally starting to realize that not all the memories of him and Dad are bad. And maybe, just maybe, he's beginning to see that our father really was on his side.

"You know the other day, in Cash's truck when you said you were staying?"

I meet Tripp's tentative gaze, and I nod once.

His eyes flash down to the third glass of whiskey in his hands. "Are you really gonna stay?"

I consider his question for a long moment. And in that moment, I think about everything. I think of Tripp, and the moment we shared earlier today, when he pulled me into a hug so tight, I forgot just how much I missed him over the years. I think of Colt and our time together last night, how right it felt lying in his arms, falling asleep to the rhythmic thrum of his heart that beats only for me. But I also think back to New York, to where I've spent the last ten years of my life, wondering if it really came down to it, could I actually give that all up?

My eyes meet Tripp's once again, and I'm fixed within his deep, penetrative stare, and I suddenly remember back to this afternoon, to what he said to me.

I cock my head to the side, studying him carefully. "Hey, what did you mean today?"

His brows knit together at my question.

"You said to be careful with Colt." I arch a brow. "That a lot of shit has happened . . . What did you mean by that?" I ask with a shrug. "What happened?"

Tripp suddenly looks uncomfortable, his hand grasping his glass so tight I'm worried it's about to shatter in his palm. He shifts in his seat, doing all he can to avoid my gaze. He runs a hand through his hair, blowing out a heavy breath between his lips, but then he fixes me with a serious look, studying me for a long moment.

"What?"

"You still love him, huh?"

I nod without hesitation. "I never stopped loving him."

His gaze moves over my head. He watches the lights flicker up above, clamping his bottom lip between his teeth. And I can see the thoughts racing through his mind. He's battling with what I can only assume is right and wrong. And it leaves me feeling very uneasy. But then, as if he can sense my anxiety, Tripp's shoulders sag as he shakes his head, his gaze settling upon me once again. "Talk to him about it," is all he says, finishing what's left in his glass, his eyes moving back toward the bar. "I'm gonna get another round."

And before I can question him, before I can grab hold of his arm and force him to stay right where he is and demand he tell me exactly what he's obviously trying to avoid, he's gone, and I'm left there alone, my mind reeling.

Tripp has been caught up playing a game of pool with some of his buddies, and I've been all but ditched, receiving no more than the occasional glance from across the bar as I remain on my own, nursing my beer, trying so hard to make sense of my brother's cryptic ramblings and conflicting actions.

I look up in time to see his eyes on me, staring in my direction unseeingly, a crease etched between his brows as if in deep thought, and I've had enough. I can't take this anymore. I can't take the secrets. The confusing snippets of information. The cautious glances. I need some air. I place my half-empty glass of beer onto the table and grab my purse. I walk away, snaking my way through the swollen crowd as I head to the bar for a water, which is when I crash face first into a hard body.

A familiar scent envelops me, causing the hairs on the back of my neck to stand on end as memories of last night suddenly inundate every particle of my hazy mind. I tilt my head back, finding Colt looking down at me, a blank, unreadable expression on his face that contradicts the blatant look of heat blazing within his green eyes. A small smile ghosts over his lips, one that he tries to hide by raking his teeth over his bottom lip, and he takes a step closer, completely closing the distance between us.

"W-what are you doing here?" I stammer, and I'm not sure he can even hear me over the shrill sound of an electric guitar solo currently ringing through the saloon.

I can feel his breath fan down over my temple, his hand reaching up, gently stroking my arm as he leans in so close. "Isn't that skirt a little short?" he whispers, his voice gruff and raspy as his lips graze against the shell of my ear.

I look down to my jean skirt, unable to stop myself from grinning before plastering a look of faux innocence on my face. "You don't *like* it?"

His eyes burn as they implore mine, and I see nothing but a wanton desire in his steady gaze. And suddenly, all I want right now more than anything is to kiss him. But I'm not sure I can do that. I'm not sure we're there yet. He said this morning that he needs time. Time for what? I have no idea, but time all the same.

He grabs both my hands, holding me close, his gaze imploring, and I can see an internal conflict within his eyes, one that he masks with a small smile that causes his dimples to pop. "Dance with me," he says so close, his lips grazing my temple.

Before I can even answer him, we're moving toward the dance floor, as the electric guitar and drums fade into the gentle melody of a soft acoustic song playing around us, causing us to sway to the tune, our movements almost involuntary. Colt pulls me flush against him, one hand holding mine against his chest between us, the other gripping my waist before snaking around and resting upon the curve of my lower back.

We don't speak. We don't even look at each other. My head is bowed, resting against his chest. His hand holds mine against his heart, the pad of his thumb stroking the sensitive spot on the inside of my wrist, causing me to shiver, my breath catching at the back of my throat. I'm wholeheartedly consumed by everything Colt Henry right at this moment, and it's almost too much. I don't even know why he's here, or how he even knew I was here. I don't know much right now. All I know is his scent, his touch, his lips grazing against my forehead in the lightest yet most meaningful of kisses. And I could actually cry with just how right this feels. It's all so much, but I really wouldn't have it any other way.

I pull back after a moment, finding his eyes watching me, fixed on me with so much sentiment and emotion, and the look is both breathtaking and heartbreaking.

"Why are you here?" I ask.

"I needed to see you," he whispers into my ear, his lips brushing against the lobe.

I study him a moment.

He offers a gentle smile. "You wanna go for a drive?"

"A drive?" I question.

He nods, swallowing hard. "I wanna show you something."

"But I'm here with Tripp." I glance back in the direction of my brother, which is precisely when I see him standing there by the pool table, watching us intently, and suddenly something doesn't

186

feel right. Between the look in Colt's eyes, and the way my brother is just hanging back watching us, my heart sinks low in my belly, dipping uncomfortably. Something's going on.

"He'll be fine." Colt grabs my hands, linking his fingers through mine, flashing me his dimples. "Come on. Come with me."

I want to ask him why. Where does he want to take me? Why does he want me to leave with him right now? What shit has happened over the years that I've been gone that no one will tell me? But, of course I don't. Instead, I nod, managing a tentative smile that doesn't reach my eyes, and Colt ducks down, capturing my lips with his in a sweet yet chaste kiss, squeezing my hands. And then he turns, holding on to me with everything he has, leading me with him as he navigates the way through the thick crowd.

# Chapter 22

The liquor I consumed with Tripp back at Duke's is nothing more than a long-forgotten memory. I'm suddenly stone-cold sober sitting in the passenger seat of Colt's truck as we drive through the darkness of the night. Colt has barely spoken more than two words to me, his hand resting upon my thigh as he navigates the big pickup down a pitch-dark backroad in the middle of nowhere, a soft song playing through the radio helping to fill the void between us.

I cast a glance across the cab, studying Colt. His grip on the steering wheel is obviously tight, causing the veins in his forearms to move beneath the surface of his inked skin. His sharp jaw ticks, as if his teeth are clenching painfully with everything he isn't saying. His brow is set in a deep furrow as he stares ahead at the road illuminated only by the headlights. And I want to ask him if he's okay. But I don't. And I don't know why. I think I'm scared. Scared he'll say he isn't okay, and that last night was a mistake he wishes he could take back.

"You quite finished staring at me?" Colt chuckles unexpectedly, causing me to startle.

He flashes me a mischievous look, and I almost breathe a sigh of relief when I notice the way in which his eyes twinkle

188

beneath the glow of the dash. He smirks knowingly to himself, his hand squeezing my knee. "Keep lookin' at me like that, and I'm gonna have to pull over on the side of this here road, Quinny," he rasps, his voice suddenly huskier than usual, causing a flurry of butterflies to erupt in my stomach.

I can't stop my own smile as it claims my face, my cheeks flushing.

Colt's hand reaches for mine, pulling it to his lips. He kisses the backs of my fingers as his eyes remain trained on me for a moment longer, and in that instant all my breath is stolen from me. He gently places my hand onto his jean-clad thigh, and goes back to watching the winding road ahead as we continue through the night, wherever it may take us.

About fifteen minutes later, down a beaten old track, with nothing but the intermittent light of the moon breaking its way through the smattering of clouds guiding our way, Colt's truck bumps and grinds to a rolling stop at the top of a clearing.

"Where are we?" I ask, only slightly concerned as I stare out through the windshield. Rolling valleys and fields as far as the eye can see, all the way down to a river, the same river that runs through Black Canyon, all the way up through the middle of Wagner Ranch.

"This is the place I was telling you about. The place I'm thinking of buying," Colt says, switching off the rumbling engine. He casts me a reluctant, nervous smile, unfastening his seatbelt. "C'mon. I wanna show you around."

I follow suit, unfastening my belt and getting out of the truck. I meet him in front of the grill and he takes my hand in his, leading us down a rocky slope, through some overgrown, bushy spruce trees until we come to a clearing, to a small log cabin that looks like it might fall down if the wind picks up enough.

"This is it." Colt holds his hand out, indicating the tiny structure.

I stand back, taking in the cobwebs hanging down from the eaves. Windows boarded up. A giant gaping hole in the rusted tin roof. I try so hard not to outwardly frown because I can feel how excited he is just being here, but I can't help casting him a wary once-over, quirking a brow. I don't want to hurt his feelings, but come on.

"I know it needs a bit of work," he says with a light chuckle, nudging me playfully with his elbow.

"A *bit* of work?"

He rolls his eyes, ignoring my tone. "But it's a damn steal. Your brothers said they'll help me. They said they'll let me use the ranch hands for a lot of the grunt work."

"How much?" I ask, averting my eyes from the dilapidated cabin, choosing instead to focus on the real value of the property, which is the sprawling land that climbs all the way up into the foothills.

"Just over a hundred acres," Colt says, continuing, "just over a million."

I shake my head almost immediately.

"What?"

"There is *no* way you're paying that," I say with utter confidence. "For a million dollars, you want more than a pile of rotted logs and spiders' webs to call home." I point at the dwindling cabin. "They can't even list this as a livable dwelling."

Colt lets go of my hand, shoving both his into the front pockets of his jeans. "You don't think I should buy it?"

I look up at him. "Of course you should *buy* it! If that's what you want to do. The land is perfect for cattle."

"I just want something that's mine," he says, bowing his head a moment. "I ain't never had nothin' of my own, before."

My heart aches from his words.

Growing up, Colt Henry came from a dirt-poor family. His father, if you can even call him that, would drink and gamble the money away, often leaving Colt and his grandmother without the bare necessities they needed to survive. His father ended up in prison when Colt was nine, which is where he should have been the whole time. When we were kids, Colt spent a lot of time at our house. I always assumed it was just because he and Tripp were best friends. But then I found out it was because his grandmother didn't want him home when his dad rolled in drunk from a night of gambling. She bore the brunt of her son's despicable behavior, sparing Colt, and he stayed at our house, where he was safe. When his grandmother died, Colt had no one but us.

"I'd be offering no more than seven and a half. Best and *absolute* final." I glance at the cabin one last time, waving my hand in its direction. "And I'd be demanding that they demolish and remove this whole . . . *situation* . . . before you even consider signing anything."

Colt regards me for a moment, looking me up and down, the hint of a smile ghosting over his lips.

"What?" My brows knit together.

The moon shines through a break in the clouds, illuminating his face, dimples and all. "You're pretty damn sexy when you go all businesswoman-like."

I bite back my smile, my cheeks flushing, but he just laughs quietly, moving behind me. His arms come around my waist and he ducks his head down, his lips pressing against my neck, causing my skin to prick with goose bumps, butterflies erupting in my belly, doing somersaults and cartwheels. I sigh contentedly, relaxing back against his chest, my eyes closing a moment as I bask in his closeness, against the gentle lull of his heart.

"Can I ask you something?"

My eyes open when his hold of me tightens almost instinctively, adding to the hesitation within his question. I turn in his arms, looking up at him, finding his gaze fixed on me, full of a nervous fragility.

"Of course. You can ask me anything. Always." I place a hand against his chest, over his heart, where I know my name is permanently etched into his skin.

191

He swallows hard, his eyes flitting down to my lips and lingering for no more than a second before fixing on mine again. "D-did you mean what you said? About staying here?"

I stare at him, studying him so closely I can see he's holding his breath, and I nod.

His hands on my waist grip me even harder, his fingers digging into my skin painfully. But it's a bearable pain because it's full of his unrelenting fear, and I hate that there is clearly something going on in that head of his that is causing this unexplainable anxiety.

"I'm not going anywhere, Colt." I shake my head, staring deep into his eyes. "I'm staying right here."

He releases the breath he's been holding, closing his eyes a moment as if to fully allow my words to sink in. He rests his forehead against mine, wrapping his arms around my waist and holding me flush against him.

"Promise me." His voice is quiet, hushed, hopeful.

I snake my arms around his neck, my fingers dancing through the longer lengths of his hair as they curl at his nape. "Promise you what?"

He pulls back just enough to gauge me with a look so all-consuming, so penetrating and full of an almost unbearable weight. His brow furrows as he studies me, studies every single part of me as if he's looking inside of me, right through to the very fiber of my being. I've never been looked at like this before.

"Promise me, no matter what, you won't leave me again." His voice is barely a whisper, but it's a whisper I don't miss. Between the pain laced through each one of his words, the way he's holding me so desperately, and the fraught look of trepidation in his eyes, my stomach twists painfully.

"Colt, I promise." I shake my head again, never once breaking the intense gaze he's set upon me. "I'm not going to leave you." And, in an attempt to break the somewhat uneasy air that's settled heavily between us, I manage a wry smile, leaning in even closer. "I'm sorry, but you're stuck with me."

Colt's shoulders sag, and he releases another sigh, pulling me closer. He holds me against him, burying his face into my hair, muttering how much he's missed me, how much he loves me, how he can't bear the thought of ever losing me again. And although I've wanted nothing more than to hear him say these words, it's these same words I've been desperate to hear that suddenly terrify me more than anything as Tripp's warning flashes through my mind.

*Be careful. A lot of shit has happened. I don't want either of you to get hurt.*

It's after two when Colt pulls up to the main house once again.

The night is silent. Cold. Dark and still.

I glance up at the sprawling home I spent the first eighteen years of my life growing up in, the windows softly aglow against the black of the night sky. And I smile when my eyes land upon my bedroom window, the delicate lace curtain doing nothing to conceal the soft pink walls inside.

"Do you remember that first night you scaled the verandah railing and tapped on my window?"

I don't even have to look at Colt to know that he's smiling.

"Yeah," he says, his voice hushed through the silence of the truck cab. "I remember lying there, on the top bunk in Tripp's room, staring at the ceiling, listening for his breathing to even out. Man, my heart was racing, each beat was deafening. It echoed in my ears; I was sure he'd be able to hear it. I knew that what I was about to do would risk everything, but I did it anyway."

I grin at the memory. I'd been lying in bed all night staring up at the ceiling, just like Colt had been. I remember thinking what I might do in the instance it ever happened, if my schoolgirl fantasy actually came true and he knocked on my door in the middle of the night, or tapped on my window. I doubted it would ever happen. I was certain it was all just a stupid teenage dream. But that night, it did happen. And it was that night everything changed.

"Your dad knew."

At that, I snap my head to the side, finding Colt smirking to himself, his head ducked low as he stares up at my bedroom window through the windshield.

"What?" I balk, gaping at him.

He chuckles lightly, meeting my eyes. "He knew. He told me. He knew everything we did. Every night I came sneaking into your room. Every morning I crept out before the crack of dawn. He said he let it slide back then because he knew, no matter what he did, no matter how many times he kicked my ass, we were gonna be together whether he liked it or not."

I huff an incredulous laugh, searching Colt's eyes. "He *actually* told you this?"

He nods. "Yeah. A couple years back. He was always rooting for us. Back then, and . . . after everything that happened."

I look back out at the house, thinking back to all the times my dad threatened to take Colt out to the back paddock, to the same back paddock he used to take his old, lame horses and put them out of their misery. All the times he used to clear his throat excessively loudly when he would walk into the room to see Colt with his arm draped around my shoulders, glaring at him until he removed it, reminding him that he had a shotgun and a shovel. All the times he made our adolescent love lives a living hell. And all I can do is smile to myself.

I reach over, taking Colt's hand in mine, casting him a shy smile. "Do you want to come up?"

But suddenly, his smile is gone, and it feels like a slap to the face when he moves his hand away from mine, choosing instead to place it onto the steering wheel, gripping tight.

My brow furrows in confusion. What the hell just happened?

"Actually . . . I-I have to go."

I blink at him. "Go? Where? It's two o'clock in the morning."

He avoids my dubious gaze, raking his teeth over his bottom lip, his telltale stalling sign.

"Colt?" I press. "What's wrong?"

"I've gotta sleep . . ." He shrugs, still not meeting my eyes. "Cattle drive tomorrow, all the way up to Eagle Hawk Neck."

I study him for a long moment, glancing from his death-like grip on the steering wheel, to the way his teeth are so obviously gritting together, causing his stubbled jaw to tense painfully tight. His eyes are hard, conflicted, full of a haphazard plethora of emotion that I just can't seem to decipher.

"Colt? What the hell is going on?" I shake my head, grabbing his arm, forcing him to look at me, but when he does, I see nothing but defeat, and it causes my stomach to sink.

He quickly averts his eyes down to his lap, and panic begins to course through me.

"What is it? Mere seconds ago we were laughing about sneaking up into my bedroom. Less than an hour ago, you were holding me so tight like you couldn't bear to let me go, making me promise that I'll never leave you, kissing me with all you had beneath the Canyon moon." I'm incredulous and desperate as I continue. "Now, you can't even look at me!"

Colt hesitates a moment, cursing under his breath before reluctantly and tentatively taking my hand in his, staring down at our intertwined fingers, but he still won't look at me. "I spent so long missing you, Quinn. So long," he hisses, shaking his head.

I watch as his eyes squeeze shut so tight, as if his mind is clouded with memories of the pain he went through all those years ago. The pain that is still very much real, like a wound that just won't heal no matter how long it's been.

"Every day I missed you. Every night I missed you even more." He continues, "I can't bear the thought of going through that pain again, of losing you, *again*."

I shift in my seat, placing my other hand over his and holding him so tight. "I'm not going anywhere, Colt. I promise. You *need* to believe me. I know it's difficult to trust me again after what I did to you, but you have to—I'm here. Now!"

"This isn't about what *you* did," he interjects, his voice slightly

195

raised, hoarse with emotion and painfully raw, echoing through the silence.

I stop, snapping my mouth shut as I watch him.

Slowly, he looks at me, his eyes glossy and cautious. "I've done some . . . some shit I'm not proud of . . . And I'm so scared that you're gonna . . . you're gonna *hate* me."

His words and the starkness of them render me breathless. He's serious. Whatever he's done, is serious. This is his past. This is what I've been waiting for. But could it really be that bad? I stare at him, my mind reeling with what it is he could have possibly done that would make him even think it might make me hate him.

"Colt," I begin, pausing to think of what I can possibly say to make him believe me. "I could *never* hate you. You're the love of my life. I've spent ten years missing you more than I ever thought was possible to miss a person. Ten years of my life were spent with this giant, gaping hole in my chest where my heart once sat." I gauge him closely, squeezing his hand. "Whatever it is you that *think* you've done, we can get through it. *Together.* You just need to talk to me. *Please?* Please just talk to me." I plead with all that I have, and the tone in my voice is almost pathetic. But I no longer care.

After a few seconds, Colt nods just once, still avoiding my eyes, his gaze firmly set on our hands. He lifts both of mine to his lips, kissing the backs of my fingers, my hands, my wrists, each kiss a little more desperate than the last. When he finally does look at me, he's still so deeply conflicted, but there's something else. Something I've never seen. He reaches a hand out, cupping my jaw, and he edges closer and closer until his lips press against mine in a kiss so full of raw sentiment, it's both breathtaking and heartbreaking at the same time, and it ends just as abruptly as it began.

"I've gotta go," he whispers painfully, pulling away from my lips.

I stare into his eyes, which are so contradictory it's infuriating, but he gives me nothing more.

"Fine." I sigh, shaking my head in frustration.

I pull away, cursing under my breath, my fingers fumbling as I try quickly to unfasten my seatbelt and get the hell out of the truck before I allow my emotions to get the better of me and say something I don't mean. But he grabs me once again, forcing me back to his mouth, his lips and tongue relentless with every assault, each kiss drawing more and more of that emotion out of me until I taste the all-too-familiar bitter tang of salt as my tears fall into our heated exchange.

This time, it's me who pulls away, holding a hand against Colt's chest in an attempt to keep him at arms' length, despite my want and need objecting from deep down in my core. I swipe violently at my traitorous tears with the back of my hand, avoiding his eyes. I don't want him to see my hurt.

He grabs my wrist, trying so hard to stop me from getting out of the truck. "Quinny, don't—"

"Colt, just go!" I yank my hand free from his grasp, looking away and jumping down from the cab. "I need you to talk to me, to trust me enough to open up to me. You come find me when you're ready."

And, without even risking so much as a second glance in his direction, I slam the door shut, blocking him out before he can say something that will make me change my mind. I cross the front lawn with my head down, taking the porch steps two at a time, warning myself not to risk glancing back over my shoulder. And once I'm safely inside the warmth of the house, I fall back against the front door, collecting myself as best I can. But that's when the real tears start to fall. The tears of fear. Of loss. Tears of knowing that no matter how strong I try to act, maybe I'm not that strong after all. And, right now, all I want in the world is my dad.

# Chapter 23

I didn't sleep much last night. Understandably so. I tried everything. Tea. A warm shower. Soothing music. A boring-ass book. But nothing worked. All I kept thinking every time I tried to close my eyes was what exactly Colt thinks he did that is so bad. I know it's serious. I've known him almost my whole life, and I've never seen him as scared as he was last night in his truck. But what the hell has he done that he feels is so bad he's going to lose me again?

I yawn on my way down the stairs, every bone in my body aching with every movement I make. When I step into the kitchen, I find Tripp standing at the island, his back to me.

"Morning." I walk past him, stopping at the coffee machine, and I see him turn in my periphery, his gaze heavy as it fixes on me.

"Hey . . ." He clears his throat.

I place a pod into the machine, sitting a mug underneath and press the button. When I glance over my shoulder, I find Tripp watching me, eating his toast, his eyes studying me carefully with an unreadable expression.

"What?" I ask, folding my arms over my chest.

"You okay?" he asks, and I can tell he's taking in my puffy eyes, my splotchy skin, the telltale signs of a woman who's spent the best part of her night crying herself to sleep.

I sniffle from the cool morning air, my jaw clenching as I nod, looking away from him.

"Did he tell you?"

My eyes widen and I snap my head back, gaping at my brother. And from the look in his eyes, to the memory of what happened last night, Colt coincidentally showing up at Duke's. My brow furrows in confusion as some of the pieces start to come together. "Did you tell him to come get me from the bar last night?"

Tripp says nothing, his impassive gaze trained on me; he's always had an enviable poker face.

"You told him to come get me, to tell me the truth," I say more to myself than to him. The look of painful conflict in Colt's eyes last night, the contradictory softness and desperation in his touch as he danced with me before almost pleading me to go with him.

"Did he tell you?" Tripp asks again, his deep voice slightly more demanding.

And I could lie right now. I could tell him that Colt did tell me whatever the truth is . . . and I could trick my brother into divulging everything right here, right now. But I don't do that.

"No." I shake my head. "He didn't."

Tripp releases a heavy sigh, a muttered curse hissed beneath his breath.

"What is it, Tripp?" I ask, my voice raised slightly higher, wavering through my own emotion. "You're my brother . . . my *twin* . . . Why can't *you* tell me?"

He just shakes his head, clearly unable to risk meeting the beseeching look in my eyes. "It ain't my shit to tell, Quinny."

"I am your *sister*," I cry, slamming my hand against the marble countertop in a show of fury. "For once, can't you just have my back over Colt's?"

"This shit is bigger than just you and him!" Tripp's voice booms loudly, violently.

I cower, shrinking against the threatening tone in his words.

199

"W-what do you mean it's bigger than just *him*?" I ask so softly, scared of my own question.

Tripp throws his half-eaten toast into the sink, shaking his head before tearing his fingers through his hair. "I'm late for the cattle drive . . . I gotta go."

I stand there, frozen to the spot, watching as he storms around the island, grabbing his hat and his jacket from the table. His boots heavy with every footstep as he continues out through the glass doors, disappearing into the cold and dreary morning. And I stare at the door as it slams shut with such force, the glass panels rattle. I blink hard as my tears make a frustrating and unwelcome return, trailing down my cheeks, fear and dread consuming me.

Running on coffee and not much else, I sit outside Duke's before it's even open, waiting for Rylie. She's really all I have in this town, the only person I can talk to who seems to get the kind of turmoil my mind is currently facing. I need to speak to her. I need her to offer me some semblance of reasoning because right now, after last night with Colt, after this morning with my brother, I'm on the verge of losing my shit altogether. And I know if I lose it, I'll do something stupid, something I'm going to regret.

My knee bounces with every tap of my foot as an insufferable combination of anxiety and apprehension courses through me. My heart races, but I do all I can to try to keep it all together. The last thing I need right now is to break down right here in the middle of the main street of town and give the unforgiving people of the Canyon something else to talk about.

After a few minutes longer, the doors to the bar unlatch, opening wide, and I find Rylie in the doorway, her brows climbing slightly higher in surprise when she spots me right there, a small smile of confusion pulling at her lips.

I stand tentatively, biting down nervously on my bottom lip.

"Hey, doll," she says, looking me up and down, a slight crease pulling between her brows. "Everything okay?"

Almost before she can finish her question, I shake my head, glancing furtively up and down the street to check for prying eyes before I allow my emotion to get the better of me, and when I find the coast is clear, I allow my tears to fall, sniffling them back as best I can to no avail.

Rylie gauges me a moment, looking at me long and hard, her face blank, yet full of an unspoken understanding. And before I can fall to the ground beneath the weight of my emotion, she closes the distance between us, wrapping her arms around me and pulling me into an almighty, crushing embrace that I never knew I needed until right now.

Duke's Saloon is dark and empty and cold, and it reeks of disinfectant and stale beer. I've never been here while it's closed to the public, and without the flashing lights, the flat-screens displaying a whole heap of different football games and baseball games, the jukebox playing some old tune long forgotten, the place lacks its normal charm. It's cold and dingy. And it fits my mood just perfectly right now.

"You take a seat, doll." Rylie points to one of the barstools before moving behind the counter and placing her handbag up onto one of the shelves. "I'll make us some herbal tea."

I watch as she busies herself with finding two mugs in one of the high-up racks, a canister of tea bags coming down with it.

"My secret stash," she says with a smirk, winking at me as she pours boiling water into each of the mugs.

Peppermint wafts from the steaming mug placed onto the counter before me, and I quickly wrap my icy-cold hands around the porcelain, holding it close in the hope it might help to warm the crippling cold racking through me. I release a trembling sigh, which is when I meet Rylie's sad eyes watching me from across the bar.

"Talk to me," she says softly, reaching out and gently touching my arm.

"I'm so scared," I admit. "He won't tell me the truth. No one will tell me the goddamn truth!" I shake my head incredulously. "We had the best night of our lives the other night. We shared so much. I fell more in love with him than I even thought I could. I realized that I want to be here. I want to be back here with him. This is where I belong, with Colt."

Rylie takes a sip of her tea, nodding once and listening to every single one of my scrambled words.

"Then yesterday Tripp warned me to take it slow with Colt. He told me that a lot of shit went down after I left. And then last night, Colt came here to get me because Tripp told him to! Tripp told him he needed to talk to me, to tell me the truth!"

Rylie nods again. "I saw you two leave together."

I shake my head. "But he didn't tell me the truth, Rylie! He won't tell me the truth. He just keeps telling me that he's scared I'm going to hate him, that I'm gonna leave him when I find out!"

I place my mug of tea down onto the counter before my trembling hands drop it. Wiping at my tear-stained cheeks, an unexpected sob rattles through me, and I cover my face with my hands, crying quietly. "I love him so much." I glance up at Rylie through bleary eyes. "What isn't he telling me?"

She just watches me with an obvious sadness in her eyes, shaking her head slowly.

"I'm sorry to come here and lay this all on you." I grab a napkin from one of the holders on the countertop, wiping my eyes and my nose. "I just don't really have anyone else I can talk to." I laugh a derisive laugh, shaking my head at my own pathetic ridiculousness. "You're literally all I have."

I expect Rylie to laugh at my admission. To say something equally as pathetic. To lighten the mood. But she says nothing. And when I look at her again, I notice the gleam of unshed tears in her eyes as she stares at me, gripping her mug with everything she's got, as if it's her lifeline.

"Rylie?" I steady her with a serious look. "Are you okay?"

She snaps out of her daze, shaking her head once at herself before forcing a smile onto her face, blinking away the tears. "Yeah. Sorry." She sniffles. "I guess I just know how you feel, is all."

I study her for a long moment, taking everything in from the sadness in her eyes, to the way she appears so confident and flawless. I could tell when I first laid eyes on her that there was so much more to Rylie. She's a woman with a broken past and there's an obvious sadness she tries so hard to mask. She hasn't just had her heart broken before; her heart is broken, now, and I suddenly feel like the worst person in the world.

"I'm sorry, I shouldn't have come here and just—"

She stops me, holding her hand up in the air. "Don't you dare apologize, Quinn." She continues, her emotion causing her voice to waver ever so slightly, "Just promise me one thing."

I regard her a moment, her seriousness cutting through me. I nod.

"Please don't give up on him," she says so quietly, I almost miss it.

My brows pull together in confusion. She's talking about Colt.

She smiles softly at me, nodding. "You deserve to be happy. And so does Colt. Y'all are meant for each other. I can tell."

But there's so much more to her words. So much more that she isn't saying. But she doesn't continue. And, for some reason, I know not to press her. She's right. I can't give up on Colt. We are meant for one another. And I know that no matter what he's done, nothing can be so bad that I wouldn't want to be with him. I need him. He's a part of me. I've already lost my father. There's no way I can risk losing Colt. Not again.

I spent the afternoon racking my brain with everything Colt could possibly be keeping from me. By the time I hear the familiar sound of the wranglers banging around in the far barn, music blaring from the bunkhouse, signaling they've returned from their cattle drive, I'm an utter wreck of emotion.

I need to see Colt.

I need him to talk to me.

I won't leave him until he tells me the truth.

Hurrying downstairs, I stop in the foyer to pull my jacket on over my sweater before continuing out into the cool dusk air, following the rocky trail down between the stables, toward the bunkhouse, trying so hard to psych myself up the entire way, repeating over and over again in my mind exactly what I'm going to say when I see him.

When I make it to the bunkhouse, to the patio out back where the ranch hands are sitting around a fire drinking beers, I spot Cash across the way, talking to one of the wranglers, Tripp sitting on one of the logs in conversation with Bernie, an older cowboy who has worked here at the ranch since I was a little girl.

Tripp notices me through the flickering flames of the fire, his eyes meeting mine, and I stand there watching as he excuses himself from Bernie, standing up and coming toward me. He glances off to the side a moment, and I can tell he's considering his words before stopping right in front of me, steadying me with a knowing look.

"Where is he?" I ask, looking around.

Tripp's jaw tightens with his hesitation.

"Tripp?" I ask again through gritted teeth, my voice slightly more demanding.

"He's at the cabin."

I nod once before turning, but before I can leave, Tripp grabs a hold of my wrist. I look down to where his big hand holds me tight before flashing him a warning glare, and he quickly lets me go, his eyes warily regarding me as he holds his hands up in surrender. He shakes his head once. "Quinny, please. You shouldn't go there, you—"

I ignore my brother's pleading warning, continuing on my way back up the path. With everything I have, I know it's now or never. I need to find out what the hell is going on, and not my brother, nor anyone else who seems to know the truth, is going to be able to stop me.

In what feels like less than a few minutes, and such a blur I can't even remember the drive over here, I find myself pulling in to the makeshift parking bay outside the cabin, but my brows knit together in confusion and my eyes narrow when I find a shiny Mercedes G-Class parked right next to Colt's truck.

*What the hell?*

Taking a few deep breaths in through my nose to try and calm the anxiety coursing through me, I stare up through the windshield, to the lights illuminating the windows, and a million and one conflicting thoughts race through my mind.

He's up there with someone.

This is why Tripp was just warning me.

I shouldn't be here.

What if this is his secret?

What if Shelby was wrong?

Oh my God, what if he's secretly married?

I feel sick to my stomach; the pain almost unbearable.

But I deserve to know the truth. And with one last deep, fortifying breath, I force myself out of my car, glancing dubiously at the Mercedes on my way past. But I continue despite my reluctance. And I don't allow myself to even breathe until I'm at the top of the front stairs, standing right on the other side of the door, staring at it for a few beats. I consider knocking. I work up the courage. And I actually have my hand hanging in the air, knuckles prepped and ready to tap against the stained glass, but then, what will I say? What will I do? I don't know if I'm ready for this.

Against my better judgment, I do knock. Once. Then once more. Then again. I force my hand away before I go for a fourth, pulling my thumb to my mouth and nervously chewing on my nail as I wait, my heart wreaking havoc in my chest with every excruciating second that passes. I actually consider turning and running. Maybe this is a truth I'm not ready to deal with. Maybe I should just leave, pretend I never even stopped by. But then the handle dips, the latch clicks, and slowly the door opens, and my heart jumps up into the back of my throat when I find a familiar face staring back at me.

No. It can't be.

What feels like the insufferable pain of a million knives suddenly starts to stab me right in my back. I can't breathe. I feel weak in the knees, and in that moment, I'm afraid I'm going to fall. But somehow, I find the strength I need to stand tall, my eyes pricking with tears as the realization comes over me in shocking, unrelenting waves.

Of course. How could I be so damn stupid.

"R-Rylie . . .?" I stammer, my cracking voice wavering.

Rylie's face falls in stark realization, and she takes a tentative step over the threshold. "Quinn, it's not what—"

"Who is it, Ry?" Colt's voice calls from inside.

I watch Rylie close her eyes, bowing her head just as the door is pulled open, and suddenly Colt appears over her shoulder, smiling obliviously, Rylie's daughter, Emmy, giggling in delight as she balances precariously on his shoulders, squealing with laughter. And it's at that moment I realize just how stupid I am. I should've known. And I guess a part of me did know. I saw it in that little girl's eyes, those eyes that are so much like his it's actually scary.

I tear my gaze away from Emmy, meeting Colt's, and the sudden heaviness in his stare tells me all I need to know.

"Hey, I know that lady!" Emmy points at me with a dimpled smile as Colt places her carefully back down onto the floor. She waves at me. "Hi!"

I want to wave back. More than anything I want to wave and to smile, because none of this is her fault. But I can't find it in

206

me to even move. I'm frozen. Hell, I can't even fake a smile right now. I can't do much at all as I look from Colt to Rylie, to Emmy who is a heartbreakingly beautiful combination of the both of them. And, as we stand there staring at each other in some kind of awkwardly silent stand-off, my heart comes to a sudden and crashing halt, shattering into a million jagged pieces in the pit of my belly, the crushing reality setting in.

Time stops.

Everything stops.

Hell, it almost feels as if the world itself stops.

"I'm sorry, I shouldn't . . ." I take a stumbling step backward, staggering unsteadily. I reach for the railing, gripping onto it for dear life as I turn and hurry to the stairs.

"Quinn, wait!" Colt yells.

I stop. I don't know why. Maybe it's the pleading desperation in his voice. I don't know. But I stop long enough to glance over my shoulder, watching as he tears his fingers through his hair, glancing momentarily down at Emmy, his daughter. But I shake my head, dismissing whatever it is he's going to try and tell me. I can't deal with this right now. I turn and hurry down the stairs as fast as my feet can carry me. He doesn't need to tell me a single thing. I get it. I don't need his words.

"Quinn!" Rylie's voice calls after me.

I ignore them both, running across the yard to my car with everything that I have, desperate to get the hell away.

# Chapter 24

By the time I make it back to the main house I'm an emotional wreck, I don't even know how I made it here in one piece. Between the racking sobs and the blinding tears, I had my foot down on the gas the entire way, barely dodging trees, fences, bumps in the road.

With tears streaming down my face, I ran straight into the house, up the stairs, and into my father's bedroom. I threw myself onto his bed, curled up into a ball, and hugged his pillow so tight. I needed something, anything, to remind me of him. And I've been here for what feels like an eternity, crying inconsolably, my tears soaking through the sheets.

To be honest, I don't even know why I'm crying. It just hurts. It's an unimaginable pain, like nothing I could have ever been prepared to feel. I can barely breathe through the overwhelming emotion, consuming me as it courses through my entire being in waves.

Colt has a child. A beautiful, six-year-old little girl. She is his. And Rylie is her mom. I should have realized when I looked into Emmy's eyes, the moment I noticed something within her green gaze. Now it's blatantly obvious. Those eyes are exactly like her father's. Her smile, her dimples. That was the connection I initially felt with her; the pull I felt when I was with her. She is a tiny version of him. God, I feel like such an idiot.

*You're that girl?* Rylie's words and the stark look in her eyes when she must have realized who I was, flashes through my mind.

She knew. Everyone knew. Everyone, except me.

My father knew . . .

I swear, I've never felt more betrayed in my whole life.

But it isn't the fact that Colt has a daughter.

It isn't even the fact that everyone knew, and yet nobody saw fit to tell me, despite the fact that they had seven years to do so. None of that even matters.

What does matter, what hurts like hell, is that I know now, regardless of how we feel about one another, Colt and I can never be. He may love me, but I saw that look in Rylie's eyes, I saw her heartache, I felt her pain. She's in love with him. With the father of her child. Who am I to stand in the way of Emmy's parents being happy together?

A gentle knock sounds upon the bedroom door, and I squeeze my eyes shut, taking a few deep breaths. Maybe if I don't say anything, whoever it is will just go away and leave me alone. But of course that doesn't happen, and another knock sounds against the wood, before it opens ever so slightly.

"Quinn?" Tripp's voice is hushed as it breaks through the silence.

Gripping the pillow tighter, I say nothing as a sob bubbles in the back of my throat, desperate for release. But I hold it in.

Tripp sighs heavily from the doorway, and a second later I hear the sound of his boots creaking over the hardwood floors, coming closer. I keep my eyes shut tight, even when I feel the foot of the mattress dip, even when I feel a hand gently rest against my knee.

"Quinny," he begins in a whispered voice so unlike him. "Quinny, please look at me."

I bury my face into the pillow, sniffling back that same pesky sob that's threatening me. "Will you please just tell me now?" I

209

plead, my voice muffled. "After everything, can you just tell me the truth?"

He sighs again. "It started about a year after the accident," he finally says, his voice gruff and reluctant. "Colt was going through rehabilitation. Learning to walk again. But he was so depressed. He barely ate. Hardly slept. He got addicted to these pain pills, and no matter what, the damn doctor kept prescribing them." He pauses, sniffing once. "We tried to get him clean. Hell, Dad even got him a place at this exclusive spot in Utah. But he refused to go. Nothing worked. He was in a bad place, and . . . Well, I guess I feel partly responsible, because if I didn't force you to leave . . . if you'd been there when he woke up in hospital, then maybe everything would have been okay." He releases a trembling breath, and I turn my head, glancing at him to see him scrub a hand over his weary face.

"It wasn't until he met Rylie that he started to clean himself up."

At the mention of Rylie, I exhale a shaky breath, resting my cheek on my forearms, settling my gaze straight ahead at the big bay window that looks out into the darkness of the night.

"Rylie didn't know nothin' about what happened. All she knew is that he'd been hurt by a girl. He did something stupid. And he needed someone. And, for a while, the two of them were good."

My stomach twists at that thought. I close my eyes momentarily, and my mind is inundated with visions of Rylie and Colt together. And it makes me feel sick, because now that I see it, they're almost perfect for one another.

Tripp continues, "Rylie fell hard for Colt. But then, after a while, Colt changed. He started being horrible to her. Treating her like shit. And I knew why. It was because, no matter how hard he tried to pretend, Rylie wasn't you. He used her to try and forget about you, about everything he lost."

I rake my teeth painfully over my bottom lip, listening to the sad story that breaks my heart even more. For Colt. But for Rylie, mostly. That poor girl.

"For a long time Colt wasn't a good guy, Quinny. He was an asshole. A sullen prick, completely against the world and everyone who only ever wanted to help him. Including Rylie."

I close my eyes again as another sob racks through me.

"Eventually, Rylie woke up to herself, and she realized that Colt would never want her the way he would forever want you. So, she ended it, and she was going to go home to New Mexico, but then she found out she was pregnant. So she stayed until she had the baby, but then Colt changed. It was Emmy who finally made him wake up. And he was his old self again. So, Rylie decided to stay."

Tears burn my cheeks, sliding down over my lip, and I wipe them away with the sleeve of my sweater, sniffling back the overwhelming emotion as it tries so hard to get the better of me.

"I know I should have told you. I wanted to. But I didn't . . . And I'm so sorry. I really hoped Colt would have told you over the years."

I shake my head. "Nope. He didn't tell me. But I guess . . . why should he? I was just the girl who broke his heart."

"But you weren't just the girl who broke his heart, Quinny," Tripp argues, pulling my hand and forcing me to look at him. "You were the love of his life. He cried every damn day over you, over what he lost. All he wanted was you. You've always been the love of his life. He just made some shitty mistakes in the time it took him to get you back. You can't hold that against him."

"I'm not angry with him," I admit. "I'm angry with myself."

"Yourself?"

I sniffle again, forcing myself to sit with a heaving sigh. I nod. "I'm the one who left. I've been gone for so long. I never called. Never anything. And I just expected to come back and everything would be the same." I scoff, scrubbing my hands over my face. "If I had stayed, this never would have happened. Hell, if I didn't leave the love of my life at the altar because I was too damn focused on chasing my dreams, none of this would have happened. Everything would be so different."

211

"Maybe. Maybe not," Tripp offers, ever the voice of reason. "But Colt still loves you more than anything." He ducks down, catching my eyes. The tiniest smile pulling at his lips. "You can't deny that."

I stare down at the rug on the hardwood. "Yeah," I say with a shrug, wondering now if love is really enough. I don't doubt Colt loves me. And I love him more than anything. But everything has changed now. I bury my head in my hands.

"You need to talk to Colt," Tripp says, gently patting my back.

"I know," I mutter into my hands.

And, like clockwork, the sound of footsteps echoes through the house, pounding up the stairs, and after a few seconds the bedroom door swings opens, followed by panting, breathless gasps. But I don't look. I already know it's him. I can feel him. Sense him.

"Quinn?" His broken voice pleads through the silence of the room, and it's almost heartbreaking.

All I can do is close my eyes tight, my hands still covering my face.

"Quinn, please?" His footsteps come closer. "Please talk to me!"

With a deep, racking breath, I force myself to look up, opening my eyes, staring straight ahead at nothing in front of me. I can feel Tripp's intense gaze on me, his hand remaining on my back in a show of support. And, probably against my better judgment, I find myself moving, standing on jelly-like legs, turning to see Colt gaping at me, looking like half the man I know him to be.

"Please, Quinny . . ." He shakes his head, his glassy eyes red-rimmed and full of desperation as they implore my own. "Please let me explain."

I bite down hard on my bottom lip, staring at him for a moment. From his wayward hair sticking up every which way, which looks as if he's been tearing his hands through it. Tired, weary eyes full of dismay. The haphazardly fastened flannel shirt he's obviously just thrown over his T-shirt in haste. My heart

212

breaks for him, for his current state, and I know that I owe it to him to hear him out.

I offer a small nod to my brother, walking around the bed, and I step past Tripp, avoiding his eyes, leading Colt back out of my father's bedroom, waiting momentarily for him to follow me. When I hear him behind me, I continue down the hall, mentally preparing myself for whatever it is he feels he so desperately needs to explain to me.

He's so close behind me as I walk through the door and into my bedroom. So close, in fact, I can feel his breath on the back of my neck, smell his intoxicating scent, feel his fraught hopelessness as he stays so close, yet carefully keeps what little distance he can bear to keep from me.

A big part of me wants to turn around and wrap my arms around him, cry with him, and kiss him, tell him that everything is going to be okay, that we can get through this. But, a bigger part of me doesn't do that, because she knows the truth. Everything isn't going to be okay. I don't know if this is something we can get through because I don't know if I can be that woman. The woman who comes back into town as if nothing ever happened, and turns everyone's life upside down. Colt has a life here. He's a father. He has a family. I don't know if I can put myself in the middle of that, knowing how in love with her baby-daddy Rylie truly is.

I step into my room, moving to the furthermost corner from him. I don't say anything as I stand at the window, wrapping my arms around me in an attempt to stop the shivers from coursing through me. He remains tentatively by the door, watching me. Too close, yet so far. He lingers. I can almost hear his mind working overtime with what he should or shouldn't say.

"Say whatever it is you need to say," I murmur with a casual shrug as if I don't care. But I do care. More than anything. So much so, I close my eyes, waiting with bated breath.

"I need you to look at me," his raspy voice whispers, so broken each word cracks.

I just shake my head, keeping my eyes closed. "I can't."

I hear him sigh, a defeated sigh full of torment and torture, and the sound alone is almost enough to crush my stubborn resolve. But I stand my ground. I can't risk looking at him, for his sake as much as mine.

"I wanted to tell you. I swear to God, I wanted to tell you. Years ago. I had your number memorized in my head, and I was gonna call you, and tell you when I first found out she was pregnant. But . . . I didn't."

Tears prick my eyes, but I keep them shut so tight as I repeat his admission, "But you didn't."

"At first, I stopped myself from calling to tell you because I fucking *hated* you and, as far as I was concerned, you didn't deserve to know. It was none of your damn business."

I swallow hard, steadying my breath. I reach up and grab hold of the wall, gripping it tight when my knees go weak.

"When I finally moved past that hate, I was going to call you after Emmy was born to tell you, but I stopped myself then because . . . because I was fucking terrified that *you* would hate *me*."

I hear Colt sniffle, and that sound causes my own tears to seep through my lashes, spilling onto my cheeks.

"I'm sorry for not telling you, Quinn. I made the biggest mistake of my life. I'll never forgive myself. But I won't apologize for Emmy—God, I fucking love that little girl more than I ever thought I could ever love anyone. She's the best damn thing to happen to me in—"

I open my eyes at that. "You think I'm upset because of your daughter?"

He blinks at me, his own cheeks damp, eyes red and swollen.

"That's what you think of me?" I sob. "You think I'm upset because you have a kid?"

He goes to speak, but I cut him off, raising a trembling hand in the air. "This isn't about Emmy, Colt." I shake my head. "It's been ten years. For all I know you could have gone and had a whole bunch of kids in that time, and that would be none of my business." I take a moment to really collect myself, to gather my thoughts and my emotions. "Yeah, it would have been nice to have been told, but I'm not mad at you for that. And, in fact, I'm not mad at you at all. I'm just . . . I'm sad."

A fresh wave of tears falls as I take a seat on the very edge of the window box. "I'm sad because all I ever wanted was to be with you. And I could've been with you. But I gave it up. And I left because I had this stupid notion in my head that I had to chase my dreams so I wouldn't wind up like my mom. But after a while I realized that my dreams were just that. Dreams. I was so hell-bent on getting out of this town that I forgot what I had here. I lost everything. I had my happy ever after in the palm of my hand, and I threw it away."

Colt drops down onto the chest at the end of my bed, his head in his hands, his shoulders trembling from his own sobs as he tears violently at his hair, muttering, "We can still have our happy ever after, Quinny."

I shake my head. "No, because now it just feels like too much has happened, too much has changed. I missed so much. I missed years with my dad. I missed everything with you. Everything is different now. And maybe . . . maybe I belong in New York, and you belong here with Emmy and—" I stop when he jumps up from the chest.

Crossing the room to me, his hands break through my invisible barrier, cupping my face, the pads of his thumbs wiping at my tear-stained cheeks. He crouches down so close, his eyes flaming as they bore into mine, and the look within them is almost feral, I can't help but gasp. I grab at the hem of my sweater, my fingers twisting at the wool, tearing at it, anything to stop myself from actually reaching out and touching him. I can't. I just can't risk it.

"Please, baby. Please! You promised me you wouldn't leave me again," he hisses through gritted teeth, so close, our foreheads touching. "I should've told you. I wish I could go back and tell

215

you. But I didn't and I can't. But I need you, Quinny. I need you to please stay. I can't lose you again. I can't. I won't. I'm fucking shit without you." He's sobbing through his words, and he closes his eyes, his nose touching mine, his lips less than a hairsbreadth from my own. I can feel his tears mix with mine as our cheeks graze together, his breath hot and hushed. When he edges just close enough for his mouth to brush against my own, that's my undoing.

My hands grip his shirt, fisting the flannel when our lips crash together. I pull him even closer when his tongue pushes inside my mouth, allowing him all the access I can give him. But still, it doesn't feel enough. I need him, more than anything. All of him. Right now he is all I need. My fingers tear blindly at the buttons on his shirt, pulling and yanking them until they either snap or pop. I don't care, nor do I have time to wait. I don't care that I'm a mess of emotion and pain and heartache. I don't care that I can taste Colt's tears on my lips. I don't care about much at all right now, except how bad I need to feel him, and only him. I pull away from our kiss just long enough to pull my sweater up over my head, leaving me in just my bra and jeans.

Colt's heavily hooded eyes are fixed on me. He runs his tongue along his swollen bottom lip, a soft, animalistic growl coming from the back of his throat as takes the moment to just appreciate me, worshiping me with his gaze, memorizing every square inch of my body. In one swift move he shrugs out of his shirt, tugs his T-shirt up over his head, and his hands are on me once again, guiding me backward toward my bed, his lips slamming against mine, hard and desperate, his kiss full of raw emotion and wanton need.

Colt takes a seat on the mattress and I climb onto his lap, wrapping my arms around his neck. I moan into our kiss when his hands trail down my sides, stopping at my hips and pulling me flush against him. He groans when I grind against his need, our tongues lashing together, teeth clashing.

"Fuck, I love you," he murmurs through a racking sob, his emotion tumbling into our heated kiss. Abruptly, he pulls away from my mouth, his lips finding my neck and kissing my skin, suckling and licking, skating down over my throat. "You're mine, and I will forever be yours." His breath is hot against me as he whispers over and over again how in love with me he is, how much he loves me. "I've always loved you. I always will."

I've waited so long to hear him say these words, but now the sentiment behind them feels slightly tainted, because I keep thinking of Rylie. Did he say these words to her? Did he tell her he loved her? They have a child together; theirs is a love I'll never be able to compete with. I find myself squeezing my eyes shut tight, trying so hard to block out his voice.

"Always and forever," Colt whispers, his teeth gently grazing against the sensitive skin at the base of my neck. "You and me. Always."

"Stop!" I yell, pushing him away before I even know what I'm doing.

He rears back, the look in his eyes one of horror, as if I've just slapped him.

"I'm sorry, I can't do this." I slap a hand over my mouth in an attempt to stifle my sob. "You should be with Rylie!" I say against my palm.

"Rylie?" He pulls my hands down from where I'm covering my face. He steadies me with a hard look. "What are you talking about?"

I bite down on my trembling lip, remembering the look in her eyes earlier. The look of sadness, and the painful heartbreak that she tries so obviously to hide behind her confident facade. Her heart is broken over this man because she's so clearly in love with him. He's her one. The one she wants, and the one she knows she'll never have. But she should have him. They should have each other. For Emmy's sake.

Colt's eyes widen as if he can hear my thoughts. He gauges

217

me. "No, baby, Rylie and me . . ." He shakes his head, as if he's searching for the right words. "It was never about . . . *love*." He sighs heavily. "It was just sex, Quinn. And I fucking hate myself for admitting that, but that's all it was. It was nothing more than—"

"I can't hear this." I cover my mouth again with a shaking hand, moving to get off his lap.

"Quinn, stop!" he hisses, holding me where I am.

"Colt, let me go," I warn him, unable to look in his eyes.

He pulls his hands away, holding them in the air in surrender, and I move off his legs, wrapping my arms around myself as I take a few steps back, away from him as far as the room will allow, still unable to face looking at him, unable to face the rejection I know I'll see if I meet his eyes.

"Quinny?"

I shake my head. "Don't."

"Quinn!" Colt yells, his voice hard and raw.

And, at that, at the stark, shrill sound of his pleading, desperate tone, I do meet his eyes, because I owe it to him. "Leaving you was the biggest mistake of my life. I'll never forgive myself. But it was so stupid of me to think that I could just come back and that everything would be how it always was." I shake my head at my own stupidity. "It's been too long. Everything has changed." I stare at him, allowing my tears to sting my eyes, unable to look away from him. "Colt, look me in my eyes and tell me that Rylie means *nothing* to you?"

He says nothing. He just gazes painfully into my eyes, his stare heavy and unwavering as he remains deafeningly silent.

And that's all I need.

"You should leave." I avert my gaze, looking down.

A long and stifling silence ensues, but I keep my sights fixed heavily upon the floor.

Colt sighs, and I hear the rustle of the bedcovers as he stands up. I see him in my periphery as he goes about collecting his shirt and T-shirt from the floor. All the while, I can't look at him. If he's even half as broken as I feel right now, I don't know what looking at him will do to my already fragile self-control. I want him, but I shouldn't want him. I need him, but I know I can't need him. I love him, but I can't love him. He's no longer mine to love.

His footsteps are slow as they sound upon the wooden floorboards, moving closer to the door. But he stops, and I listen as he releases another heavy sigh of defeat, and I just know he has his hands in his hair, his fingers tearing at the lengths in frustration.

"I won't ever tell you that Rylie means nothing to me," he says, his voice so steely and gruff. "I can't say that. She's the mother of my fucking kid."

His words hurt me because they're the heartbreaking truth, and I rake my teeth hard over my bottom lip in an attempt to take my mind off the crippling pain this truth is inflicting upon me, staring down at nothing as tears blind me.

"But what I will tell you, Quinn, is that . . . it's *always* been you. It always has been and it always will be. If that's not enough for you, then– then *I'm* not enough, and for that I truly am sorry, because all I ever wanted was to be enough for you."

I listen as his footsteps start again. The door opens, and then it closes. And another heavy silence follows. But this silence is sad, and empty, and cold, and lonely. I wipe my cheeks with the palms of my hands, looking around the room, taking it all in, from the mess of the bedsheets where we sat only moments ago, entangled with passion and need, to the door, which the love of my life, my heart, just walked out of.

Reluctantly, I collect my sweater from the floor, pulling it on over my head. And despite my best efforts, my tears continue, and all I can depend on is the only thing I know for sure right now; I was wrong. This is no longer my home. It's been too long. Too much has changed. I don't belong here anymore.

# Chapter 25

I can't tell you how long I've been staring at the brick wall in my bedroom. Hours probably.

I should be getting up. I should be almost ready for work by now. Hurrying out the door with my phone in one hand, my purse in the other, half a toasted bagel clamped precariously between my teeth. I should be facing the morning with gusto. *Seize the day*, and all that shit. But I just can't bring myself to care enough to bother with any of that. I don't have it in me. I'd like to think it's just a moment of weakness, that "time" of the month, something I'll get over sooner rather than later. But it's been like this for the entire five weeks I've been back in the city. I'm scared this is just how it's going to be forever.

Every morning at precisely six-forty-four, my eyes open of their own accord, and I just lie here, counting sixty excruciating seconds in my head until the shrill sound of my alarm pierces my soul. I don't press snooze. I don't pull the sheets higher. I don't roll over. I don't compromise with myself to take a shorter shower for an extra five minutes more in bed. I just lie here, not moving, barely breathing, listening to the sound of New York City's morning chaos carry up into the air and through the double glaze of my windows three stories above street level as

I stare at the red-brick wall across from my bed, trying so hard to convince myself that this, this is the life I was meant to live.

But eventually I do get up, forcing myself out of bed like I always do. If I don't, my phone will ring, and it will be Oliver asking me where I am. If I don't answer his call, he'll show up at my door and ring the buzzer for three minutes straight until I give up and let him in. He'll proceed to sit around, watching me while I go about my business of getting ready. He'll sip his iced frappe or iced latte, or something equally as laden with whipped cream and chocolate powder through a straw, despite the late November chill hanging frigid in the air, eyeing me dubiously when I choose a pair of last season heels to wear. He'll make some smart-ass comment about needing to get my jiggly thighs back to spin class, and I'll throw him the occasional middle finger.

But it's Oliver who makes me get up in the morning. If he wasn't his annoying, relentless, and downright infuriating self, I would spend all of my days in bed, nights too, just wasting away while staring at that same wall as if it alone has done me some kind of unforgivable injustice. And, despite my objections, my eye-rolling, my dramatic sighs and muttered curses, I'm eternally grateful that Oliver cares enough to harass me the way he does. He doesn't know what happened while I was away. He doesn't know why I came back. He has no idea why I am the way I am. But he still won't give up on me. He's a true friend. The only one I've got.

"Hey, Quinny, it's Tripp. I called you yesterday but you didn't answer. Can you please call me back? I'm trying to help Cash with the December forecast, but he's fucking clueless and he keeps screwing up the formula cells!"

*Lies.* I created that spreadsheet for my brothers to use without fail. Dad had been running the business on paper since he took over the reins and the outdated books from Grandpa in the Nineties, and when Cash emailed them to me, it was a disaster, so I designed a new accounting register for them. Easy to follow. Impossible to break. It's an Excel spreadsheet, for God's sake. There's no way Cash is messing up the figures. This is just Tripp being Tripp. Every time he calls me, he creates some new excuse for me to call him back. I know I should call, but every time I do, we get into the same old argument, and I end up feeling worse after we race to see who can hang up on the other first.

I roll my eyes while brushing my teeth, skipping to the next voicemail on my cell.

"Hey, Quinny, it's Cash. Just checking to see if you're gonna come home for Christmas. Shelby's planning a big traditional dinner and she wants numbers soon. I don't know why she needs the numbers so soon, but she's always gotta be prepared . . . Anyway, give me a call when you can. I miss ya. Oh, and if Tripp calls, the spreadsheet is fine. I deleted one column by mistake. But I figured it out. He's so dramatic."

I can't help but laugh, my heart clenching in my chest at the sound of Cash's gruff, monotone voice. I miss him. I miss them all. This time the distance feels almost too far.

I walk through to my bedroom, tossing my cell on my bed as I continue through to my closet.

I trail my fingers over the myriad clothes hanging in my closet, trying to decide between a navy suit and a gray dress when the next voicemail comes through, but when I hear the unexpected voice playback from the bedroom, I freeze on the spot, clutching at my chest.

"Hey . . . Quinn. It's m-me . . . umm, R-Rylie."

I walk back out into the bedroom in some kind of a daze, my brows knitting together as I stare at my phone lying on the mess of my tangled bedsheets. And I sit down. I contemplate ending the message. Deleting it. But, I don't. Instead, I wait for her to continue.

"I know, you're probably thinking what the hell? What does *she* want?" Rylie laughs lightly into the phone, and it's a nervous laugh, void of any humor. "Well, the thing is, I . . . I don't really know *why* I'm calling. I don't know if it's my place to call you, but I needed to tell you that Colt is miserable. I'm really worried about him, as a friend and as the father of my daughter, nothing more, I swear. I've never seen him like this before. But people are starting to tell me that he's going back to the way he was when you first left. Before the accident. And . . . I'm scared. Even Emmy is worried about him, and she's not even seven years old."

I drag my teeth over my bottom lip, staring out through the big windows, to the gray morning outside, deftly toying with the fluffy collar of my robe.

"Colt told me what you said to him that night. You think he and I should be together. But, Quinn, Colt and I are never going to be together like that. Was I in love with him? Yeah. Did he break my heart? Yes. Is there a tiny part deep down that wishes things had turned out different? Of course. I know you're hurt, Quinn. You have every right to be. But Colt really loves you. More than anything. He always has. And right now he needs you. I know it's difficult, but I really do hope you can at least consider giving him another chance. You two are meant for one another. You always have been . . .

"I remember the way he used to talk about you, about the girl who broke his heart. He tried so hard to act as if he hated that girl. As if she was nothing to him. But even through the hate he tried so hard to hold on to, his love was always there. I wanted him to love me the way he loved that girl. But he didn't. And that's okay. Please just don't give up on him. Like I said, a love like the one you and Colt share, it's rare. Don't let it get away . . . Well, look, you have my number. You know you can call me anytime." Another nervous laugh rings through the phone, followed by silence. "I-I miss talking to you, Quinn."

The voicemail ends and Siri comes on to tell me there are no more new messages. But I don't move. I can't move. I can't even think straight. I just sit here, staring down at the blank screen on my phone, my mind left reeling from Rylie's call.

Suddenly, all I can think about is Colt.

Rylie sounded genuinely concerned about him.

What if he's sinking back into that same dark place he was in years ago, the place that almost killed him?

He wouldn't. Surely he isn't that selfish. He has Emmy to think of. He told me himself—he's never loved anyone the way he loves that little girl. He lives every day for her. But what if it all becomes too much? What if . . .

I jump when my cell begins vibrating once again. I glance down, my heart racing at the thought of yet another call from home. But then I see Oliver's face, the selfie he took with my phone when we were day-drinking at a party in Montauk last Labor Day, flashing upon the screen, and I clutch my chest, sagging in relief. I catch my breath as I reach for the device, pressing the accept button.

"Hey, Ols."

"Hey, girl," he chimes through from the other end, far too cheerful for this time on a Tuesday morning. "I'm almost at your building. You have approximately seven minutes, depending on the traffic on Broadway. We have to be uptown by nine o'clock, so you better be dressed, preened to perfection and waiting on that damn curb in six and a half minutes."

"Shit!"

"You *forgot*?" Oliver panics.

"No, of course I didn't forget!" I lie.

I totally forgot. I'm the worst. Today, Oliver and I are pitching for an eight-million-dollar brownstone on the Upper West Side. Oliver's first potential listing over ten million. A huge feat for any agent. And, since I'm back on the sales floor, I suppose it's my first, too. Mr. Hawkins was kind enough to reluctantly take me back. I can't screw this up, for myself or for Oliver.

I spring up from my bed, hurrying back through to my closet, grabbing the first thing I can. "I'll be ready and waiting outside in four minutes, I promise!" I yell back in the direction of my phone, and thankfully the call ends in time for me to race breathlessly around my room while I scramble to get dressed in record time.

When we arrive at the office after our meeting uptown, Oliver parades through the sales floor as if he's just won an Academy Award. He points his fingers at people, popping off shots of victory. He does a spin every few feet. He even slides his Gucci sunglasses down over his eyes as if he's a celebrity faced with a swarm of paparazzi.

I trail behind, rolling my eyes. We didn't even get the listing. Yet. We will. The seller is the ex-sister-in-law of one of my most loyal clients—a businessman from Japan who once took me out with his associates and got me so drunk on saki I was unable to get out of bed for two days straight. We've remained friends ever since. Oliver was recommended to this woman because of me. But, he's excited, so I let the kid have his fun, and I just smile and nod before sneaking away and hiding out in my cubicle to waste the rest of the day away.

I have six messages waiting on my desk phone. Three barely legible Post-it Notes stuck to my monitor. A whole heap of unanswered emails. But all I keep thinking about is that voicemail from Rylie saved on my cell, and I find myself staring at the device for what feels like an eternity, which is precisely when Colt's name appears on the screen, flashing wildly, in sync with each vibration.

*Shit.*

I fumble with the device, in the process juggling it from one hand to the other like a hot potato, but then I drop it, and it falls to the floor with a thud, the call coming to an abrupt end when the whole damn thing shuts down.

"Dammit," I hiss, reaching down and picking it up.

I look at it closely, from the crack still shattering the screen from when I dropped it to the pavement after Cash originally

225

called me to tell me about Dad, to the various chips and dents on the corners and the sides. I really should have invested in a new phone, by now. But it's been the last thing on my mind.

I press the power button and wait while it loads. After a few excruciating seconds, the Apple logo appears, and a few moments later it's asking for my passcode, which I quickly enter while holding my breath. After another couple of beats, the iPhone vibrates in my hand, a new voicemail notification illuminating the screen, and my heart suddenly rears its way up into the back of my throat. I can almost taste it.

I cast a glance around the office. Everyone looks busy, or makes themselves appear busy. A few brokers are crowding around Oliver as he tells some elaborate story about our pitch meeting. The place is as it should be, and almost everyone is none the wiser of the emotional battle currently occurring in my cubicle as I nervously dial the number for my messages. I hold the phone against my ear with a trembling hand, chewing nervously on my bottom lip as I stare at the screensaver on my computer monitor while Siri tells me I have one new voice message.

"Hey, Quinny. It's me. Colt." His voice is rough and raspy as it reverberates through the line, and I find myself closing my eyes, allowing his words to warm through me, followed by a smooth yet slightly awkward chuckle that makes me smile. "I guess you knew that already since you just rejected my call."

*No, I didn't. I swear. I dropped my phone. Please don't think I rejected your call.*

I listen to his heavy sigh, and it only breaks my heart even more.

"Look . . . I just . . . I was calling because I really wanted— no, *needed*—to hear your voice. I guess your message recording is the best I'm gonna get. But it'll do for now. I just . . . I miss you. Like crazy."

I begin chewing on my thumbnail, my eyes still closed. His voice is so deeply conflicted, so gruff, so broken. It's painful. But, in a way, it's almost as if he's right here beside me. And I find some unexpected solace in that. I can pretend, even if only for the moment, that we're together, and in that moment it's pure bliss.

"I've never needed you more than I need you right now. It hurts like hell. Like I've lost you all over again. Only this time, I don't have that anger roiling inside of me to mask the pain. I just have regret, and this hollow, empty feeling in my chest where my heart used to beat."

I hunch forward a little, feeling like I've just been kicked in the stomach.

"I love you, Quinny. I'm so sorry. If I could take it all back . . . I– Well I probably wouldn't, because then I wouldn't have Emmy. But if I *could* go back and change everything, I would. I would have told you about Emmy the moment I knew Rylie was pregnant. Hell, I would've put my pride aside and followed you to New York in the first place, and I would've begged you to realize that you belong with me. I wish you believed in me enough to know that if you stayed, I never would've let you wind up like your momma. I would have done everything different, and maybe . . . maybe you'd still be here." He pauses momentarily a derisive chuckle sounding through the message. "But that's the thing about hindsight. It's full of the could'ves, should'ves and would'ves, and it only makes you feel a million times worse."

I smile through my tears.

"Look, I'm not gonna call you again. I know I messed everything up, and I'm so sorry. But I just wanted you to know that I meant every word I said to you that night at the cabin. Just know that I'll never stop loving you. I tried, but it only ended badly. I can't stop loving you. I couldn't even if I wanted to."

The message ends with a shrill bleep, but I'm frozen, and I just sit here with my phone at my ear, staring straight ahead at nothing in the air before me, as a million thoughts swirl around my head, none of which are doing me any favors.

I needed to hear his voice. More than anything. But now that I have, I'm at a complete and utter loss with my feelings.

I'd hoped it might hurt a little less by now. Five weeks is a long time. Enough time to move on and at least pretend to get over it. But it still hurts like hell, and every time I'm alone, it's all I can think about.

"Hey! You okay?"

I realize I'm on the verge of some kind of panic attack when I feel Oliver's hand on my shoulder.

"Hey, breathe!" He crouches down beside me, his eyes full of concern as he studies me closely, his brow pinched with worry. "Quinn, what's wrong?"

Tears sting my eyes, and I look around to see that, thankfully, I haven't drawn any unwanted attention to myself other than Oliver. I clutch at my chest, breathing in deep through my nose, trying so hard to placate myself, watching as he coaches me with a gentle wave of his hand. In and out. In and out. In and out.

"Come on," he says, reaching over and grabbing my purse from the top of my cabinet. "Lunchtime."

I choose not to argue. He's right. I need to get the hell out of the office before I completely break down and cause a scene I can't explain. I'm already the woman who lost a one-hundred-million-dollar deal. The woman who got fired. The woman who collapsed on a sidewalk in SoHo in front of her archnemesis. The woman who came crawling back. I can't also be the office nutcase. That's far too many unsavory titles for one person.

Standing, I keep a hand on my chest, feeling my heart race beneath my skin. I grab my coat, and follow Oliver with my head cast down, as he leads the way through the bustling sales floor. I'm desperate for some semblance of reprieve from the suddenly stifling air.

228

# Chapter 26

Oliver and I don't end up going back to the office for the rest of the afternoon. Suddenly, it's dark out, and we're perched at the bar in a dive on the Bowery, drinking the night away while a grunge-revival band plays a Nirvana song to a college-aged group of die-hard fans.

We went for lunch at a bistro off Fifth Avenue. Well, it was lunchtime, at least. And we ordered food with our wine, but we didn't eat too much and ended up consuming two whole bottles of Sauvignon Blanc between us.

Then, with a buzz on, we proceeded a few blocks up, stopping in at Bergdorf's, where I ended up spending an obscene amount of money on a pair of completely gaudy heels I doubt I'll ever wear but were far too pretty to pass up, and the latest handbag for my collection that I've been waiting months to hit the shelves. I bought Oliver the leopard-print Louboutin loafers he'd been eyeing the entire time we were there. He didn't know I bought them. He would have stopped me. So I added them to my purchase when he went to take a phone call, and I waited to give them to him until our Uber dropped us off in the Lower East Side. We'd come too far to take them back, and I tore up the tax receipt right in front of his face and threw it in the trash, so he couldn't return them later. He was angry with me, but totally in love with his new shoes. He refused to even set them down on the floor next to my shopping bags, fearing someone might take them. And that put a smile on my face for the first time in what felt like forever.

So, now, here we are. Two uptown real-estate agents in a dive bar on the Bowery. Completely out of place. Perched at the bar, drinking surprisingly decent French martinis while college kids cooler than I'll ever be, mosh to "Smells Like Teen Spirit". All the while, I'm spilling my guts to Oliver, trying not to be that drunk woman crying in a bar on a Tuesday night.

"So, wait a minute . . . Let me get this straight." Oliver interrupts my rambling, shaking his head to himself as if to process my slightly slurred words. "You . . . You were *engaged*?"

I blink at him.

After everything I've told him about Colt. Me leaving him jilted at the altar. Running away from home. The accident. Leaving again and never returning. My family. My brothers. My father. Everything. And *that's* what he chooses to focus on?

I offer a droll look, rolling my eyes. "Yes. I was engaged," I say with a sigh.

"And you left him . . . *Colt*?" He looks at me as if to check he has the name right.

I nod.

"And then he almost *killed* himself."

I nod again, feeling that same tug in my belly that I always feel when I think back to what Colt almost did. To the state he must have been in to have done what he did. To what Rylie said in her voicemail; I truly hope he doesn't go back to that dark place again. I swear, I'll never forgive myself.

"And now he has a daughter . . . with Rylie?"

I've never seen Oliver look so overwhelmed. He's utterly bewildered. This is far too much drama, even for him, and he watches all the reality shows on E! religiously.

"Yes!" I throw my head back, huffing in exasperation.

"And it's been ten years since you and Colt were together?"

"Yeah . . ." I answer a little sheepishly.

"So, I hope I don't sound insensitive," he begins, before continuing quite abruptly, "but what's the big goddamn deal?"

I gawp at him, his hands thrown in the air in confusion, and I must admit his reaction is completely justified. He's right. I glance down at my drink, watching the bubbles rise to the top. And, for the first time, I actually consider his question as it hangs in the air, lingering like a bad taste in my mouth. What is the big goddamn deal?

Am I angry that Colt has a child? No. Does it hurt? Yes. Am I jealous? Insanely, and shamefully so. Growing up, being with Colt, I'd always imagined starting a family with him. I wanted babies. A whole heap of them. And I wanted them with him. Now he has a child with someone else. And she's beautiful, perfect, sweet, and everything in between. And I'm not her mother. It hurts like hell to think what could have been. It could have been me having Colt's baby girl, and we could have lived our happily ever after. But I was too damn focused on my dreams, on not turning out like my mother, and now the last ten years is one big regret I doubt I will ever move past.

I look up from my drink, staring straight ahead at the shelves of liquor bottles behind the bar, to the mirrored wall behind them. I find my reflection staring back at me, and at that moment, it's as if it suddenly dawns on me. Realization at its finest. But with that heartbreaking revelation comes the weight of the world crashing down upon me like a ton of bricks. Tears sting my eyes, and my heart physically hurts.

"Quinn?" Oliver places a hand on my shoulder, gently squeezing me.

Slowly, I force myself to look at him, sniffling once as a hot tear hits my cheek the moment I meet his eyes.

"What is it, honey?"

231

"It's all my fault." I shake my head. "I should've never left. I should've stayed. I should've gone back. But I didn't do any of that. And now, this is what I get . . . It's ten years later, and the dreams I selfishly spent the last decade chasing have all come true. But what are realized dreams when you have no one to share them with?"

A small, sad smile pulls at Oliver's lips and he moves in, wrapping his arms around me and holding me a moment. And I don't care that we're in a dive on the Bowery. I don't care that we're surrounded by college kids dancing to not-Nirvana. I don't care that I have mascara tracks streaming down my cheeks. None of that matters right now.

"Perspective, huh?" Oliver says in my ear, kissing my cheek before pulling away.

I nod again, resting my chin on my hand with a heavy sigh as I swipe my tears away.

"That's the great thing about home, Quinn; you can always go back." Oliver nudges me with his elbow. But I don't look at him. I can't. I can't risk seeing the trite look of a twenty-four-year-old who knows better than me right now.

"But everything's changed. Nothing is the same. I was stupid to think that I could go back, and things would be just like they were."

"But home is where the heart is, girl. And your heart sure as hell isn't in New York City no more. That's for sure."

He's right. Annoyingly, he's always right. That's one of the traits I both love and hate about dear Oliver. He's younger in years, but wise beyond those years.

"I'm going to go to the bathroom." I slide off my barstool, handing him my cell as I adjust my dress. "Can you order me an Uber. And a water from that bartender when he stops flirting with the woman with the awesome cleavage."

Oliver laughs at me, and he goes about ordering my Uber, and I continue to the bathroom to relieve myself, and wipe the streaky makeup from my face.

# Chapter 27

When I woke this morning, I was planning on calling in sick. I *was* sick. Hungover with a seriously bad case of broken heart. Surely that's a valid sickness, right?

But Oliver needed me. He'd accidentally double-booked himself, and was supposed to be in two places at once. Brooklyn Heights, and Gramercy Park. I had nothing on for today. No client meetings, nothing. I would have happily stayed in bed and slept the day away. But I just couldn't let Oliver down; I might no longer care about any of this—for me, it's just a job to pass the time it takes for me to decide what my next step is going to be—but he's young, and he's going to be a really great agent. So, I forced my sorry ass out of bed and, here I am. In an historic, cast-iron building on Gramercy Park West, overlooking the park, hungover, more disheveled than I care to admit, racking my brain with all the possible reasons Colt hasn't yet returned my drunken, cringeworthy phone call from one o'clock this morning.

I stand in the foyer of the eclectic and grand three-bedroom duplex, twirling the brass door key around my finger as I look up to the twelve-foot ceilings, studying the cobwebs hanging from the crown moldings, the dust particles as they float aimlessly through the air.

The place is empty. Silent and still. Not long vacated by the flamboyant ninety-two-year-old woman who lived here since the day she married her husband in the early 1950s. She made this place her home. Her children were born here, raised here, grew up here. Then her husband passed away. Her children moved out. But still, she stayed, making this place more of a home for herself and her three poodles, than for anyone else. And as I stand here in the dusty, empty expanse of the apartment, I can almost feel the energy that once lived here. This was a place of love. A real home. And I can't help but smile to myself.

A knock on the door pulls me from my musings, and I jump to action, nervously tucking my hair behind my ear, smoothing my hands down the front of my dress. I clear my throat, crossing the foyer, and I plaster a big smile onto my face, one I'm sure doesn't even come close to meeting my eyes as I pull open the door.

"Good afternoon." I beam, looking from the man to the woman who both appear to be around my age. "You must be Mr. and Mrs. Sawyer."

"Please, Joey and Victoria is more than fine." The man dismisses my formalities, pointing to himself before indicating his wife. And I like him already. Not the Gramercy Park type, that's for sure. A young Fintech éntrepreneur looking for a place in the city to begin a family.

"I'm Quinn Wagner. Oliver sends his apologies." I shake his hand, before moving to his wife, which is when I notice how heavily pregnant she is. "Oh, goodness! When are you due?"

She offers a comical deadpan expression, clutching a hand to her swollen belly. "Next Friday. But I'm getting out and walking around as often as I can in the hope she gets the hell out much sooner!" She smiles through obviously gritted teeth.

I laugh out loud. I like this woman. She reminds me of myself.

Joey chuckles, pulling his wife under his arm. He presses a sweet kiss to the top of her head, and I watch on with a fond smile as they share a loving glance with one another. But I'm also unable to mistake the painful lump balling in the back of my throat. I turn away quickly.

"Okay." I clap my hands together. "Let's have a look around, shall we?"

"Well, we like what we see so far," Joey says from behind me.

"Do we *really* get a key to the park if we buy this place?" Victoria asks, a smile in her voice.

"Yep. Sure do," I say over my shoulder. "There's an annual fee, of course. But it's a beautiful park. Nice to sit and relax. It will be perfect for your little one."

"Oh, this is actually our third." She giggles.

"Third?" I turn, gawping at her. "You look so . . . so *young*."

Victoria looks up at Joey with an endearing smile. "We met in high school. I got pregnant in my first year of college. So, we decided, why wait? Let's get married, have our family young, and we can all grow up together."

"I finished college. Went on to grad school. Vic went back and finished after Sadie, our first, was born," Joey explains further, looking down at his wife as if she's the only woman in his whole world.

"I got pregnant with Henry in my final year. But I was able to at least graduate before he came. I'm an interior designer. It's a good job to have as a stay-at-home mom."

I look between the two of them, their hands clasped together, fingers intertwined, and I feel a painful pinch of jealousy at the base of my spine. This could have been me and Colt. I could be as happy and satisfied as Victoria appears to be. She's glowing, and I know it's not just the pregnancy. This is a woman with everything she could ever want. And it could have been me, but I was too damn stupid.

"The duplex is thirty-seven hundred square feet." I turn around, getting back to business as I lead the sickeningly happy couple through to the large formal sitting room. I don't mean to be abrupt in my change of topic, but it hurts, more than I could have ever imagined a random couple's happiness could hurt.

"Twelve-foot ceilings. Original floorboards throughout, but you could always pull them up and lay tile, or restored flooring if you wanted to brighten it up a little. As you can see, there's a lot of natural light, which is a must-have on the East Side. We're south-east facing here, so you get the beautiful morning sun, but this helps to provide light through the afternoons, especially in the winter." I point out the chef's kitchen and the family dining area with a solarium roof, through the French doors to the patio. "There's a small, private courtyard, perfect for entertaining during the warmer months, and a great place for the kids to get some fresh air if you can't get out to the park."

"Wow, this kitchen is almost brand new." Joey gasps, looking closely at the sleek, top-of-the-line appliances. He offers a wry smile over his shoulder at me. "I fancy myself a bit of a novice *chef*."

Victoria casts me a wide-eyed look, stealthily shaking her head.

I stifle a laugh. "Yes. The seller had the kitchen redone a few years back. And all three bathrooms have been renovated, too."

"It's so beautiful." Victoria holds a hand to her chest. "How much is she asking?"

I nod. "It is beautiful. And for under seven million, with a private courtyard *and* overlooking the park, it's an absolute steal at just under nineteen hundred a square foot."

"Well, I love it!" she exclaims, positively beaming at her husband.

"It's a lot of money, V," Joey says under his breath with a nervous smile, but I'm not worried. I can already tell *she* wears the proverbial pants in the marriage when it comes to these kinds of decisions, and her mind was made up the moment she stepped foot over the threshold.

"Yes, but for our forever home, *this* is perfect."

I smile. "Shall we head upstairs to see the bedrooms?"

We proceed up the stairs, and I take Joey and Victoria through the master suite, which earns a chorus of praise from both of them. But it's when we come to a smaller room, next door to the master, with a beautiful view of the park across the street, Victoria begins discussing her design plans, imagining the bedroom as a nursery, showing where she'll put the cot, and the dresser, explaining what color she'll paint the walls, and what curtains she'll hang up. And that's when I find myself violently blindsided.

"Do you have any children, Quinn?"

I snap myself from my daze, looking to see both Victoria and Joey watching me.

"Oh." I offer a small laugh. "No. No children."

In the flash of an instant, so quick I almost miss it, she frowns, a pitiful look in her eyes before recovering almost immediately. "A husband? Partner?"

I press my lips together in a tight-lipped smile. "Nope. I'm single." *And almost thirty.*

She looks me up and down before casting a glance at Joey, a devious smile curling her lips. "Joey, babe? Don't you think she'd be *perfect* for Miles?"

My eyes widen. *Oh my God. Please tell me this is not actually happening right now in the middle of a goddamn showing.* I bite my tongue so hard, I'm almost certain I can taste blood in my mouth.

Victoria glances at me, offering an apologetic laugh. "I'm sorry. Miles is Joey's business partner. He's *perpetually* single. But I think he just needs to meet the right lady. And you're perfect!"

"V! Stop!" Joey chastises with a light chuckle. "I'm sorry, Quinn. You'll have to forgive my wife. I think she's going baby-crazy. Is it weird if I tell you you're not the *first* woman she's accosted this with?"

I feel heat prick at the back of my neck, my stomach pulling tight. And I'm worried I might bring up one of last night's drinks.

"It's f-fine . . ." I manage, smiling curtly. "Why don't I leave you both to look around some more, and I'll wait for you downstairs?"

I don't wait for them to agree or decline. I turn on my heel so fast, taking the stairs quickly before I do or say something to jeopardize Oliver's commission and my reputation. As I burst through the French doors, the bitter cold air slaps me in the face the moment I step out onto the patio. But I need it. It helps to calm my burning skin, my racing heart. Helps to stifle the sick feeling bubbling deep in my belly.

I wrap my arms around myself, my coat inside by the front door, and I walk over to the furthermost side of the courtyard, staring up at the leafless trees, their jagged branches entwining overhead, high up into the miserably gray sky. And as I stand there, reeling with every overwhelming emotion wreaking havoc on my mind, I've actually never felt so alone.

And suddenly, I'm crying, and the tears won't stop.

Somehow, by way of a miracle, Victoria and Joey put an offer in on the duplex.

I'm assuming they felt sorry for me when they found me—a grown-ass woman, a real-estate broker—crying at their private showing.

"I told you, you can't go around asking random women if they'll date my best friend, Victoria!" Joey had hissed angrily at his wife.

"I'm *so* sorry!" Victoria cried, pulling me into an awkward embrace.

Thankfully, they made an offer. I texted it to Oliver straight away who called his client, and by the time I arrived back at the office, the all-cash, zero-contingency deal was already signed.

Oliver didn't come back to the office from Brooklyn Heights. So, I stayed late and finished all the paperwork for him so all he'd have to do when he came in in the morning is sign on the dotted line and have them couriered to the lawyers. I asked if he wanted to meet up for a celebratory dinner, but he apologized, telling me he had something else on. And I can't help but feel a little deflated, and even more alone, if that's possible.

So, as I sit in the dimly lit back seat of a cab driving at a snail's pace down Broadway, dreading going home to my empty apartment, I scroll through my cell, trying to decide between Indian and Chinese. Or maybe pizza. Hell, maybe all three. My mouth is actually salivating at the thought of food, so I shoot off a text to Oliver, asking if we're going to go back to spin class in the morning.

**Oliver**: *Maybe . . .*

*What do you mean, maybe?* I reply. And then it dawns on me, and my fingers can't tap out a follow-up text fast enough. *Is this why you ditched me for dinner? Are you on a date?*

I smirk to myself as the dots appear in our text window, indicating his reply. But then, no reply comes. Nothing. The dots disappear. Radio silence. And for some reason, I can't help but wonder if he's mad at me. He found out about my crying at the showing. Maybe he's pissed at me for allowing my emotion to get the better of my professionalism. But I got the deal, didn't I?

With a huff, I sag back against the uncomfortable vinyl seat, folding my arms over my chest. I watch as the city lights fly by in a blur through the window, and I sigh heavily in resignation. I can't be angry with Oliver. He has a life of his own. I refuse to resent him for living it, and it sure as hell isn't his fault I'm sad and single and desperate for reassurance. I can't keep expecting him to be here for me. He's been by my side for five whole weeks. He's twenty-four. He has to live his life or else he'll end up like me.

It isn't long until the taxi is rolling to a stop, and I glance up to see the familiar exterior of my cast-iron building come into view. With a small smile, I pay the cab driver and grab my things from the seat next to me, unfolding myself from the cramped back seat.

A cold wind barrels down the empty street, and I fight with my purse, clasping my coat lapels together to shield from the iciness. I hurry across the sidewalk toward the secure external door, but when I look up from the pavement, I come to a sudden and crashing stop, my handbag and satchel falling to the ground with a clutter at my feet.

My eyes bulge and I gape at the shadowy figure waiting at

the entrance to the lobby, a big duffel bag on the ground beside his scuffed boots, a sad-looking bunch of gas station flowers in his hand.

It can't be.

My eyes have to be playing tricks on me.

Surely I'm seeing things.

It has to be my imagination, or my questionable sanity.

"C-Colt?"

He lifts his chin, his face illuminated by the soft glow of the lights shining out from the lobby. He reaches a hand up, tentatively removing his Stetson, raking his fingers through his hair, his eyes dark yet blazing through the muted light as he stares down at me with an unreadable expression on his face.

"W-what . . . are you d-doing here?" I stammer, my voice breathless and broken.

He takes a step closer, effectively closing the distance between us.

Hesitating, I reach a trembling hand out, my fingers grazing his coat as if at any moment he's about to disappear into a cloud of smoke. But when I touch him, he doesn't disappear. He's real. And I find myself grasping at him, holding him so tight, releasing the breath I've been holding as my shoulders sag in relief.

"Hey, Quinny." A small, nervous smile tugs at his lips.

"W-what . . .?" I shake my head, looking him up and down. "H-how?"

"I got a call from your friend Oliver, last night," he begins, pausing to study my reaction.

My brows knit together as I gape up at him.

"You were in the bathroom . . ." He shrugs. "I told him you'd be pissed at him if you knew he was calling me, but he said he didn't care because your happiness is worth a day or two of moodiness." He chuckles softly.

I think back to last night, when I naively handed Oliver my cell to order me an Uber. Of course I knew he would do

240

something stupid. But I thought maybe he'd post a fake status on my Facebook page, or tweet something inappropriate like a fake dick pic. I didn't imagine he'd actually call Colt.

"Oh my God . . ." I sigh, bowing my head a moment, making a mental note to kill Oliver, or buy him another pair of Louboutins; I can't decide.

"Quinn, I wanted to come here so bad. I just . . . I didn't think you'd want to see me."

I meet Colt's eyes again, searching them, and I see a frail hopelessness within his gaze that hurts my heart.

"What I did, I . . . I should have told you about Emmy, I just couldn't . . ." He shakes his head, unable to finish. "I'm sorry . . . I don't even know where to start."

"Just say whatever you need to say." I encourage him with a nod.

"I should have told you about Emmy. About Rylie. About everything. I was just so thankful that I finally had you back in my life, and I was terrified of losing you again, for good."

I watch him a moment longer as he struggles so openly to find his words.

"Quinn, when you left me all those years ago, I lost everything. You were my all, my reason for waking up every goddamn day. Without you, I had no reason for living. After the accident I had no idea what I was going to do with my life, whether or not I was even gonna keep going on. But I did go on. Because I knew one day, maybe, just maybe you would come back to me. It was that hope that kept me going." He implores me with his eyes, his hands reaching for mine, gripping them so tight. "I never loved Rylie. I tried. But I couldn't. She wasn't you. I didn't love her, I just missed you. And, now that I've got you again, I can't let you go, Quinn. I won't. I don't want anything else in my life. You're it."

I blink at him. Taken aback by those words.

He shakes his head, steadying me with a look that touches my heart. "Despite what's happened, whether it's right or wrong, you're my one, Quinn Wagner. All I want in my life is you, and our happy ever after."

I'm breathless. The world around me dissipates, fading into the blackness of night.

"I . . . I love you, Colt." I blink back the tears threatening me. "I don't care about what's happened. Well, I do . . . but I care about us more. And I'm just sorry it took me so long to realize that you're all I want, and that you're enough for me, and so much more than I could have ever hoped for."

He closes his eyes, releasing what appears to be a breath of relief. "You don't know how badly I needed to hear that." He opens his eyes again, finding mine. "I missed you these last few weeks. Hell, I've been missing you for ten long years."

"You're actually *here*," I say more to myself than to him, thinking back to the last time he was here, when he proposed to me all those years ago. "Here, in New York."

He makes a face, scrunching up his nose in mock disgust, and I can't help but laugh.

Colt hates the city life. He's always been a country boy. And as I glance up at him, dressed in his riding boots, his worn jeans, a pearl-snap shirt beneath a suede jacket with a fluffy wool collar, he sure does look out of place on the cobblestone streets of Tribeca. But I really wouldn't have him any other way. He's not *just* a cowboy, he's *my* cowboy. New York City be damned.

"I love you, Quinny. And I don't want to be apart from you." He grabs my hips, holding me close. "If I have to move out here . . . I will. I'll do anything if it means being with you."

I shake my head. "I don't want you coming out here."

His face falls momentarily as he tries to process my unexpected words.

"You don't have to come to New York City, Colt." I smile. "Because I'm coming home."

"To the Canyon?"

I nod.

A smile claims his entire face, his eyes lighting up, dimples pulling into his cheeks. "You're serious?" he asks. "Like, for real?"

I nod, laughing at his reaction. I swear, I've never seen him so happy.

"You're coming back for me?"

I nod. "It's always been you, Colt. It always will be."

He takes a moment, allowing my words and the sentiment behind them to fully sink in, but then his strong arms come around me, enveloping me so tight, I almost can't breathe. When his lips crash against mine it feels like with just one kiss I'm suddenly brought back to life. I instinctively wrap my arms around his neck, sighing into our exchange before giggling against his mouth like a damn schoolgirl, when he actually sweeps me up off my feet and twirls me around and around, mid-kiss.

When I find my feet again, I pull back, gaping up at him, taking him in from his glassy eyes full of wonderment and happiness, to his swollen lips glistening from our kiss. He's the most beautiful man in the whole word. He takes my breath away. And he's all mine.

"You know, I'm still pissed you left me in the middle of a field with a pack of wolves lurking in the bushes . . ." I quirk a brow at him.

His jaw drops, and he gauges me a moment. "Yeah? Well, I'm still pissed you left me at the altar on our wedding day."

I open my mouth to speak, but then I realize he has a point. I press my lips together, staring into his eyes as a moment passes between us, one where each of us is obviously trying so hard not to laugh.

"Call it even?" I ask with a nervous, hopeful smile.

With an indulgent roll of his eyes, Colt shakes his head, smirking at me as he ducks to rest his forehead against mine, staring deep into my eyes. "Just shut up and kiss me, Quinny."

And I do. I kiss him again, and again, and again, right there on a darkened sidewalk, in the middle of New York City, my one dream finally coming true.

# Epilogue

The sun beams down from high in the summer sky, shining down over the entire valley, casting an effervescent glow upon everything in its path. A gentle breeze sweeps through the long grass, causing the leaves to rustle in the trees, birds singing, butterflies floating aimlessly through the air.

I breathe a contented sigh, looking out over the endless view of Wagner Ranch winding through the hills and the mountains, as if it goes on forever. Smiling to myself, I place a hand over the small, growing bump beneath my dress, and for a moment I just exist in this one place, feeling so overwhelmed with love and happiness, and joy, I could cry. *Damn hormones.*

"Hey, Dad," I say, glancing at my father's tombstone beside me, to my mother's right next to his. "Hi, Momma," I say a little more softly. "I'm sorry I haven't been up to see you guys in a while. But I'm here now."

I stretch my legs out, getting comfortable. "Dr. Munro says I have preeclampsia, which is why I haven't been feeling well. He said I need to take it easy for the remainder of the pregnancy. So now Colt won't even let me lift a damn finger. I swear, he actually stands outside the bathroom door while I'm peeing, just to check I'm okay. I'm going to lose it if he keeps this up for the next sixteen weeks. I can't even work on the books without him watching me like some kind of weird, creeping stalker. As if I'm going to spontaneously combust while carrying a remainder . . ." I roll my eyes. "He's doing *everything*. Working here at Wagner. Building our house at the Henry Ranch. He wants it done in time for the baby, but that's probably not going to happen." I shake my head. "I'm worried he's going to burn out, but you know him. He won't stop until *everything* is done."

I pick at a long piece of grass, twirling it between my fingers, listening to the sound of the afternoon as it goes on around me. I glance up at the tall pine trees, glimpses of the sky flashing through the leaves. I look out at the mountains in the distance, and I sigh a slightly defeated sigh, reaching out and stroking my fingers over Dad's face in the marble of his headstone.

A sad smile curls at my lips. "I guess I really just needed to be with you today. Of all the days, this is the one I knew I would spend missing you the most. I wish you could be here. I really need my dad today." A solitary tear wins the battle of emotion deep within me, slowly trailing down over my cheek, and I wipe it away, sniffling once. "I'm in such an emotional state at the moment. It's so unlike me. It's embarrassing!" I scoff at myself.

"Hey, Quinny?"

I startle, turning to see Tripp walking in through the small gates.

"You ready?" he asks, tapping his watch.

"Oh, yeah." I quickly wipe my cheeks once again, not wanting to give myself away. "Sorry. I didn't realize that was the time."

I begin to push up from the grass, but Tripp quickly swoops in, his big hands on my shoulders.

"Stop!" he mutters. "I'll help you."

"I can get up, you know!" I roll my eyes when he grabs both of my hands, carefully craning me up onto my feet.

"You don't understand." He steadies me with a serious look. "Colt said he will kick my ass if I don't get you there in one piece."

246

I laugh under my breath, shaking my head at my brother as I wipe the dry grass from the back of my dress.

"You okay?" Tripp asks, looking closely.

I nod.

"You've been crying?"

"Yes. I'm pregnant, remember," I deadpan, quirking a brow. "I've been crying for four months."

This time it's Tripp who rolls his eyes, but instead of saying anything, he just pulls me in for a hug I wasn't expecting, pressing a kiss to the top of my head.

I stand there for a long moment, just basking in my brother's embrace, smiling to myself.

"You ready to do this?"

I look up at him, meeting his eyes, and I nod with a small smile.

"It's about damn time." He smirks down at me.

Grabbing my hand, Tripp leads the way back to his truck parked down the hill, and we say nothing more as I take a few extra-deep breaths, my heart suddenly racing in a way I've never felt it race before.

"You *sure* you wanna do this?" Tripp asks from the driver's seat after we pull up at the main house.

I look across at him, obliging him with a droll smile. "For the last time, *yes*, Tripp."

He flashes me an impish grin, moving to get out of the truck. Before I can even get my seatbelt unfastened, he's opening my door and holding his hand out for me. I stifle my own eye-roll, taking his proffered hand and hopping down from the truck.

My brother holds my hand as we walk through the front yard of the main house. And I'm glad he's here. If I can't have my dad, Tripp is the next best thing. He's probably the only other person in the world who can stop me from freaking out at a time like this. He's always been that person for me. Even now, as if he can hear my thoughts, he offers me a knowing, reassuring smile, squeezing my hand gently in his as we continue around the house, toward the tiny gathering congregated by the edge of the hill that overlooks the rolling fields and paddocks.

And that's when I spot him.

And my breath is momentarily stolen from me.

He stands with Reverend Jackson, the two of them sharing a hushed conversation. And even from here, with his back to me, I can tell he's as devastatingly handsome as always. Dressed in a pair of dark-wash jeans, with a crisp white button-down, his hair swept wild, in its usual and adorable disarray. His hands are clasped behind his back, and I can tell he's nervous just from the way his thumb is tapping an imaginary and relentless beat against his wrist. Beside him, right there by her father's side, is Emmy wearing a pretty navy dress, holding a posy of wild flowers, her blonde curls wild, just like her daddy's. And I smile, my heart clenching in my chest the closer we get.

All heads turn in my direction, and all attention is focused solely on me as Tripp walks me down the path lined with flowers, his hand never once faltering from mine.

Rylie greets me with a beaming smile, dabbing at the corners of her eyes with a Kleenex. I return my best friend's smile with one of my own. I don't know where I would be without her. Since I've been back, she's been my biggest support. I know she'll always love Colt. She's the mother of his daughter, and they shared something during one of Colt's darkest times that no one else, not even me, will ever be able to take away from her. But their love is different. And I am so happy that she's still here. Because without Rylie, I might not have my Colt.

Shelby pulls me into a big hug. Cash wraps his strong arms around the both of us. CJ stands on a chair so he can see, grinning mischievously. God, I love my family.

Lastly, I come to a stop at Oliver. And I can't help but laugh. In a sea of neutral, country folk, he's dressed in a loud silk shirt

248

and a pair of bright fuchsia skinny trousers. He's so flamboyant, so extra, so out of place, but so, so him. I love it.

"You look beautiful, girl," he says, pulling me in for a hug.

"Don't you know it's in bad taste to upstage the bride at her wedding?" I pull back, offering him a dubious once-over.

Oliver smirks, winking at me, playfully popping his collar. "You know it."

"Thank you for coming all this way, Ols," I whisper. "I have a feeling if it weren't for you and what you did, I—"

He stops me with a wave of his hand. "This is all you, Quinn."

I smile at him, fighting what I can of my tears, hugging him once again and taking that moment to just breathe him in, his slightly overpowering Tom Ford cologne causing my head to spin.

"Come on, Quinny." Tripp tugs on my hand.

I go with him, continuing until we reach Reverend Jackson. And it is then that Colt finally turns to look at me. And what a look it is. One of incredulity. One of pure adoration. One of awe. One of almost every emotion that makes me weak at my knees. I smile, and his eyes turn glassy, reflecting the afternoon sun as he looks at me, down to our bump with such a loving tenderness I can feel it with every beat of my heart. He reaches out, placing both hands on my waist, cradling our baby boy.

"You finally made it," he whispers with a smile, a lone tear trailing down over his cheek, one he doesn't even attempt to wipe away.

Barely holding back my own tears, I nod, swallowing that pesky lump at the back of my throat. "I'm sorry it took me so long."

# Acknowledgments

This book was written during the time when my entire country was burning down, at the very beginning of a pandemic when I often found myself wondering, "What's the point? We're doomed. Who's going to even bother reading a book, right now?" But I moved past those thoughts, and I continued writing. Because what I've learned over my thirty-something years is that books have the power to help people through some of the darkest days, pulling them from the horrible state of reality and taking them away to another life, where, even if only for a few hours, they can forget. My dream was to write something that might one day help someone through a tough moment in their life, a horrible day, a bad week, something to help put a smile on someone's face. Books have helped me, and now I am so grateful that I have that ability to help others, particularly during these times.

If someone had told me two years ago that I would be writing my acknowledgment for my second book right now, I probably would have laughed. But, here I am. It's been a dream come true for me, to be able to do what I love, to put words on a page and share them with people all over the world.

My dream would never have become a reality without the one person who has stuck with me through everything. My love. My

Michael. Thank you for doing the mopping and the vacuuming, for taking Niall to the park, for cleaning up after Louis, for doing everything you have done to allow me the time to sit down and write all the words. You're my rock, and I'm so thankful to have you on my team.

Thank you to HarperCollins, but especially to my editor, Abi, for helping me through these dark days, when I felt lost and confused through this process, while it felt as if the world around us was quickly beginning to fall apart. I'm really happy with this book, and I'm so thankful that you believed in it, too. I hope to work with you again in the future.

I have a whole heap of people to acknowledge. Jacki and Karryn, my two writing buddies. Zoe, for all her advice and encouragement along the way. Kristi M for setting me straight and finally being the one person to be able to explain "show vs tell". Ruby Charlot, for being my go-to. All the friends I've made along the way, and those who've stuck by me. Margie and LJ for being my two biggest fans (LOL). My family for their support. So many thanks, unfortunately not enough word count.

Lastly, to you, the person reading this, thank you. As I mentioned above, I hope what I do makes a difference in your life. I'm not solving world hunger, I'm not curing disease, I'm definitely not changing the world. But I hope my words have helped in one way or another. Let's face it, this world is bad enough right now. All you need to do is read a newspaper or watch the news to see heartbreaking reality after heartbreaking reality. But it's stories that allow us to escape, that remind us that not everything in this world we live in is bad and horrible.

For now, I'm going to sign off with the words of Brad Pitt, because well, hello . . . who doesn't love a bit of Brad Pitt? But, also, because right now these words couldn't be more fitting: "If you see a chance to be kind to someone tomorrow, take it."

Keep reading for an excerpt from

*Where We Belong* . . .

# Chapter 1

I push my glasses up my nose for the millionth time, and while holding my breath and with one eye narrowed, ssI wipe a tiny smudge of frosting from the silver turntable holding Mr. and Mrs. Robertson's fiftieth wedding anniversary cake. It may have taken me two full days and most of last night, but I've finally finished. Exhaling the breath I've been holding for a beat too long, I take a step back to really appreciate my craftsmanship. Four layers of lemon and blueberry perfection, covered in a fluffy whipped buttercream frosting, decorated with beautiful red roses, delicate peonies, and a smattering of baby's breath, all of which have been hand-piped by yours truly.

I place a hand on my hip, smiling proudly. "Alice Murphy, once again you've outdone yourself," I whisper under my breath, mentally high-fiving myself.

The bell above the door to the shop jingles, pulling me from my musings, and I walk through from the kitchen to the front of the store, still smiling at the thought of my latest masterpiece.

"Welcome to Piece O' Cake," I sing in a cheerful customer service voice. "How can I help yo—" Stopping dead in my tracks, my eyes go wide as I gawp at the unexpected figure standing in the middle of the shop. He's shadowed by the afternoon sun shining in through the windows, backlighting him to nothing more than a darkened silhouette, and I blink hard, unsure whether or not I'm imagining things. But then he speaks. And I would know that voice anywhere. This is definitely not my imagination playing tricks on me.

"Hey, Murph." The shadow takes a step forward, coming in to the glow of the overhead lights, and I'm immediately enamored by that all-too-familiar grin.

"N-Nash?" I gasp.

His smile is bright and those eyes. I'd remember those eyes anywhere after spending such a big part of my life dreaming about them.

"Oh my God!" I scream, covering my mouth with trembling hands until I finally come to, ripping off my apron before practically throwing myself over the counter. Jumping up, I wrap my arms around his neck, and emotion gets the better of me as I stand there in the familiarity of his warm embrace with tears of happiness streaming down my cheeks.

He's here.

The love of my life.

He's home.

The May sun simmers gently upon my shoulders. Birds chirp in sync, their chorus singing through the air. Butterflies flutter aimlessly, whisked away by the gentle breeze. And, in the distance, a child is giggling full of an infectious happiness that I can feel through to my soul. I can't possibly wipe the smile from my face. I couldn't, even if I wanted to. Nash Harris is actually here, by my side, as we walk beneath the canopy of the lush magnolia trees. The moment couldn't be any more perfect.

"What are you doing here?" I ask incredulously, my cheeks stinging from smiling so hard.

"I wanted to see you." Nash stops, turning to me and pulling my hands into his. "Actually, Murph, I *needed* to see you."

I look up at him, our eyes meeting as his thumbs gently stroke the backs of my fingers. But when I catch sight of something unfamiliar in his gaze, something unsettling, my heart sinks a little in my chest. I know Nash. Something is wrong. He continues smiling that same beautiful smile, but I can see it in his eyes.

"Nash, what's wrong?" I ask, suddenly worried. Is he in trouble? Oh, God. Is he sick? I wouldn't be able to handle it if something happened to him. Not to my Nash.

"I'm fine, Murph." He shakes his head once with a light chuckle, dismissing my concerns, and then, letting go of one of my hands, he reaches into the back pocket of his jeans, causing my eyes to widen of their own accord. For a moment my mind begins to get carried away with itself. Between the chirping birds and the fluttering butterflies, the beautiful warm sun, and the backdrop of the inky river reflecting the fluffy white clouds in the sky, it's all too perfect. And, as he reaches into his pocket, I begin to wonder if Nash Harris is about to drop to one knee and make all my dreams come true.

The realization that Nash doesn't have a ring box in his hand snaps me from my reverie. Instead, he presents me with an envelope. And not just any old plain white Staples envelope, but a sparkly gold one, made of real fancy paper. My brows pull together in confusion as I look back up at him, meeting his eyes once again.

"What is this?" I ask, tentatively taking it from him. But he doesn't answer. He just takes a step back, letting go of my other hand and scratching at his lightly stubbled jaw as he watches me, waiting. He's nervous. So am I. And, right now, I almost wish something *was* wrong with him, because I have a terrible sinking feeling in my belly that whatever this is, I am not going to like it one bit.

I lift the tab with my index finger and pull out a single piece of card. Looking closer, I push my glasses up my nose, and it takes my eyes a while to adjust to the dim light of the shadows cast by the overhead trees. But then I manage to read the words embossed into the card in my hand, and in that moment, it feels as if my whole world comes crashing down around me.

*Mr. and Mrs. Howard E. Hutchins request the pleasure of your company . . .*

I stare at it—the invitation—reading the words over and over again as a painful ball of emotion wedges itself into the back of my throat. Suddenly I find it difficult to breathe. "W-what is this?" I finally ask, trying so hard to keep my voice from quavering. I glance up with a tight smile I know doesn't even come close to reaching my eyes. "You . . . You're getting m-married?"

Nash nods slowly, the ghost of an uncertain smile playing on his lips.

A flush heats my cheeks, and I know tears are imminent, but I try to keep what little composure I have, looking down at the invitation in my trembling hands in an attempt to avoid his eyes.

"I wanted to tell you in person," Nash says. His words are soft and gentle, as if he knows what they're capable of doing to me.

"Wow." I try so hard to sound excited and happy, but I know I'm not even close to pulling it off. My heart is breaking. Actually, no. It's already broken. And then I do a double take, looking closer at the invitation, and I actually can't even believe my own eyes. "Next *week*?" I shriek, finally forced to meet his gaze.

"Yeah." Nash tucks his hands into the front pockets of his jeans, shrugging a little sheepishly. "I know it's sudden. But with my final year of med school coming up, and Anna studying for the bar, if we don't do it now, we'll probably be waiting another whole year, and we really don't want to wait any longer."

"Anna?" I ask, looking down at her name embossed in shiny black lettering on the invitation. *Annabelle Victoria Hutchins.* I can only imagine what she looks like. Her name is elegant enough. I bet she's tall and beautiful. Thin and probably blonde. Nothing like me, Alice Murphy. I once thought Alice was a beautiful name. Beautiful like Alice in Wonderland. But Murphy?

Bleh. When all the guys started calling me Murph, I just went with it. Because, let's face it, I'm certainly no Annabelle Victoria Hutchins.

"Yeah." Nash's wistful smile is enviable as he ruffles a hand through his sandy blond hair. "Murph, you're gonna love her. She's great. She's a lawyer. Well, she will be once she passes the bar. She's so smart. And funny, and kind, and . . . Well, she's just perfect." His blue eyes actually glaze over for a moment while he gets carried away with himself, and I wince as the bitter taste of bile begins to rise up the back of my throat.

Thankfully, before he can gauge my reaction, Nash turns, continuing to tread the stone path that trails down to the board-walk at the river's edge, and I follow, still speechless as he proceeds to talk. "I was coming out of my favorite juice shop. You know, the one on the same block as my dorm? And Anna was walking with her head down, looking at her phone." He chuckles, scrubbing a hand over his smiling lips. "She collided headfirst with me, and my smoothie spilled all over the both of us."

I smile, but really, all I want to do is cry. But I swallow the emotion, clearing my throat. "B-but, isn't it a little soon?" I ask, adding a casual shrug to try to lighten my question. "I mean, when I came up to visit you for New Year's you were . . . *happily* single." I meet his eyes with a knowing look. He and I slept together after a drunken night of celebrations on New Year's Eve. It had been a night of promises, the night I thought everything was going to change. I thought this was going to be our year. And now he's marrying some woman named Anna?

"What's it been? Like, a few months?" I guffaw, shaking my head in exasperation.

Nash looks at me, and I can see he wants to say something, but he's hesitating, considering my question. "I guess . . . when you know, you just know." He shrugs, looking down to the ground a moment before tentatively meeting my eyes.

Never before have I imagined someone's words could feel like such a brutal kick to the stomach, but he's just about crippled me with that.

"Yeah." I look down at my hands as they twist together. "I guess I wouldn't know."

We continue along the boardwalk and, despite the obvious shift in the air between us, Nash keeps talking about his wonderful, perfect Anna, and their impending nuptials. All the while I'm considering whether or not to just jump into the murky water of the Chelmer River and save myself any further torture. He's killing me, and he doesn't even know it. Or, worse. Maybe he knows exactly what he's doing, and he just doesn't care.

The thing about Nash and me is that we have a past. It's more than just the occasional New Year's hookup. He's not only my best friend, he was my first crush, my first kiss, my first love, my first everything. He and I were childhood sweethearts who actually thought our love would last forever. But life managed to get in the way and, after we left for college to live our happily ever after together in New York City, my mother's illness brought me back to Graceville, and our love suffered. I literally went from seeing him every single day, to every third weekend of the month, then every other month until we finally ended things and visited one another when we could.

Now, he's marrying someone who isn't me, and I'm still stuck in Nowhereville, Georgia, running my dead mother's bakery. Suddenly I begin to wonder how different things could have been if she'd never fallen sick. It's not like I haven't thought about it over the years, but now the what could've beens are as real as my broken heart.

"So? Will you do it?"

Realizing I haven't been listening, I glance up from the wooden planks at my feet, meeting his hopeful blue eyes, and he offers me a knowing smirk. "Our wedding cake! Will you *please* make it?" He nudges me playfully with his elbow. "I know it's late notice, but I always did love your cooking."

So, not only has he flitted into town on a whim to tell me he's marrying another woman, he also wants me to make his damn wedding cake? I . . . I . . . I can't even. I swear, it takes everything I have not to give him a piece of my mind. But the longer I gape at him, finding nothing but innocence and sincerity within his eyes, the more I know I have no way of saying anything but yes to this boy. I've never been able to say no to him, and I can't start now.

"Of course." I smile with a nod. And then, because I need to get the hell away from him, I glance down at my watch, not even really paying attention to the time. "Actually, I have to get back to the store," I say all flustered and pathetic. "A customer is coming by to pick up their order."

"Okay." Nash grins. "I have to head into Chelmer to pick Anna up from the airport."

At the mention of *her* my stomach twists at just how real this whole situation is.

"We're having a small get-together tomorrow night at the club."

"The club?" I ask, quirking a brow.

"Harrington Country Club." He nods. "That's where we're staying for the week to prepare for the wedding."

My face scrunches up at the thought. Nash Harris at a country club. It doesn't make sense. We used to make fun of the rich kids who came into town every summer to stay at Harrington's. We'd sneak onto the golf course through the pine forest, steal their golf balls before they could get to them, and laugh at how long they would spend looking for them. Now, Nash is one of them, and I feel sick at the thought.

I'm suddenly brought back to the now by a pair of strong arms wrapping around me in an all-too-familiar embrace, and that unsettling feeling in my belly is immediately gone. I find myself smiling as I rest my cheek against his shoulder, closing my eyes and breathing him in. He smells like him, like he always has, like home.

"You're my best friend, Murph."

My eyes fly open as I remain in his hold. Best friend? Those two words are suddenly like a slap to my face. I slowly pull back, finding him looking at me with that same innocence he's had his whole life and I sigh, forcing another smile onto my face as the realization comes crashing down upon me like a ton of bricks. I've lost the love of my life.

Dear Reader,

We hope you enjoyed reading this book. If you did, we'd be so appreciative if you left a review. It really helps us and the author to bring more books like this to you.

Here at HQ Digital we are dedicated to publishing fiction that will keep you turning the pages into the early hours. Don't want to miss a thing? To find out more about our books, promotions, discover exclusive content and enter competitions you can keep in touch in the following ways:

JOIN OUR COMMUNITY:

Sign up to our new email newsletter: hyperurl.co/hqnewsletter

Read our new blog www.hqstories.co.uk

🐦 : https://twitter.com/HQStories

f : www.facebook.com/HQStories

BUDDING WRITER?

We're also looking for authors to join the HQ Digital family!
Find out more here:

https://www.hqstories.co.uk/want-to-write-for-us/

Thanks for reading, from the HQ Digital team

**If you enjoyed *Sweet Home Montana*, then why not try another delightfully uplifting romance from HQ Digital?**

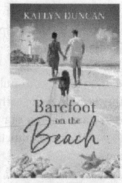